SWAY

SWAY

A NOVEL

AMY MATAYO

Sway
by Amy Matayo

Okay Creations Cover Designs © Sarah Hansen www.okaycreations.com
Cover photo by Todd Moncrief Photography
Author photo by Amber Lanning Photography
Represented by Jessica Kirkland of The Blythe Daniel Agency
www.theblythedanielagency.com
jessica@theblythedanielagency.com

This book is dedicated to my kids.

The four of you sacrifice the most in order for me to achieve my dreams, and I will forever love and adore you.

ACKNOWLEDGEMENTS

I would like to thank my readers for coming back for my third book. It was a humbling and thrilling experience every time anyone bought my first two, especially when someone would take the time to give a nice review or sweet face-to-face comment. I appreciated every single one, and I'm forever grateful for you.

A huge thank you to my fantastic agent, Jessica Kirkland. Without your guidance I would still be staring at a screen, wondering what the heck to do with the finished manuscript stored inside my computer. Thankfully you always know what comes next. You're savvy when I am clueless, sharp when I am dull, excited when I am lifeless, a marketing genius when I am not (which is always since I hate marketing). I'm eternally blessed by you.

Thank you to my awesome editors—Taryn Albright, Kristin Avila, and Jenny B. Jones—for your willingness to read this book and for taking my very rough manuscript and turning it into something (hopefully) worth publishing. Your selflessness means the world to me, and you girl's rock.

To Nicole Deese for every encouraging word you've ever spoken. If words came to life and I tried to stack them in a room, all your kind ones wouldn't fit inside. You cheer me up when I'm down and eagerly volunteer to slap me when I'm filled with self-doubt. Only a real friend would do something so sweet. God made a great person when He made you, and I am privileged to know you.

To Stacy Henagan, Joy Francoeur, and Nicole Deese for reading this unedited manuscript and offering advice on how make the story better. It's not an easy thing to read a first or second or third draft, but you always volunteer and never complain. At least not to my face.

To Zoie Piazza for your awesome selfie-taking skills, because if they didn't exist, where would I be now? With a boring book cover, that's where. Thanks for being so pretty.

To Alec Stockton for sharing my love of creating things from nothing but imagination and a computer. It's nice to know someone who shares my weirdness. Or coolness, as I prefer to call it.

To my sisters, Tracy and Emily, for being my best friends and for not giving up on me when I'm under a deadline or going through last-minute freak outs. I love you both. Thank you for loving me.

To my awesome family—both the Millsap side and the Matayo side. I couldn't ask for a better group of people to belong to.

To my husband, Doug, for loving me, sticking with me, and encouraging me through the craziness.

And to Jesus Christ, for saving my life. I'm messy and ridiculous and constantly screwing up, but your grace makes all the difference.

1

Caleb

"A Boy Like Me, A Girl Like You"

—Elvis

There's something inherently pure about the sound of a needle on vinyl—the crackle, the static, the rich undertones of music playing in its most basic, unprocessed form—especially rare vinyl that only a handful of people own. Which is precisely what I was thinking an hour ago while thumbing through the latest issue of Rolling Stone *in my apartment. The Million Dollar Disc, the headline proclaimed, the article outlining in detail the rarest vinyl in today's market—from Lennon and Ono's* Double Fantasy *to Elvis Presley's* Stay Away *to The Quarrymen's* That'll Be the Day*—each worth a minimum of twenty-five thousand dollars. For a moment, I lost myself in the dream of owning just one of those albums. Just one.*

Now, I'm stuck in a Starbucks drive thru at nine o'clock on a Tuesday morning, dreaming about nothing but getting out of this stupid line.

I hate Starbucks. More than that, I hate Tuesdays. I hate staff meetings and dress shirts and endless mounds of paperwork. I hate traffic and stoplights and horns blaring at the slightest hesitation. Of course people hesitate, because Tuesdays make people jittery. Nervous. Filled with dread and apprehension and skin-crawling regret. Even history hates Tuesdays. Normandy was bombed on a Tuesday. Nine-eleven happened on a Tuesday. Johnny Cash was thrown in jail on a Tuesday.

I was thrown in jail on a Monday, as if I need the reminder. But I'll take a Monday over a Tuesday any day of my life. Tuesdays come with memories. And memories come with nightmares.

I hate the nightmares worst of all.

Shifting in my seat, I flip on the radio, cringing when the chorus of Katy Perry's Wide Awake *blares back at me like a taunt—jabbing at me, poking, as if even she knows that I didn't sleep again last night.*

It's Friday night and I, Caleb Stiles, have completely lost my mind. I knew this ten seconds after walking through the door—the dumbest move I've had in the five years since I started my job. Then again, my other ideas didn't involve alcohol, mosh pits, and women dressed in nothing more than belts and well-positioned triangles.

It's the triangles that have me questioning my sanity, because they're the hardest to ignore. I would try to figure out a way if I could think straight, but the woman to my left keeps rubbing against me as she orders a drink, her skin pressing so close I can almost feel her pores. Among other things.

I shift in my seat, turning my back on a desire that still comes more natural than breathing. But the desire won't undo me. Nowadays, thanks to a whole lot I can't even begin to list, I'm pretty sure there isn't much that will. That's the way I want it.

I upend my Coke and take a long pull, ignoring the way the carbonation nearly chokes me, wishing for a split second it actually would. Whiskey. With its strong bite and powerful burn, it would be smoother going down, and I find myself longing for a glass. It's that old wish that has me setting my tumbler back on the counter and raising my finger for water.

"What can I do you for?" The female bartender flashes a sultry grin and leans across the bar, propping her arms under her chest. This classic move gives me a personal invitation to ogle her ample cleavage, though I'm fairly certain most of it was bought and paid for. In all my time spent getting familiar with the opposite sex, I've never come across one who looked like her that money didn't buy. God makes things perfectly, but He darn well didn't make those.

I force my eyes upward and answer.

"Water, please." The control it takes to keep my eyes locked on her blue irises and not dip south is ridiculous. You'd think I would have conquered this by now. Apparently not. I push my empty soda glass across the countertop.

She raises an amused eyebrow. "You came into this bar on a Friday night for water?" Her red fingernails grab hold of my empty tumbler. She dumps out the ice and scoops in a fresh batch. "Pardon me for saying so, but you don't look like the water-drinking type." She slides the water toward me.

I stir the ice with my straw and look up at her face. Only her face.

"What type do I look like?" As soon as the words leave my mouth, I want to kill my own stupidity with a quick stab to its invisible side. The question is only a curious one, but even I hear the flirtatious undertones. From her slow smile that promises hours of pleasure in its lilting curve, it's clear she hears it too.

"You look like a man that needs some company." Reaching for a square bar napkin, she scribbles a few numbers in blue ink and tucks the paper in my front pocket, giving my chest a pat that sends my pulse reeling. "I get off at midnight," she purrs. "Call me and we'll work something out."

My voice goes dry. When I say nothing, she gives me a slow wink and moves on to the next customer. I take the napkin from my pocket, crumple it, and let it fall to the floor, wondering how I still manage to get myself into these situations. Thankfully, in an answer straight from heaven itself, Scott sits down on the stool next to me looking even more on edge than I am.

With mousy brown hair that needed a scrub two days ago and his polo shirt tucked too tight into his Levi's to be considered cool, he isn't as pretty as the woman. But he's a whole lot safer. And safe, for me, is what keeps me accountable. It's what keeps me on the path I've chosen.

"Tell me again why we're still here," Scott says, eyeing the woman next to me with a look best described as distain. Scott was a sheltered kid. Scott did church on Sundays and Wednesdays and any other day the door was open. Scott pot-lucked with old women. Scott didn't do bars. "The kids didn't show like you thought they might, so now would be a great time to leave. You know, since we could have ditched this place nearly an hour ago."

Sarcasm doesn't become Scott. And if the way his gaze keeps darting around the room is any indication, neither does nervousness.

"It's early—they still might. Besides, we're also here to get to know people. It's a good experience for all of you. Life doesn't only happen at the center, you know." I look around at the other guys we came with. Matt, Jordon, Kimball…all playing a game of pool in the back of the room. All, I notice with a pang of disappointment, keeping to themselves. I'm not sure any of them have acknowledged anyone but each other, and I'm *positive* the art of mentoring was lost on them three rounds ago.

This was definitely a bad idea. Obviously Scott agrees.

"It's good for us." He says with a raised eyebrow. "A bar. With barely-dressed women. And majorly drunk people. Is good for us?" He fingers the corner of a napkin. "If you don't mind, I'd rather be at the center."

Of course he would. "Tell me, Scott." I drain my water and eye him over the rim. "Besides the guys we came here with, who have you talked to tonight?" I spent the evening talking to a group of guys from Tulsa going to the university on scholarship. Nice guys, the sort I might have been friends with in another life, but they left nearly an hour ago. It's that one conversation that keeps me from feeling like a hypocrite. I set my glass down and silently thank God I didn't completely keep to myself all night.

The way Scott's mouth hangs open, and the way his eyes dart away tells me everything I need to know. They've talked to no one, making this night pointless. A waste of time. One that will probably garner all kinds of complaints by nine o'clock in the morning.

I stand and cuff him on the shoulder, intending to see if the other guys want to leave. "Yes, it's good for you. But from the looks of things, I can see none of you agree with me. So what do you say we pack up and go?" There isn't much here anyway. None of the kids showed up, and the band playing off to the side is giving me a headache. A throng of heavily-tattooed devotees are screaming around the make-shift stage, and the cheap spotlights and cheesy smoke machines make it hard to see.

A blast of cool air hits me in the back as a door slams behind me. I turn to seek out the source and eye a leggy blonde standing at the entrance. She shrugs out of her jacket, her *pink* jacket—an awful cotton-candy hue with a ring of fur around the collar. It covers her outfit except for a tiny strip of black material sneaking out of the hem. A skirt in the most liberal term, since it barely covers her butt.

Half of her ensemble screams innocent. The other half screams I'm Not Buying It. Who comes to a bar in a fuzzy pink coat, bare legs, and four inch spikes in late November?

The girl hooks the jacket around the back of her seat and sits down. Four chairs dot the table in a full moon-shape, and just as I spot her similarly clad companions, they sit down with her in a quadruple ring. Spray tans, lotions, and beauty products practically hover over them like a halo. I would roll my eyes, but it seems like a thing only a chick would do. Besides, something about the blonde draws me in, like she's familiar somehow.

Aware that Scott is rounding up the rest of our group, I press my back into the bar. Bad idea or not, I change my mind about leaving. Something tells me to stay.

I stare at her as the familiar pressing feeling starts in my head. It moves to my neck, then works its way to my heart. It's the heart that tells me I'm doing the right thing. I'm supposed to stay. Not sure for how long—maybe just an hour—but I know I can't leave.

I ask for another water, a somewhat disappointing order considering the scent of whiskey hovers all around me.

2

Kate

"Confessions on a Dance Floor"
—Madonna

If scientists ran an infrared germ test on this room, there probably wouldn't be a clean spot anywhere from floor to ceiling. That's what I'm thinking as I gingerly pull back my chair and sit down, aware that tonight, I'm the only one who doesn't know what she's doing. I'm also aware that I could really use a Handi Wipe. Apparently seedy taverns are a rite of passage—something every twenty-one-year old must do to be declared an official adult, along with getting out-of-your-mind drunk and hooking up with a stranger. It's the hooking up that has me scared, if only for my friends. I have no plans to follow their lead.

"It's like, eighty degrees in here, Kate. How can you possibly be cold?" This comes from Lucy, my best friend since eighth grade and the only girl in Oklahoma who can wear a bikini in sub-zero temperatures without as much as a shudder. I'm not kidding. Last year at this time, we both participated in the seventh annual Polar Plunge—a local event held on Hefner Lake that benefits cancer research. The idea is to plunge into icy, usually snow-topped water—in nothing more than a bikini— swim to a pre-placed buoy a few yards out, then jump out and rush into the pre-heated towels held up by volunteers. Lucy did all that, except for the towel. While I was plagued with uncontrollable convulsions for the next half-hour, she spent every minute of that time parading

7

through the crowd completely unaffected. Granted, the television cameras probably helped, but the girl didn't have a spot of goose flesh on her. I've hated her ever since, except for the obnoxious fact that I love her like a sister.

"There's snow right outside the door, Lucy. Of course I'm cold. I don't know why you picked tonight to go out when I could be at home under a blanket right now."

"She picked tonight because no self-respecting twenty-one-year-old should spend her birthday watching *Friends* reruns," Iris, our friend since the beginning of the semester, says. "It's lame, Kate. L-A-M-E."

"You know what else is lame? Sitting here with you guys when there are a dozen men here waiting to make my acquaintance," Ashley says with a flip of her hair. With silky blonde locks and legs that stretch for miles, she's the type who will have a guy on her arm in seconds. We've timed this before. Her record is eight.

Not one to miss an opportunity staring her in the face, Iris hops up and rushes after her. Following Ashley around is a sure-fire way to find a last-minute hook up.

Not that I know this. If given a choice, I would much rather be watching *Friends* right now. I don't mind admitting it. Just not out loud.

I sigh and look around the bar, trying not to grimace at the horrible band playing near the back of the room. The members look punk-rock underground with a hint of psycho—all spike haired with scary-looking piercings. But the sound quickly unravels their tough-as-nails image. With their high-pitched whine and upbeat rhythm, they resemble early Hall and Oats…if Hall and Oats added a background singer who screamed random, bizarre lyrics. *Death to Nemo! Slice the carrot!* Maybe these aren't the actual words coming from the screamer's mouth, but that's what they sound like. The band is awful. Grating. Desperate to convey a Straight from Hell image that isn't quite working.

Kind of like me in this ridiculously short dress. An hour ago, Lucy yanked it out of her closet and shoved it over my head, practically ripping me out of my sweatpants while she worked. I didn't ask if she'd washed it since her last wearing—Lucy already thinks I'm a germaphobe, which I'm totally not unless you count hating to touch things that have been previously touched by others. Instead, I reluctantly let her dress me. The sweatpants are still lying on my bedroom floor, calling to me, begging to be worn. Lucy would kill me if I tried. I tug on the hem of the world's most uncomfortable dress, hoping nothing is showing that shouldn't be.

I blink and look away from the band, taking in the ridiculously dim lighting. It's so dark in here, I can barely see my friend's faces. How will I possibly order off a menu? Scanning the table for one, I see nothing but paper coasters in front of me. Empty paper coasters, since no one has been by to take our drink orders.

Lucy doesn't seem the least bit concerned as she smirks across the table from me. "Well, I guess we need to find someone to help warm you up. Someone you can climb under a blanket with before the night is over." Her gaze sweeps the bar, then snaps in a double take at something behind me. A slow smile drags her lips upward. I've seen that smile a million times before. She's spotted something she wants, something she will soon describe as...

"Yummy. That guy is hot," she says. "The one standing over at the—don't look now, Kate! At least wait for me to give you the signal."

But I don't. I whip my head around before I can stop it, a compass pointing in a direction that may or may not lead toward a wrong turn. He leans against the bar a few yards away, one foot crossed over another, close enough to make my staring obvious. Low slung jeans encircle his hips, held in place by a studded leather belt. A chain hangs from it, disappearing mysteriously inside his left pocket as though it might connect to knife, a gun, a wallet...depending on how on-the-edge the guy lives. Everything about his image screams danger. Good danger. The kind of danger that might make a good girl like me consider sharing her blanket tonight. A tight black t-shirt defines the most amazing muscles, easy to see, despite the pale blue button-up shirt hanging loosely at his sides. A hint of a tattoo peeks out at his collar-bone, black and gray and feathering upward. And his hair…his perfect chestnut hair. It's messy in the best imaginable way, the way I've seen in magazines, in hit movies, on Abercrombie billboards hovering over the middle of Times Square.

I've been to Times Square only once.

But I've never forgotten the billboards.

Still, there's something about the guy that unnerves me. It isn't the outfit. Or the image—because he's beautiful. He doesn't seem menac-ing or threatening, despite the rough exterior. In fact, if the guy standing next to him is any indication, he seems almost…normal.

Open.

Too open.

He's been staring at me the whole time.

I raise one side of my mouth in half-hearted acknowledgement and turn back to Lucy, wishing for a glass of water to quench my suddenly dry throat. As if conjured up by pixie dust, a waitress appears and begins dispensing glasses. One for me, one for Lucy, one for Ashley, and one for Iris, whose chairs still sit empty. I give a once-over to the room and spot them next to the stage. Here barely ten minutes, and they've already found dates. Leaving me and Lucy alone at a table with four cups of water, two empty chairs, one giant headache, and a hot guy still staring at me. I chance a tiny glance at him just to be sure.

I'm right. Happy Birthday to me.

3

Caleb

"If I Never See Your Face Again"
—Maroon 5

A *s a kid, I spent hours dreaming about what I would be when I grew up, childish dreams that involved jumping off buildings or driving fast cars or moving to the speed of sound while wearing only a Speedo and a cape. After I saw the movie* Rocky, *I dreamed of being a boxer, of taking down all my enemies with a hard jab of my fist and a clean swipe to the legs.*

On my first day of elementary school, the kid next to me punched me in the nose for breaking his pencil. That day, I discovered that getting hit hurts.

I also discovered that even if you don't instigate a fight, you still might be labeled a troublemaker. And once that label sticks, it takes years to peel it off.

More often than not, it's too much trouble to try.

In the ten minutes she's been here, I've already changed my mind about the blonde. My first I'm Not Buying It impression was totally inaccurate. The girl is innocent. Quite possibly naive. In my twenty-four years of living—eleven of which would make even the most compassionate nun question my ability to be redeemed—I've discovered that usually the two are one and the same.

Sure enough, as I'm sizing her up, Trouble in a dark red shirt walks up behind her and rakes over her legs, zeroing in a little too long on her barely-there skirt. I watch with a mix of fascination and disgust. Fascination, because the guy is so dang confident. Disgust, because even though he carries a beer and wobbles sideways, I've been here long enough to know he hasn't had a drink all night.

Falsely inebriated and cocky, an often lethal combination. I, of all people, know this.

I'm contemplating intercepting this little exchange until the guy gets stopped by a genuinely drunk buddy who shouts something about needing another drink and "why the heck aren't you out here dancing with us, Man?" Except the friend doesn't say heck. He doesn't say hell either. Use your imagination.

The girl in the puffy pink coat still doesn't notice the two guys behind her, just sips her water and swings a toned leg back and forth to the music. The sound is generally unpleasant, verging on outrageous. A couple of the band members need to take more lessons or stop playing altogether, particularly the guitarist who wouldn't know rhythm if it pounded a beat straight into his brain. I'm surprised the girl likes it. Then again, I've been surprised by a lot lately.

The guy starts moving again just as Scott bumps me from the side.

"Caleb, we have a problem," he says in his overly excited, anxious way. This would worry me, except this is how Scott talks all the time. High pitched and nervous, as though something is chasing him, as though he is one breath away from an anxiety attack. I've seen him have one once—when the stock market took a dive last year and took most of his penny-stock earnings with it. Twelve hundred dollars, but you might have thought it was twelve million. He didn't stop wringing his hands for a solid week. Didn't stop talking about it for another two. When it comes to Scott, he's more fifty-year-old man than twenty-two year old computer genius slash financial planner.

Still, he keeps the books for us at work, and makes sure everything follows the letter of the law. That's why I like him—he's straight and narrow in all the places I'm twisted and mangled.

"What is it?" I ask him.

The hand-wringing commences. "Well, it seems Kimball took the whole 'coming to the bar and mingling with the locals' thing a bit too seriously, and…"

"And…?" My stomach plummets, as though it knows Scott's next words before my ears do.

"He's drunk. And not just a little."

I take a few steps away from the bar, thinking about the trouble I'm going to be in tomorrow. Sure, every one of these men is of age, every one of them is old enough to make their own decisions and live with the consequences, but I'm in charge. It's my butt on the line if something goes wrong.

"Where is he?"

"In the men's room, hugging the toilet."

"How did he get drunk?"

"I believe he consumed too much alcohol." Most people would say Scott deadpanned the words, but the guy wouldn't know a joke if it fell on his tongue.

I roll my eyes. Chick thing to do or not, it's the only appropriate response. "I get that he drank too much, but why? I specifically remember telling you guys not to order anything."

"I know, but it seems that someone bet him in a game of pool…"

For the love of Mary and Joseph—gambling and drinking. I'll be lucky if I have a job left tomorrow. I push through the bathroom door and catch sight of a moaning Kimball, lying in a puddle of his own vomit while Matt works to clean the mess up. He's going about it all wrong and making everything worse, but I say nothing. Bending down, I meet Kimball at eye level.

"What part of 'don't drink anything' did you not understand?" Sympathy, I've discovered, is something I'm fresh out of.

I'm greeted with an even louder moan and a lunge for the toilet. Knowing he's about three inches off the mark, I take the back of his head and pull it forward, trying to be gentle. But if I hurt him a little, I really don't feel bad about it. Kimball purges, this time landing on the target. The smell of puke hovers in the air like a cloud of sulfur. It might make me sick if I wasn't so used to it.

"Feeling better?" I say as Kimball leans back, eyeing me like a puppy in trouble. I feel like whacking his nose with a newspaper.

"A little." His lips are green around the edges.

"Good enough to stand up? We need to get you home."

He nods and tries to lift himself up, but falls back down in a heap. I sigh and grab him under his armpits, lifting at the waist. The only thing worse than a severely drunk guy is a severely drunk guy who's never been drunk before. Kimball is completely out of his element. This hangover might last for days.

"Was it worth it?" I ask, a little louder than necessary, but I figure it's my job to drive the pain home. Maybe he'll think twice next time.

"No. Not at all." He shakes his head before seeming to think the better of it, and groans. "My head hurts so bad. I need a Tylenol."

"You need about three of them. But first you need coffee. A big cup. The blacker, the better." Scott opens the door and we leave the bathroom. Jordon's nowhere around and I'm annoyed, but then I spot him across the room and see the reason why. He's chatting up a cute redhead near the dance floor who looks very much into him. Too bad his good time is up.

"Jordon! Get over here." I don't even try to hide my irritation.

His head snaps around, his complexion quickly matching the red-head's hair. He doesn't look happy, but he listens to me. "What's wrong?" he says as he walks up. At least he has the decency to look chagrined.

I square my jaw and swallow about a dozen foul words just itching to make an appearance. "I need you to bring your car around. Kimball went and got himself drunk, and we're going to sober him up before anyone finds out. Think you can peel yourself away from the enter-tainment and take care of that for me?" My words have a sharp bite and covey a whole lot of implication, but I can't help it. What started out as a way to help other people has turned into a disaster.

I royally screwed up. And now, thanks to this, I'm royally screwed.

He fishes his keys out of his pocket. "Sure thing. Give me a couple of minutes." Jordon sprints toward the door, Matt and Scott following behind him. I'm left alone with the slurring, drunk guy. Lucky me.

Kimball's knees grow weaker by the second, and consequently he grows heavier. Kicking a chair out with my foot, I lower him into it, taking care to stand in place so he can lean on me, knowing that if I move, he'll drop to the floor. His head will pound uncontrollably tomorrow. He doesn't need a bash to the skull from the hard concrete floor to add to the pain.

While Kimball snores below me, I scan the room. The bar has grown more crowded; apparently its faithful clientele doesn't arrive until midnight. It doesn't take me long to spot the blonde, whom I've all but forgotten about in the drunken fiasco. Maybe fifteen minutes have passed since I left, but she's still sitting at the same table. Yet everything else has changed. Her friends are no longer with her, and she's been joined by the red-shirt guy. The two of them are drinking, flirting across the table. His arm is draped across her back and his left hand caresses her wrist. She slaps it away and takes another drink, laughing hysterically at something he's said as beer bubbles over the cup and slides down her chin. The laugh is a little too loud, obnoxious in the sheer magnitude of the sound. He dabs at her chin with a napkin and leans in to kiss her. She leans in too, but just before their lips touch, she abruptly stops. After a moment, her face contorts, like she's experiencing the world's biggest headache. Or, like she's confused.

It's my first clue that something isn't right.

Her eyes close for a moment and her body slumps sideways.

That's my second.

I've seen hundreds of drunk people in my life. First-time drunks and long-term drunks, and though nothing about the two are even remotely similar, one thing holds true in both situations, no matter a person's level of tolerance:

Headaches…confusion…unawareness…none of them *ever* start this early.

The guy whispers something in her ear, but this time she doesn't crack a smile. He stands up and takes her hands, pulling her out of her chair. She practically lunges toward him and falls into his waiting arms. As he does, a little white pill slips from his pocket and falls to the floor. It skids toward me and I lean down to palm it. Blood rushes between my ears as the old familiar anger sets in.

And this is my third.

Feeling something akin to panic rising up to meet the anger, I search the room. There's no sign of the friends she came with. There's also no sign of Jordon, and only Matt is left by the window. Scott, with his low tolerance of the sinful nature of bars, has clearly ducked out already.

My earlier thought comes back with a vengeance. This night was definitely the world's biggest mistake. Where is everyone?

My heart rate picks up speed as the front door opens and the guy walks through it, leading the blonde in her short dress behind him, not even bothering to slip that ugly pink coat over her shoulders. From behind them, I can make out the faint drift of a light snowfall. It's cold. It's cold and dark and isolated and heading straight toward a bad ending, with her in trouble, alone—and to top it off—sick. I can see it now, like a bad novel I've read a dozen times and memorized the ending.

God, please.

It's the only thing I can think. The only thing I can feel. The only thing I can do.

Until finally Scott walks through the door and makes his way over to me, his head dusted with white, his black coat dripping melted snowflakes onto the concrete floor below him.

"You ready to go?" he asks.

But I barely hear his words.

"Here, take him." I hand off Kimball and walk away without looking back, knowing time is running out and feeling my gut twist because of it.

"What am I supposed to do with him?" Scott yells back, sending my already bad mood plummeting even further.

"Get him in the car! Then figure out the rest!" I swear, sometimes it's exhausting being in charge of so many people, especially the ones who can't seem to think for themselves. And though I know Scott is a good guy, and though I know I'm supposed to be here, sometimes I hate it just the same.

"Hey!" I yell as I burst through the front door. Just as I thought, the guy from the bar is stuffing the girl inside a silver Mazda coupe. Just enough of the door is open to see her dark figure splayed across the front seat, completely passed out. He closes the door and walks around the front of the car, either unaware that I'm talking to him, or in a rush to leave before I catch up. I make it to the trunk. "Hey!" I say again, too close to ignore. This time he has to turn. His eyes are flaming arrows shooting straight through me, but I can take it. I've taken worse.

"What do you want?" He opens the driver's door and slips one foot inside as though challenging me to stop him.

So I do.

"I want you to back away from the car." I look him straight in the eyes when I say it, so I'm a little surprised when he laughs and slides into the seat.

Laughs. Sits down and laughs, which are both completely unacceptable. So I do the thing that comes naturally. Automatically. It's been five years, but as they say about picking up an old, abandoned habit, it's like riding a bike. I yank him forward by the collar and slam him into the back door, metal crashing against skin in a familiar crunch. His head snaps forward as his eyes burn a hole into my skull. They're clear, focused. My suspicions were right. He's stone, cold sober. "I said, back away from the car. Since you didn't do it the easy way, I'll give you a little help."

I see his fist coming a little too late. It smashes against my jaw, knocking me to the ground. The bone doesn't break, but it misses a golden opportunity. I think about remaining there when the ground begins to spin, but the sound of the girl's moan from inside the car brings me back to my feet…feet a lot less steady than they were moments ago. Before I can meet his eye, another blow lands in my gut.

Which totally ticks me off. A familiar adrenaline rush kicks in and I lunge for him; I haven't been this mad in years.

That bike I'm riding once again becomes a pimped-up Harley Davidson as my fist connects with his face, his jaw, his ribs. I punch anything that moves until his body falls to the ground, only vaguely aware of the words "Caleb, stop!" sounding in the background. But for two more blows, I don't.

Until the sickening thud of bone meeting gravel brings me to my senses.

Until the arms of Scott and Matt wrap around me and pull me away. Like cold water dumped into a pool of boiling hot rage, my anger fizzles as my eyes meet the writhing form lying on the ground below us. It takes me a minute to figure out what happened…a minute to break through my haze of rage…a minute longer to recall what had me so angry in the first place.

But then it comes back.

"Check on the girl," I say to Matt, touching the back of my hand to my mouth and drawing back a ring of blood. It's coming from my nose, I think, though my left eye feels kind of wet, too. Glancing at the guy on the ground, I see that he's fared worse than me. There's barely a spot of unmarred skin on his blood-stained face. The thought brings me more satisfaction than it should. Especially when guilt quickly follows.

Dear God, I whisper under my breath, knowing that for a split second, I let anger control me…the very thing I surrendered years ago. I embraced it. Let it take over. And enjoyed every moment of it.

I hear the car door open and forget about the guy on the ground, then limp my way toward the passenger side. Another moan greets me when I arrive, but the girl only turns and slumps into the console.

"What happened?" Matt asks, with more than a little concern on his face. He looks at me like he's seeing a stranger...like the past five years have been erased in an instant. In a way, I guess they have. Most of these guys know me as their leader, their boss. In some ways, a saint.

They're only now seeing the guy who's danced face to face with the devil.

I nod toward the ground. "He drugged her. I didn't see the whole thing since I was stuck in the bathroom cleaning up Kimball's mess." I glare toward the waiting van where Kimball now sits hunched in the passenger seat. "But I saw enough. He gave her this." Fishing the pill out of my pocket, I hold it up.

"What is that?" Matt asks, leaning closer toward my fingers. Scott joins him, a look of confusion lining his eyes. What I wouldn't give to be that innocent, that sheltered. But life didn't deal me that same hand. Not even close.

Instead of answering, I walk toward the battered guy, now attempting to sit up. He's groaning in pain, but that doesn't stop me as I lean down and hold the pill in his face. "Do you want to answer that?" I spit the words out. "My friends want to know what this is."

In spite of his swelling face, his eyes still manage to go wide. He holds up a hand to block another blow, but I'm way past that. The anger I felt before has been replaced by something else. Something once described to me as a holy fury. The words are right, because even though I could lay my fist into the guy again, I won't. I'm too eerily calm now.

"Look man, I didn't mean anything by it," he says.

I lean closer, our faces only inches apart. "Nothing by it. Is that right?" We can both hear the threat in my tone. "You just meant to get her drunk, add a few drugs to her drink to get her good and passed out, then stuff her in your car, and drive somewhere to take advantage of her in peace. Is that the 'nothing' you meant by it?"

He stumbles to his feet, clearly thinking I'm one word away from killing him right here. What he doesn't know is that in another life, I might have.

"Look, just let me go." He's walking toward his car, tripping over his leather lace-ups as he goes. I spot the brand as Prada. A rich boy, and he needs to drug a girl to score. The thought only adds to my nausea, gluing my feet to the pavement.

Maybe I should call the cops, maybe I should hold him hostage, but right now, my only concern is her. Getting her out, keeping her safe. After that...I have no idea.

"Not with her, you're not. Scott, help me get her out of the car." He takes one side, I grab her from the other, and we lift her out. Shooting a prayer toward heaven that she remains blissfully unaware, I grasp her under her legs swing her up against me. Once she's secure, I glare toward the pervert, already situated inside the car. "Get out of here. And if I ever see you here again..."

I don't get to finish that sentence, because his door slams shut at the same time his engine roars to life. A small bag flies next to my head and lands on the pavement next to me. Two seconds later, he's out of the parking lot. I stare after his taillights, conflicted in a dozen different ways. The girl is safe, unharmed. But who's to say he won't be back at it tomorrow? Slap a little make-up on his face to camouflage the broken skin, whip out the pills once again, and use them on another unsuspecting girl. I glance down at the one settled in my arms and slowly exhale. I can only pray that what almost happened to her won't happen to someone else.

The sound of Scott's voice stops that prayer before it's complete.

"So, is that a date-rape drug you're holding? And he gave it to her?"

I look down at my hand, only just now aware I'm still clutching the pill. It burns into my palm until I release it. When it settles onto the pavement, I crush it under my hiking boot, grinding it into powder that disappears into the gravel. "I'm pretty sure he gave her a few. Enough to keep her knocked out until he got the job done. Probably more than once."

I see the grimace that crosses both of their faces at my harsh words, but sometimes life isn't pretty. Sometimes, it's ugly and scarred and brutal. And right then and there, I decide these guys should know it. After a moment, Scott's eyebrow slides up.

"I have a feeling this isn't what you had in mind when you said 'let's go to a bar.'"

Whether he intended the words as a joke or not, I can't help the smile that tilts my lips. I shake my head. "Not even close. I'm going to be in so much trouble tomorrow."

Scott and Matt look at each other and shrug. "For what? We're not saying anything," Matt says.

"I don't even know what you're talking about," Scott echoes the thought. "My lips are sealed. Except I do have a question."

"What's that?" I ask, aware that this girl is getting harder and harder to hold. She's still snoring, still passed out. Letting me do all the work while she just lays there, limp.

"What are you going to do with her?"

I blink at him. Blink at Matt. Blink down at her near-lifeless form. All that blinking has gotten me nowhere. Then I remember her bag. "Someone open that up and find her I.D. Maybe then I'll know what to do. But first, can you bring me my car? Keys are in my back pocket."

Matt fishes them out and sprints away while Scott reaches for the bag and opens it. "Are you sure I should be doing this?" he asks.

I shift my weight, and hers, to my other hip. "It's either that or we leave her here. Or I guess we could take her to your house…"

Scott rips at the bag like a tiger attacking a steak. Pulling out a rectangle card, he holds it up. "Found her license. It says she lives on third and Hudson. Apartment 213B. Hope that helps." He looks up at me. "Isn't that Clearwater apartments?"

It's Clearwater. And it helps. In the way that a pack of cigarettes helps an ex-smoker.

I sigh. "Yes, it does. Now, I just have to get her home."

On cue, my car pulls up. Scott opens the passenger door and I slide her inside, then turn to face the guys, my arms screaming in blessed relief. I rub my hands together, hoping to convey an authoritative edge.

"Alright, who's coming with me?"

4

Kate

"Heaven Knows I'm Miserable Now"

—The Smiths

'm moving. Swaying back and forth, my head giving an occasional bounce as we hit what feels like a pothole. My mind feels fuzzy, my vision is blurred, but I'm aware enough to know that I'm not in this car alone. But who is with me? I remember my friends, I remember the tattooed guy at the bar, I remember the other guy that bought me a drink and told me I was beautiful, that I was the present he'd been waiting for even though I was the one celebrating the birthday. I remember all of those people.

But I can't remember who I left with.

I'm stopping. Being lifted and carried and cradled while someone fumbles with a lock. A door opens. It shuts. It's dark inside the room, and I'm glad. I think even a pinprick of light might make my head explode.

My head.

It's spinning.

It's spinning and I'm moving and I'm twirling and I'm stopping. Someone lays me down. Someone tucks a blanket around my shoulders. I'm cold, and then I'm warm.

My eyes crack open for the slightest second, long enough to see muscle and tightness and strength and man. He's warm, too, so I kiss

23

him and giggle and kiss him again. He doesn't kiss back. I don't understand much, but this isn't how a one-night-stand is supposed to go. But then I wasn't supposed to have a one-night stand. I was supposed to drive my drunk friends home.

His presence confuses me. His reaction confuses me. My lack of friends confuses me. My head confuses me. The cold confuses me. The wetness around my mouth confuses me.

The odd sensations come all at once, overwhelming me until blood rushes to my head. I sink my head into the pillow, letting my arms and legs go limp on the mattress. This feels good, this feels normal. This is perfect.

Everything goes black.

5

Caleb

"Diamond Eyes"

—Deftones

*A*ccident-prone *was the term my mother often used to describe me. My elderly neighbor was less gracious—he often shouted "klutz!" at me across the driveway after another fall from a bike, a trip over skates, a stumble over my own two feet.*

While the cranky old man kept going with his taunts, without fail, my mother came rushing. After a wet rag and a well-placed Band-Aid and a smile, she routinely made my pain better with a kiss.

I learned at a young age that a kiss always makes things better.

It wasn't until I grew older that I quit believing that lie.

Of course I'm alone. Every one of those idiots tucked tail and ran the second I invited them along. Matt claimed a sudden sore throat. Scott blamed his curfew—the guy is freaking twenty-two but still answers to his mother. And Kimball…for all I know he's passed out cold in a garage somewhere.

My friends. What a bunch of worthless losers.

Guilt chases that thought and I kick the front door closed with the heel of my foot. Once we make it inside the empty apartment, I bump nose-first into a bedroom door, try not to curse, then lay the girl down on the first bed I can find. I reach for a blanket to cover her. Even in the dark, I can see that it's a bright shade of pink—just like her coat. This is obviously her room, which has me seriously questioning this girl's sense of taste. Pink is nauseating. Pink is shallow. Pink is sororities and air-kisses and chicks who talk about manicures—everything I despise.

Pink was my mother's favorite color.

That thought comes from nowhere, and suddenly I'm angry. I don't even know this girl and she's making me revisit things I would rather not remember…things I can't change or undo or wish back. Not that it's her fault, and not that it matters. I'm out of here in ten seconds. Hopefully less.

I tuck the headache-inducing blanket around her shoulders and stand, intending to walk out. But then she moans, rolls over, and shivers when the blanket falls off. I've seen these kinds of drugs at work before, so the coldness doesn't surprise me. The fact that she isn't completely out of it does.

Tugging the blanket up across her shoulder again, I push back a long strand of curls that manages to spread across her cheek. Her hair is silk, like lengths of gold chord that slip through my fingers, imprinting their memory long after they fall back onto the pillow. I stare for a moment, a strange longing to feel them again coursing through me. My heart picks up speed, and I know I need to leave.

Before I have a chance to move she rotates onto her back, and two soft hands slide up my arms. Her fingernails are short, blunt from a recent clipping. The edges are sharp as though she didn't bother with a file. I'm not sure if it's the absence of pink or the plainness of the cut or the fact that she's touching me at all, but it surprises me. She doesn't get manicures? As I'm mulling this thought, she yanks on my shirt and pulls me down, pressing her lips to mine. Shocked doesn't describe my reaction. I know she's unaware. I know she's out of it. But the contact rushes to my head and makes it hard to breathe.

The breaths I manage to grab turn shallow when her arms snake around my neck. Her lips touch mine again as my own hang slack. I'm stunned, but not enough to keep from noticing that her lips are soft, inviting, warm in a way I haven't felt in forever. They taste like butterscotch, rich and liquid. A longing burns in my gut, fierce in its pull, and I feel myself falling.

Falling.

Pressing into her, I lower my mouth over hers as desire numbs everything but the way this feels…the way she feels…until her teeth nip at my bottom lip and bring me to my senses. With my pulse hammering a painful beat into my neck, I rip myself away and stand, giving her a gentle push onto the mattress. She's drunk and I'm a jerk. The back of my hand instinctively moves to my mouth to remove her taste, but it doesn't quite work, and I'm mad all over again. She begins to giggle, and I blink at her change in demeanor, puzzled by her random mood swings. The sound melts away my anger, because it's musical. Funny, even. I find myself smiling down at her as she curls into the mattress and laughs. It goes on and on until I begin to think she's losing her mind.

But then she stops. Goes completely still. Turns white. And loses her dinner instead.

Twice.

All over the bed. And of course on my leg.

And now I'm right back where I started. My life could not possibly suck more than it does now. And all I can think is *why the heck didn't anyone talk me out of going to that stupid bar?*

I pull her bedroom door closed behind me, leaving it cracked just a little just in case—*in case, what?*—and walk into the living room, bumping my leg on something sharp in the hallway. It turns out to be a table, and I've smeared vomit all over it now. Finding it hard to care, I go in search of a towel, locating one lying on the porcelain kitchen sink next to a box of handy wipes and two bottles of Germ-X. I reach for the towel and wet it, and as I swipe it across my jeans, all I can think is that any minute now her roommate might show up and call the police. I could be arrested for breaking and entering, and since I have a prior record the excuse *But I used the key I pilfered from her purse* probably will not get me out of trouble. All the talking in the world would likely wind up with me locked in an eight-by-eight cell.

But I just don't care. Her friends left her at the bar. Abandoned her drunk and drugged. Entrusted her with a guy she'd never met. A guy who would have taken advantage of her in five more minutes if he'd been given the smallest chance. They left her, and I find myself hoping each one of them will walk in just so I can yell at them in person.

Seriously, why are some girls so stupid?

I pump soap into my hands and scrub them together, then flip the water off and shake them out, trying to decide what to do. Patting them on my backside, I survey the room, looking for an answer. Staying seems to be the worst option, but the girl has already thrown up once. What if she begins again? Or what if the guy at the bar slipped her more drugs than I think, and she…tries to jump out her window? Or hangs herself with an extension cord from her ceiling rafter? I have no idea if date rape drugs make a person delusional, or suicidal, but I sure don't want to read about her self-inflicted death in tomorrow's paper. I can't have that on my conscience, especially when Matt, Jordon, and Scott know I'm here.

And my concern has absolutely nothing to do with those blond ringlets I can still feel gliding through my hand. Or the butterscotch kiss that still lingers on my lips.

This is about her safety.

This is about her—

"What the heck?" My gaze lands on her white wicker bookcase. More specifically, on the rows of thin, worn cardboard lining the bottom three shelves in vertical rows. I don't need to see the sleek turntable planted above them to know exactly what I'm looking at, and my pulse picks up speed. By the time I kneel down to examine them more closely, my pulse is at a full-out sprint. Her record collection is mind-blowing. I flip through indie bands like Bon Iver, Sleeping with Sirens, The Civil Wars, The Lumineers. Classics like Buddy Holly, Etta James, Elvis, The Beatles. The ridiculous like Wham!, Wang Chung, The Bee Gees, the soundtrack for *The Breakfast Club*. They go on and on. The name Kathryn darts out at me repeatedly, her name written in black Sharpie on the top left corner of each album.

Kathryn. Kathryn's records.

Kathryn's LP's and forty-fives. Dozens of them. Hundreds. All alphabetized and categorized by genre. By size. From left to right in descending order. I can almost see her kneeling on the floor, painstakingly organizing each one until they all flowed together to offer easy access. I glance at the still open bedroom door, my mind drifting to the girl on the bed—Kathryn—currently knocked out and lying in the leftover remains of what looked like tuna on wheat.

But never mind all that. Kathryn what's-her-name has the coolest record collection I've ever seen.

I should know. I have many of these same albums at home. But not all of them. Some are way too expensive for a person living on my salary.

I'd like nothing more than to sit here for a few more hours and stoke my jealousy, but I can't. I feel like a stalker for being here this long, and this apartment has at least one other inhabitant. I don't belong here. Probably a good idea to make myself scarce before whoever she lives with decides to show up.

I'm preparing to stand when I spot one more album tucked away behind all the others. My heart, usually so even-keeled and dependable, stops cold. Dead in my chest. A weird, girly squeal comes out of my throat, and I look around, thankful the only other person in the apartment won't be awake anytime soon. The thought should make me feel guilty, but worries about my manhood usually trump everything else.

Turning back around, I lock eyes on the object as full-on lust slams into me. There, situated inside an oversized glass frame—protected and hidden from curious eyes that might be able to spot it for what it is, eyes like mine—is the only album I haven't been able to find in all my years of collecting them. Not that I would be able to own it, but I've always wanted to see one in person. With shaking hands, I reach for the frame. I have to hold it, if only for a second. My whole body goes numb as I stare at Bob Dylan's *The Freewheelin'* in my calloused hands, and it's all I can do not to let out a whoop. Websites tout this album as exclusive. Collectors tout it as impossible to find. EBay touts it as worth forty thousand dollars.

I tout it as un-freaking-believable. Some kids wished for Disney World. I've always wished for this.

I flip it over in my hands and try not to feel disappointed when I'm greeted by a sheet of laminated mahogany wood. I want to see the back, but like an idiot I've forgotten about the frame. Deciding that it probably isn't a good idea to pry it open with the pocket knife tucked inside my pocket, I study the front again, still not quite believing what I'm seeing. Why that girl keeps an album like this hidden inside an Oklahoma City apartment building is beyond me. It's ridiculous. It's irresponsible. This thing deserves to be locked inside a safe deposit box, secured by keys and bars and bank tellers with stern expressions.

I want to wake her up and tell her so, plus I'm suddenly flattened with a need to see the eyes of the girl who has the world's best taste. But I don't. I'd scare her anyway, since other than her drug-induced come-on that she'll never even remember, she has no idea who I am. Probably best to leave it that way.

With a regret I haven't felt since being hauled away in handcuffs, I return the album to the shelf. It slips easily back into place, as though it was never disturbed at all. Another pang of disappointment runs through me at leaving it behind, but I'm not a thief anymore. I said goodbye to that life years ago with no regrets, and until now, I haven't once been tempted to revisit it. Rising from the bookcase, I make another pass around the room. Kathryn might need to find her purse, so I prop it on the floor against her bedroom door. Hopefully she won't trip on it in the morning, but her morning-after hangover issues aren't my problem.

I flip off the only light I turned on and head for the door. I'm halfway outside when a moan sounds from her bedroom. I blow out some air at the sound and roll my eyes heavenward. *Why? Just… Why?* It takes me only a second to contemplate what to do, another to drop my keys and wallet on the middle sofa cushion. Shoving my hands in my pocket, I wander toward her door as another moan hits, stronger this time. Silence comes next, followed by the unmistakable sound of retching. I don't need to see it to know it's bad. I don't need to walk in her room all the way to know it stinks. I don't need to see her face to know I can't leave. I don't need to hear her voice to know she needs help.

"Please help me," she cries. I doubt she even knows she's talking.

I was wrong about my life sucking earlier this evening.

Compared to now, the first time she puked was a great big bowl of cherries.

6

Kate

"Hurt"

—Nine Inch Nails

When I crack one eye open and see a sliver of daylight, I have three semi-coherent thoughts. First, my mouth tastes like rotten maraschino cherries, and I don't remember eating any. Second, there's something dry and crusty plastered to my cheek, and I'm afraid to explore that information further. Third, I want to die. If only the zombie apocalypse would happen right here, right now and zap me of all memory and normal brain function. Because the alternative is that my head explodes into a million factions of tissue and cells. Hot. Metallic. Lethal. I gingerly lie unmoving under the pillow and try not to breathe.

I'd pay money for one of those zombies to show up.

Money.

I frown, which also manages to hurt. But...where's my purse? I search my memory, but I can't remember bringing it home last night. And I need it, because the invitation came in the mail yesterday and it's still tucked inside. I never opened it, and I can't remember the time, place, or date for my father's next speech. To call and ask would only get me a lecture about being irresponsible, self-indulgent, and scatter-brained. I could rattle off more labels from a lifetime of memories, but it pains me too much. If I could just remember what happened when I

33

walked into the house—

Then it hits me.

How did I get home from the bar?

Against my better judgment—a judgment that has served me well since the time my mother announced I would compete in the Little Miss Oklahoma pageant and I put my nine-year-old foot down; good thing, too, since the girl who won that year is currently serving time for third-degree larceny. I lift the pillow a fraction of an inch and allow one eye to slit open. This looks like my room. I can see the muted outline of three crepe paper balls suspended from one corner of the ceiling. Without moving my head, I can make out what appears to be the gorgeous face of Chace Crawford gazing down at me from the life size *Gossip Girl* poster I bought last year at Wal-Mart. Childish, maybe, but I haven't had a boyfriend in more than a year. A girl's got to live vicariously through something, and I'd rather not live through my roommate, whose idea of a long-term relationship is three consecutive nights waking up in the same bed with the same guy. It's disgusting, really. I can't believe I let her talk me into—

Wait.

Lucy. She left the bar early, after she'd snagged her potential "boyfriend." In fact, I seem to remember snagging one myself—a drop-dead gorgeous hunk of a man who flattered me mercilessly and flashed a roll of twenties to the waitress when he thought I wasn't looking. Or maybe he knew I was. Something about the move seemed deliberate. Either way, it was impressive. Stunning. And more than a little sexy. I remember talking to him, I remember telling him it was my birthday, I remember his comment about making it a night I'd never forget, I remember…

My hand lands on the mattress as I struggle to sit up. I lift it. Bring it to my face. Try not to scream. And fall back on my pillow.

I do *not* remember throwing up.

Nor do I recall, no matter how much I search my fuzzy, comatose brain, how in the world I made it to my bed. My friends all left the bar before me, so who brought me here? Who let me in my house? Who left me in this bed to rot in a layer of vomit?

That last thought makes me mad.

With my head throbbing violently, I sit up and swing my legs over the side of the bed. The person probably dumped me and left the apartment with a great, big laugh. I press my hands to my head and shuffle toward the bedroom door, stopping for a moment when the room begins to sway. It's irrational, I know, but I need to find out if everything is still here. What if he stole something? What if he's a murderer...or worse?

I'm not sure what I expect when I throw open the door and stumble into the hallway, but the person I see sprawled on the sofa definitely isn't it.

7

Caleb

"Ain't She Sweet"

—The Beatles

Waking up in a strange place requires a weird kind of detachment, one that takes much less time to develop than you might think. Unless you've had your own pillow on your own bed in your own room for any stretch of your life, waking up lying across someone else's bed doesn't come as a surprise.

But when it's been awhile, when you finally have place to call home after years and years of wishing, waking up in a strange room—especially one that smells like vomit while being ironically filled with pink—can come as a shock. A setback. A spotlight accenting your worst failure.

Funny how quickly the past revisits itself.

My eyes blink open, though I've barely been asleep for two hours. I know this because the clock on the DVD player shines seven fifteen, and I didn't make it to the sofa until after five. Sleep isn't normally a problem for me—at home, eight to ten hours is a normal stretch. But then I'm not at home. I'm at a strange girl's house. And I mean strange in the literal sense. In the past four hours, she's kissed me once, tried to slap me twice, yelled at me more times than I can count, and has thrown up on me at least double that. Until two hours ago, I spent the entire night cleaning up her puke. Off her, off her bed, off me. I was covered in so much filth from the waist down that I couldn't leave. There are a lot of things I'm willing to do—I've been to Skid Row, prisons, countless homeless shelters—but sitting my soggy butt in my next-to-new SUV last night wasn't one of them.

My gut clenches at the thought, and that's when I remember. Looking down at the thing I snatched off her hanger and slipped on a couple hours ago, I groan. It's tight, ugly, makes even *me* question my manhood, and I've got to get it off before—

"Who the heck are you? And why are you wearing my robe!" A female voice I've never heard before unless you count wailing and retching comes from the hallway, and my head spins to find her. She's fisting an iron candlestick in classic *Clue* style—*the drunk birthday girl did it with the candlestick in the hallway*—and looks ready to pounce. This would be a great time to die, but of course I'm not that lucky. I sit up slowly, fighting an unusual wave of embarrassment. It takes a lot to humble me. Just as quickly, my embarrassment fades into irritation. Who's she mad at? After what she put me through all night, she owes me big time. I give her my best don't-mess-with-me glare and settle my wrists on my knees.

"I'm wearing it because cross-dressing is my thing, and sneaking into women's houses on Friday night turns me on." Like the jerk I'm being right then, I slowly look her up and down.

For a second she looks scared. But then the fear fades, and her anger returns. With her matted hair and vomit-stained dress that used to be black but now looks like a weird shade of gray and brown tie dye—disgusting—she looks half insane. When she speaks again, she sounds it, too.

"Get your eyes off me. And get out of my house."

Now I'm mad, and since my track record is way more violent than hers, I'm pretty sure I'm better at it.

"Get out of your house? I'd love to get out of your house!" I toss my hands in the air and stand, aware that the raised volume of my voice will feel like knives to her hungover head. The fact that I'm still wearing a pink robe with ruffles at the sleeves only feeds my anger. "In fact, I wanted to leave five hours ago. But every time I moved toward the door, you started throwing up again. Did you know that when you throw up, you cry? And your nose runs like a water fountain targeting only my shirt? And you beg for strange men to stay and help you? And you whine for your mommy over and over and over? But of course you have a security code on your phone, which makes it really hard for a guy like me to find her number!" At her stricken expression, I do what a true gentleman would do. I keep going. "Know what else? I've changed your sheets twice. Not easy to do when you can't find the extra sheets and dead, drunk weight is lying in the middle of the flippin' bed!"

I'm breathing hard. And now that I've gotten it all out, I feel like crap.

When her lip quivers and she slides to floor, I feel worse. Like crap stuck to the bottom of a shoe. She buries her head in her hands. Her blonde hair that once felt so silky between my fingers is now the most disgusting mass of yuck I've ever seen, but I don't have the heart to tell her.

"How was I drunk? I only had one beer, and I don't even remember finishing it. I've never been drunk a day in my life. Last night was the first time I'd ever even been to a bar!" Despair makes her voice crack, and she sniffs behind her fingers. I lower myself to the edge of the sofa and prop my elbows on my knees, feeling the hardness of my anger dissolve beneath me. I never should have yelled at her. After the night she'd had—the girl could have been raped, for heaven's sake—it was a worthless thing to do.

Scott's mantra comes to my mind in a clarifying rush. *Acting on the moment might feel good at first, but guilt always follows right behind it.* He's talking about sex, drugs, violence and a bunch of other shameful sins, and I've made fun of him a dozen times for saying it, but he's right. It definitely applies here. Remorse weighs heavy on my shoulders, and I breathe a little prayer. I don't think she'll take this well.

"You weren't drunk. You were drugged."

Her head shoots up, pink tearstained cheeks puffed out in shock. "Drugged? By who?" But realization darkens her features the moment she asks. "The guy I was talking to? But how could he do it without me noticing? I never left the table."

I tell her everything I know, from the moment I walked out of the bathroom to find her sloshing her drink, to her confusion, to the way her body slumped sideways onto the table. When I get to the part about the guy leading her out of the bar, about witnessing the little white pill spilling from his pocket and tumbling to the ground, she visibly pales. When I tell her about the fight, about dragging her limp form out of his car and collecting the purse he tossed out of his rapidly disappearing window, I start to look around for a bucket. If this girl loses it again, I'm going to be prepared. But she gains control of herself and starts asking more questions.

"But how could I not notice? Wouldn't I have seen the pill in my glass? Wouldn't I notice the taste?"

I shake my head. "All it takes is a second. If you turned your head to look for your friends or got so enthralled by what he was saying that you didn't see his hand move toward your glass..." I shrug. "Plus, it doesn't taste like anything. That's why it's so easy for people to do."

Her eyes, now dry, narrow. It isn't hard to guess what she's thinking. "You seem to know an awful lot about it. Almost like you've used it before, yourself."

I can't help the indignant sniff that chases her accusation. "Let's just say I've had...experience."

She backs against the wall. "You know..." Her voice shakes as she says this, and once again she's afraid of me. A few years ago this wouldn't bother me. Now, I hate seeing the fear that was once so often lobbed my direction. "I don't even know who you are. Have we met before? Are you a friend of Lucy's or Ashley's or...or..." She tilts her head to study me, staying silent for so long that I grow uncomfortable. I don't remember my own mother looking at me like this, and just when I start to think about grabbing my clothes and getting the heck out of here, she speaks. "You're the guy from the bar. The guy who spent most of the night staring at me."

I don't know what I expected to hear, but this isn't it. I also don't expect the relief that seems to radiate off her for no apparent reason. It embarrasses me again, but I don't know why. "Don't flatter yourself. I wasn't staring."

Oh, I stared. And she'd just called me out on it.

"Yes you were. Every time I glanced at the bar, you were looking right at me. It made me pretty uncomfortable, if you want the truth. I don't enjoy being looked at like I'm someone's next meal."

Next meal?

Defensiveness. It's my fallback. My life raft. "I was only staring because of that god-awful coat you were wearing. I've never seen anyone wear that color of pink on purpose. You looked like a giant bottle of Pepto Bismol. Like Reese Witherspoon in full *Legally Blonde* mode, completely out of place in that nightclub. So sue me if I couldn't quit looking at you. Every guy in the bar was probably looking at you, because you stood out like a shiny pink bubble gum wrapper."

Not exactly the truth. Remembering back, I was staring at her for two reasons. One, because something told me I should be. Turns out that feeling was right. And two—the less profound reason—because she was freakin' hot. But nice to know my talent for lying hasn't died.

She bites her lip and her eyes pool at the corners once again, not the reaction I anticipated. "My aunt gave me that coat, along with the robe you're wearing. She had breast cancer a few years back—almost died from it. After a double mastectomy and two years on and off radiation, she barely made it out with her life." She swipes at her bottom lashes and looks at me.

Something twists deep in my gut. "I'm sorry. If I had known..." There's really nothing else to say. The girl has been through so much, and I go and criticize her coat. Crap on the bottom of a shoe is too kind to describe me right now.

She sniffs. "It's okay. We're all so grateful now. Since then, she's become really involved in the Susan G. Komen foundation, which is a really big organization that supports cancer research. And since they're known for the color pink..." She shrugs. "...I have a lot of pink in my closet. To support her. And all she's been through. God rest her soul."

I blink at her. And then huff some air. "You're a con woman."

She has the gall to look indignant, then adds to the drama by pressing fingertips to her eyes. "I beg your pardon? I just spill out my life's worst tragedy so far, and you call me a con woman? Just because I like to wear the color pink in my precious aunt's honor." She actually grabs her chest and gasps.

I laugh. "You belong in jail." I'm aware there's a small chance I could be wrong about the whole acting thing, but I'll take my chances. "Ten to twenty with no possibility of parole for laying it on too thick."

She tries to stare me down, but gives up and rolls her eyes. A cute grin tilts her mouth, followed by a wince that lets me know her head still hurts. "What gave me away?"

I shake my head. "The fake tears didn't help, but the "God rest her soul" pretty much sealed the deal." The robe I'm wearing slips a notch, so I tighten it and cross my arms, aware that I look ridiculous. I don't miss the way she glances at my chest, specifically at my eagle tattoo visible at the neckline. She looks like she wants to ask about it, but quickly changes her mind.

"Yeah, the moment that line came out I regretted it." She regards me with a tilt of her head before that smile returns, and then holds out her hand. "I'm Kate."

I reach for her hand, but all I can think is that she goes by Kate, not Kathryn. Kate...like the princess. Kate...the future queen. For the dumbest second, I find myself wishing my name was William. Sometimes I'm so lame, I want to punch my own self in the face. It's a disease I've never been able to shake.

"I'm Caleb."

"Well, Caleb." She eyes my chest again, which suddenly grows uncomfortably warm. If I think she's turned on by my rock-hard physique, she quickly kills that thought. "Mind if I ask why you're *really* wearing my robe?"

Like I said—lame.

"Because, Kate," I say, trying to sound as tough as standing here in pink ruffles will allow, "as much as I enjoyed taking care of you all night, there's only so much vomit I'm comfortable wearing for more than an hour or so. Three hours ago, I located some detergent and what I assume passes for your washing machine. It's the smallest thing I've ever seen and who stacks a dryer on top of a washer anyway? So a couple hours ago I threw them in, right before I collapsed on your sofa."

Her face lost its color somewhere around the word *detergent*, then recovered it in a raging red rush by the time I made it to *dryer*. "I threw up on you?"

"It's only one of many interesting things that happened."

I hoped she might laugh it off, but she manages only a groan. "Do I want to hear this?"

I shrug. "You might not like hearing it, but I'm sure as heck gonna enjoy telling it." I fill her in on the horrors of the past few hours, describing in gloriously evil detail the way she kissed me. I might have embellished a few points. Like her use of tongue and eagerly roaming hands. Hey, my life has been boring as of late, and the way I see it, the look on her face is the cheap entertainment I deserve.

Not fair, I know. And hardly chivalrous of me.

But then I keep expecting her to call me on it. To tell me to cut the crap. She never does. She also never smiles that sweet smile again. And even though I've only known her for a few short hours…

I find myself missing it.

8

Kate

"You Spin Me Right Round"
—Dead or Alive

The water runs in an icy stream, and I sit on the edge of the tub to test it with my fingers, letting it glide over my skin in a chilly cascade. Our water heater is ancient and nothing much happens. Nothing but cold, like the snow covering the ground on this late-November morning.

Slowly, it warms. It warms, and I close my eyes.

Five times. I threw up on him *five* times. And according to that long, horrifying account I just heard, he used up four towels to mop the grime off my hair and body, changed my sheets twice, and spent two uncomfortable hours curled up like a hibernating squirrel on my sofa built for two in the girliest robe I own. I didn't mention the brown terry cloth one hanging in the back of my closet that I stole from my dad before leaving for college. Something told me this Caleb guy wouldn't appreciate the humor.

Though he does seem kind. And caring. And sweet. And full of about a thousand pounds of BS with that load of crap story he just told about me shoving my tongue down his throat. And roving hands? Please. My hands haven't roved—is that a word?—over anyone, ever. Hence the birthday trip to the bar that my friends insisted we take. Their mission: To make sure I stayed sober. Their other mission: To cure me of my twenty-one-year-old virginity. As if purity is a disease. Their accomplishment: To assure with complete certainty that I will never speak to any of them again, as long as I live.

From now on, I'm only speaking to Caleb. The tattooed, not-quite-as-scary-as-I-first-thought guy I don't even know currently changing out of my pink robe in the living room. Not many guys that look like him would bring a girl home from a bar without taking advantage of her. Maybe an unfair assumption, but it's my private one. But as for this particular hell-raiser-looking guy—he's proven himself harmless. It's for that reason alone that I'm not afraid of him. Maybe I should be, but my instincts are usually right.

And right now, they're screaming that I need a shower.

I peel off my combination of sticky and crusty birthday dress and step out of it, vowing to burn the thing as soon as I exit the bathroom. It smells like a sewer. For that matter, so do I. Even Caleb in that ridiculous robe looked more dignified than I feel right now.

I sigh and reach into the cabinet for a towel as my mind grows certain of something: I will never again be able to put that pink robe on my body. Not after seeing the way Caleb what's-his-name filled it out like a Greek god in a quest to conquer my living room. And conquer it he did. Filled the entire space with his intimidating, beautiful presence, no matter how I tried to act unaffected by the vision.

I can hear the slam of the dryer door coming from the other room. At this rate, he'll be dressed long before me. That thought kicks me into motion—I don't want him leaving before I have another chance to see him—and I spring into action. Shampoo. Razor. Shaving cream. Soap. After making sure it's all lined up on the edge of the tub, I flip around for my toothbrush and a tube of toothpaste. Squeezing a little out, I pop it in my mouth and begin to work some magic.

And that's when I finally look up at my reflection in the mirror.

And scream.

"What is in my hair?"

Toothpaste sprays out of my mouth and onto the mirror, and the

Greek god in the other room begins to cackle. I stare at myself in horror through the shower of white spots.

Oh yeah—and begin to envision ways to personally toss that laughing Adonis into a black temple of doom.

"Princess, where did you get this incredible record collection?" Caleb says when I step into the living room. After washing my hair twice because one time didn't successfully remove all traces of last night's dinner—grilled cheese and tomato soup, once a favorite of mine but a meal that has now spiraled into something I will never touch again even if starving children in Africa personally serve it to me—I threw on a sweatshirt and black yoga pants, ran a brush through my wavy hair, then made a mad dash for the door despite the drum still thudding a muted beat in my head. Twenty minutes had passed. Twenty long minutes that I was certain would find Caleb tired of waiting around and long gone.

I was wrong. Right now, he's crouched down in front of my bookcase, flipping through my albums one by one. A few lay at his feet—which are expertly covered in the coolest biker boots I've ever seen, all studded and unlaced and scuffed enough to add to his already unassuming ruggedness—and it doesn't escape my notice that he's pulled out my favorites. Led Zepplin. Journey. Deftones. An old bubble-gum-pop Tiffany album that I can't bring myself to part with. Yet this isn't what keeps my mind stuck on pause, momentarily unable to process watching him as he reaches for vintage Madonna and brings it to his face. I can't think, because…

Princess? Did he just call me princess?

Something warm and tingly travels through me, but I sure as heck don't dwell on it. A lot of girls might turn to a pool of melted flesh and bones when a guy endears them with a nickname, but I'm not one of them.

"Princess, did you hear me?"

Okay, so maybe I am. My heart gives a little flip, which is nuts since I only met the guy an hour ago. He could be a serial killer for all I know. A serial killer who doesn't kill, wound, or touch a hair on his victim's head—even though said victim is knocked out and drugged seven ways from Sunday afternoon.

Clearly he's not a serial killer.

"You know, I had those records alphabetized for a reason, and now you've messed them all up." I snatch my *Like a Virgin* LP away with an irritation I don't really feel, but it gives me back some of that dignity I just felt puddle round my bare feet. At least I think it does. I shove my chin up a notch for extra emphasis. There.

My attitude seems to amuse him, and he looks up at me with a barely legal grin that has surely made countless girls before me lose their good judgment. "I might not look like much," he says, "but I did manage to learn my alphabet by my junior year in high school. Tell you what, if I have trouble with any of the letters, I'll let you put them back for me. Deal?"

I give him a look, then hand the record back and sink to the floor to join him, trying and failing to conceal a smile. "Deal. But that doesn't mean you can pull them all out—hey, slow down!" I'm sitting there with my mouth hanging open while, in a matter of seconds, a dozen more records have joined the pile. Just because I'm so accommodating doesn't mean he should disrespect the system I have going here. After all, I didn't spend an entire week last summer grouping these by name, genre, style, album color, male artists, female artists, release year, and Billboard best-sellers for nothing. It takes a lot of work—not to mention charts, graphs, and extensive case studies—to perfect an arrangement this intricate.

Kate, you are the classic description of OCD. People could do research on you.

Lucy's description of me on the first day we met comes back to sock me in my fragile ego, and I straighten my shoulders. She was so not right.

I eye the albums, hoping his hands are clean.

"What I meant to say is, be careful not to bend them. I've been collecting this particular set for years, and I would hate to see any of them damaged." They *look* clean.

"How long?"

I drag my eyes to his face. "How long what?"

Caleb's amusement only grows, as does his smile. This boy is dangerous, and I'm pretty sure he knows it. "How long have you been collecting these?" He pulls an album out of the tight space it's currently sitting in. It takes work to keep myself from gasping a little, but I'm the only person who's *ever* touched that one. "Take Velvet Underground here…" He dangles the album in question from two fingers and the vinyl slips out of the sleeve a little. He doesn't appear to notice. It's all I can do not to scream and snatch it away. These are my babies. My life's work. And he's treating them like nothing but cheap lined plastic inside old musty cardboard. What an uninformed, perfect idiot. "How long have you had it?"

"Um…" The vinyl slips a little more, and my eyes go wide. "I bought it for my sixteenth birthday, so exactly five years." My voice squeaks on that last word, and I feel my hand twitch by my side. If I could…just…grab it.

"And you're how old now?" Caleb touches the edge of the black sphere—touches it!—and pushes it back inside with one finger.

"Twenty—" I clear my throat. "Twenty one yesterday."

"Twenty one." He says it like a question, like he can't believe my oldness. What, do I look like a kid? Because most people say that I'm mature for my age, that I'm—

"Twenty one," he continues. "With a collection like this. A collection you've alphabetized, categorized, and organized with the precision of a pediatric heart surgeon. Which I find interesting. Because for someone so old and with such an extensive compilation, you don't seem to appreciate that this particular album is worth more than what some people pay for a car. So tell me, Princess, why in the world is it just sitting out unprotected on a cheap shelf that I know came from Wal-Mart?"

Now who's the idiot?

He's been playing me the whole time.

I finally reach out and take it. "That's not funny! If you knew how much it cost, why did you handle it so carelessly? Do you know what would've happened if it had slipped and cracked? Ten thousand dollars, straight down the toilet."

"Trust me, I wouldn't let it fall. I won't do anything that might result in you throwing up again. But...ten thousand dollars? And you bought it yourself?"

"Trust fund," I say sheepishly. It occurs to me that I shouldn't be talking about this to a perfect stranger, but something tells me he's honest. And except for the guy in the bar last night, my judgment hasn't failed me yet. Besides, starting now I'm no longer going to count that guy, because I'm ninety-nine percent sure that if drugs hadn't been a factor, I wouldn't have given him more than the cursory five minutes. Okay, ninety-eight percent. And maybe ten minutes, tops. Ninety-seven. Probably ninety-seven. And possibly one dance.

"Are you finished working out whatever problem you're trying to solve in your head?" Caleb says, breaking me free of my mental calculating. "Because I made three phone calls and took a short nap in the time you drifted off to sea."

"I did not drift off. I'm still sitting here, same as you."

"Well, grab a life raft anyway and answer my question." He begins slipping albums back onto the shelf, painstakingly checking name, title, and color as he goes to get them in the right order. I like him a little more.

"I already told you, I got the money from a trust fund. But don't be getting any ideas." I pick up my Tiffany album and slip it back where it belongs.

"Wouldn't dream of it. But your raft's a little leaky, because that wasn't my question."

I blink twice. "Oh. Well, what was it?"

"I said, *Princess…*" He draws out that silly nickname until I feel myself blushing. "Are you interested in breakfast? Think of it as my attempt to acknowledge your birthday a day late. Which I would apologize for, except that this time yesterday I didn't even know you existed. So sorry about the no gift thing." He tilts his head to look at me. "Think your stomach can handle it?"

On cue, it growls. Eggs, bacon, pancakes, a vat of black coffee. It all sounds good right now, especially considering the night I had.

Turns out Caleb is a mind reader.

"And just so you know, I was going to ask you before the trust fund came up. I'm not interested in your money, so stuff that thought away where it belongs."

Maybe I should be insulted, but I find myself fighting back a grin. "In that case, take me to the biggest buffet you can find. Because I could eat enough for you and me combined."

9

Caleb

"I'm About to Come Alive"

—Train

I used to spend hours and hours making my Christmas list. From the moment the last remnants of my birthday wrapping paper were stuffed into the trash—which is the first of September, by the way—my five-year-old mind would plot ways to get the latest Transformer, the newest video game, the hottest trading cards. Then the Sears Catalog would arrive sometime around Thanksgiving, and the list expanded. Skateboards. Roller blades. The coolest Ninja Turtle sleeping bag I'd ever seen—so much better than freckle-faced, red-headed loser Jason Setzer's who lived next door to me and dragged his Ninja Turtle bag out every time I came over just to rub it in my face. My Christmas list rocked. The only thing that topped it were the actual presents themselves. They were great. The stuff childhood dreams are made of.

I got that sleeping bag the year I turned six. Slept in it every night for months.

By the time I turned seven, Christmas lists were a thing of the past. By then, there was nothing left to wish for.

"Next time you'll think twice before challenging me to a contest you can't win," I say, dragging the last of my hash browns through ketchup and forking the bite into my mouth. I savor it like the four pancakes, three eggs, and two biscuits before it. Until my mouth stills, followed by my heart rate when both process the words I've just spoken out loud.

Next time.

I don't *do* next time.

Not where girls are concerned. Especially not where hot, gorgeous, keeping-my-pulse-at-an-unsteady-rhythm girls are concerned. Girls leave. *Everyone* leaves. At least that's the case for me.

But too late, I realize the implication of my words. It's a pretty big assumption, though I realize with a start, not one I'm all that averse to. This time yesterday, the mere suggestion of a "next time" where a girl was concerned would've had me howling with laughter. Look at me now. In just a matter of hours—not even enough time for the sun to make a full rotation on its dang axis—I've let this girl in the tacky pink coat turn into someone I don't want to say goodbye to. I *want* a next time. I find myself hoping for more than one.

Which is why I force myself to get a grip.

But unless she's a really good actress or just immune to suggestive comments, she doesn't flinch. Even the skin on her pretty face doesn't change color. Thank goodness.

"You are a pig," she says. "No girl alive could win a contest with a pig." She picks up her coffee and drains it, then snatches her spoon and cuts into her cinnamon apples, only half of which she's eaten. "And let me tell you something else—"

"Please do. I'm dying to hear it," I deadpan.

She spears me with a look. "Sitting across from you while you shovel food in your mouth is about as attractive as *watching* said pig roll around in manure after he's finished his dinner. It's disgusting. Vile. Too much for another human to have to endure."

"It can't be worse than watching you talk with your mouth full…" I can see bits of apple rolling around in there.

"A million times worse."

"…Or having you puke all over me. Five times." Thankfully, no apples involved last night.

That does it. The blush that eluded me a minute ago has returned full-force, along with a sudden inability to look my direction. She swallows and becomes preoccupied with making sure her dirty utensils are perfectly aligned with her equally dirty plate. Then she reaches for the salt and pepper shaker, beginning what looks like an imaginary game of chess. Just when I start to feel bad for my stupid joke, she looks up.

"I'm really sorry about that. As long as I live, I'm not sure I'll be able to get over the humiliation." The salt goes right, the pepper goes left. Checkmate.

"Nothing to be embarrassed about." I shrug. "Despite all the complaining I did earlier in your apartment, it wasn't *all* bad. Considering what could have happened to you, I was happy to be there. I'm just glad you're okay."

It must have been the right thing to say—not that I'm overly concerned with saying the right thing. Sometimes the right thing hurts, sometimes it's harsh, sometimes it isn't what another person wants to hear. In this case, it's the truth. She smiles and looks me in the eye for the first time in minutes. I reach across the table for a triangle peg board game and start playing, red jumping over white in an attempt to be the last one standing.

She still has that smile on her lips when she asks, "Why Princess?" and turns to grab a game off the table behind her. After a quick inspection that I'm pretty sure involved checking for visible amoebas—I remember the stash of handy wipes in her apartment—we both start jumping our own separate pieces and a contest ensues. I'm determined to win.

"You're kidding, right? Isn't it obvious?" I lay a white peg on the table and steal a glance at her, aware of how hot irresistible she looks competing with me.

She flips a yellow over red and discards the peg beside her. "Not to me. I've never been into super-girly things before, and no one's ever called me that."

I'm down to six pegs. I sit up a little straighter and study the board, knowing there has to be a way to make this work. "First of all, as the guy who saw you in a pink coat with fur trim and then slept in your equally tacky ruffled pink robe that your dying aunt *did not give you*, I'm having a little trouble believing the 'I'm not girly' part. Second of all, the name fits. Princess? As in, Kate?" When I glance up to see her frown at me, it's all I can do not to roll my eyes. This girl *looks* cultured. She doesn't strike me as the airhead type you often see on Jimmy Fallon who can't even name our current President. "Kate," I say, "as in the future queen of England? Geez, girl. What are they not teaching you at school? You are in college, right?"

She smiles to herself. I'm pretty sure she likes the nickname. I'm definitely sure I like that smile. "What gave me away?" She's down to four, but she is so not winning this.

"The OU sweatshirt I saw hanging in your closet. It still had the tags on it, and looked brand new. So what's your major?"

"Pre-Law with a minor in Child Development." Another peg bites the dust.

"Interesting combination. Graduation day?" Three left for me.

"Next May. If I don't bomb my term paper." Her last two pegs are three spaces apart. With a longsuffering sigh, she shoves her board away and glares at mine. In every way you slant it, the outcome of my game looks promising. "I'll need to start it after Christmas break, because it will take me all semester to write."

"For what class?" Not trying to be a jerk here, but I bite my lip on a smile, because I'm down to two pegs, and they're sitting side by side.

"Human growth and development." She narrows her gaze. "We're supposed to find a person to study—a kid who maybe doesn't have the best home life or other less-than-perfect situation. Sounds easy, but it's a little awkward trying to find someone like that without sounding rude. '*Excuse me,*' she mimics, '*are you homeless? Does your dad beat you? If so, mind if I ask you a few questions over the next three months?*—not exactly the easiest thing to ask. Anyway, we're supposed to follow them, interview them, and that sort of—" She growls at the same moment I set the last red peg on the table. "I can't believe you won that game. I've never won, not once." She sits back with a thud. "You can probably do a Rubik's Cube too." Reaching into her purse, she produces a bottle, then squirts some clear gel in her hand.

I eye her movements. "I can do one in under two minutes. Do you always use that junk?"

She gives me a look. "Bull. And this isn't junk." She drops the bottle inside and rubs her hands together. "Do you know how many lives have been saved by the ingredients in this stuff?" She holds up her hands.

"Lives are saved in the emergency room. Not inside a bottle of Germ-X." I make a face. "But if you're up for finding a Wal-Mart next, I'll buy a Rubik's Cube and show you how it's done." I sit back, thinking about flexing my muscles, but then I remember I'd be gloating over a square game designed to keep a preschooler entertained, and think better of it.

"No. I believe you. Though I'll pick one up the next time I go."

I try not to smile at the implication that we'll see each other again. It occurs to me then that I might be ruined...that in maybe another hour or so I could be whipped beyond recognition. This girl—competitive, beautiful, sarcastic, with a record collection I might die for.

That grip I had a short time ago is already beginning to come undone.

A few minutes later, we've made our way across the street to an outdoor shopping mall. With its vast blacktop parking lot and freshly lined spaces, the area smells like a country theme park—the kind that combines thrill rides and kettle corn with churned butter and nineteenth-century-style dress. I've been to Branson a few times in my life—everyone from Oklahoma has. It's our Disney World in the Midwest, and it's what I think of every time I walk these sidewalks.

The shopping center isn't the kind of place that attracts hoards of customers, since the store that keeps the whole place in business is an arts and crafts establishment that sells scrapbooking material, ceramic pottery, and Christmas trees under the same roof. But the area is buzzing with activity. Bundled-up women and a few men emerge with bags bulging with Christmas wrapping and ornaments, and I even see a few artificial trees in giant boxes being wheeled away on flat carts. The season is in full swing, and I find myself growing kind of excited.

"What's that smile for?" Kate asks, stepping off the curb with me. I look over at her, eyeing the blonde curls that frame her shoulders from underneath a wool gray hat. I can still feel the way they felt running through my hands when she kissed me...

I give myself a mental slap. It isn't fair to think about that when she doesn't even remember doing it.

"I like Christmas." I shrug, as though I'm not thinking about what her lips felt like pressed against mine. "It's my favorite holiday." Now. Again. As a kid, I loved it—the toys and the presents and the parties and the carols. But like a new Spiderman Band-Aid my mother once enthusiastically placed over some wound or another, it was ripped away with a painful sting. No more fun. No more excitement. No more color. No more anything. It took years, and a few life lessons, to get me loving it again. Now, I get wound up just thinking about the season's magic and miracles. Not something I would admit out loud, though. I *am* a guy with a reputation to uphold.

Beside me, I see Kate shiver. At first I think it's from the cold, until her next words come out. They're laced with more resignation than this pink-loving girl should ever feel. "Not me. I wish we could skip right over that holiday."

I look over at her, certain she's joking, but her serious expression blows that theory. "Sounds like someone has had one too many stockings filled with coal. Naughty kid?"

"More like a kid who never had a stocking at all." Her hands are shoved in her coat pockets—a normal black wool coat this morning—

and she's looking into the window of a furniture store, though I'm pretty sure she's not actually in the market for a sofa. Not that she shouldn't be—her current one sucks. It's more like she's looking past it, into a memory that she doesn't like. Just when I decide to file her statement into the I Have No Response folder in my brain, my mouth opens and blows that plan.

"Your parents aren't into the holidays, are they?" I kick at a chipped piece of concrete directly in my path. "Sounds like we were raised by the same type of people." If adults knew what kind of damage they were capable of inflicting on kids, no one would ever have them. Although for some so-called parents, cramming as much harm as possible in eighteen years' time—or in my case, eleven—seems to be part of the fun. If asked, I could count several right now who enjoy that sort of thing and run out of fingers trying.

Kate is quiet so long I'm not sure what to think. I look over at her and see that she's wrestling with something. Her mouth is working and her forehead is scrunched up and she looks kind of worried. Finally, she locks eyes with me. Something about that look concerns me, but I can't pinpoint it. And then she smiles, a sad smile, really. I'll admit that it's soft and warm and does all kinds of crazy things to my insides, but I won't admit much else. The word *whipped*, however, does cross my mind again for the smallest second.

"No Caleb, they weren't. They were never real big on Christmas. Still aren't, if you want the truth."

I don't. Want the truth, I mean. Because frankly, that sort of truth just sucks. No toy catalog? No lists? No cookies left out for Santa? What kind of twisted parents does this girl have? I think about what she says for a moment. I can't help it, because I'm a fixer. A schemer. Both a fault and an asset to my personality, according to my mother. I like to solve things, and this is definitely one area that needs solving, now. It doesn't take long for a plan to form. Even less time for me to announce it.

"That's the most pathetic thing I've ever heard. You need an intervention. Now."

"I never asked for one." Not the response I expected, but I can work with it.

"Lucky for you I don't usually wait for permission."

I expect a retort, but she doesn't give me one. So I take her hand and walk her across the parking lot. An innocent gesture to the outside observer, but I've never been more aware of the feel of a girl's hand in my life. I want to hold it as long as she'll let me, but she lets go too soon.

Once we're at the destination I have in mind, I reach for the door and pull her inside, ignoring the look she flashes that suggests she's seriously questioning my masculinity. Judging by the smell of artificial cinnamon and old-lady perfume currently blasting up my nose, the look isn't without merit.

"In the market for silk flowers and yarn, are you?" she teases.

"Yes, for the toilet paper cozies I'm making for Christmas gifts. Let's see, your bathroom was blue, right? I should remember, but I didn't pay that much attention in between running for more towels."

She laughs and bumps my arm as she brushes past me, unintentionally giving me a good view of her backside. I wish she wasn't so darn attractive because it makes it impossible to look away, as I should be doing right now. I force my eyes to a shopping cart filled with ninety-percent off Halloween decorations and mentally conjure up images of zombies and serial-killers stabbed through the heart to distract myself. It helps, but only a little.

"Yes, it's blue, and how do you know about cozies?" she asks over her shoulder.

In truth, I know about them from grandmas and aunts and Wednesday night pot-lucks. No way I'm telling her that, though. "Don't you wish you knew?" There. That sounded mysterious, right?

"Actually, I don't," she says.

Okay, maybe not.

Brat. I reach for her arm and lead her down one aisle, then another.

It surprises me that she doesn't tell me to let go, but she doesn't, just goes along with my seemingly aimless walking. It isn't until the third aisle that she stops short, nearly causing me to bump into her from behind.

"Why are we here?" Her voice is tight, and the expression on her face is almost anxious, but there's some wonder in there as well. Even though her cautious gaze confuses me, it's the wonder I see that tells me my decision was the right one, with or without permission. I move next to her and look up. About two feet up, if the sign in front of me is right.

"I need a Christmas tree, and I want you to help me pick one out." I don't really need one, but it seems like an inspired idea, one to get her out of the miserable Christmas slump her parents have dumped her in. "It's the first step in my three-part intervention program to cure you of your holiday aversion. Pass this one, and you get to move on to helping me choose a stocking. Pass *that* one, and you'll make it to the last one. It's a secret." I feel myself nodding as if I know what the heck I'm talking about. I made this whole thing up two seconds ago, and it appears I'm going home with a tree I don't even want. I make a mental note to hang on to the receipt.

"So go ahead, Kate. Pick your favorite."

10

Kate

"Not Myself"

—John Mayer

I must look like a caged animal, frightened beyond my comfort zone, completely threatened and twitchy. Because it's exactly how I feel. Christmas trees? Stockings? And a mysterious third thing that scares me even more than the time my father threw me off the diving board to teach me how to swim. In his defense, I was eight years old and had wasted three years of lessons. Hundreds of dollars spent and I still couldn't manage a dog paddle. In my defense, dog paddling is awkward and splashy and completely without technique. Who wants to move around in a pool using only their wrists? Not me. Definitely not me. In my younger mind, if I couldn't swim the right way, I didn't want to do it at all.

But this. *This.*

"Do you still live with your parents?" A stupid question, but it's all I can think to say. What if he says yes? How am I supposed to respond?

The look in his eyes catches me off guard, and a small part of my panic subsides. For the briefest second, he looks sad. I've seen that kind of regret before, and all at once I know there's a story behind this guy's mega-cool demeanor. I want to know what it is.

He recovers quickly. "No." He draws out the word. "Just because I want a tree doesn't mean—"

"Then what's the point of a stocking? It seems like a waste to buy one that will sit empty on Christmas morning, since no one's there to fill it for you."

When he clutches his chest and takes a halting step backward, I can't help the way my mouth involuntarily lifts at the corners. He is so darn cute when he acts wounded. "Oh Kate, Kate, Kate. You of little faith. You're killing me—first with your no Christmas and then with your blatant disbelief in Santa Claus. Next you'll be telling me the Easter Bunny isn't real."

When I raise an eyebrow, his eyes go wide in mock horror. Wanting an excuse to touch him, I slap his arm. "Stop being so dramatic. Do you want me to help pick out a tree, or not?"

"Yes, and hurry up about it. We don't have all night."

"It's noon."

"Exactly. Daylight's burning, Princess. Now choose a tree before they sell out of all of them."

I smile to myself at the nickname he's assigned to me. Something tells me it's permanent. Something tells me I'm glad about it. Something also tells me he's ridiculous—there are stacks of trees in cardboard boxes all around us. The only way they'll sell out now is if a fairy godmother waves her magic wand and makes them disappear.

Fairy Godmothers. Something else I never believed in.

Fifteen minutes later I've abandoned my apprehension, and the tree is being carted to the front of the store. I can't deny that I'm a tiny bit proud of myself. Buying a Christmas tree isn't as easy as it sounds, what with the height, the color, the shape of the branches, and the lights. And even though Caleb told me to pick one out for him, the guy is incredibly picky. He wanted a green, pre-lit eight-footer sporting thin branches. He put his foot down when I gravitated toward the tree covered in fake snow, saying nothing kills the spirit of Christmas more than dried paint trying to pass itself off as the cold white stuff.

I refrained from pointing out that fake trees with fake snow didn't seem much different than a fake guy in a red suit shimmying down a chimney. Somehow the timing didn't seem right.

Regardless, I'm now foraging through stockings, up to my elbows in all kinds of tacky fabrics while Caleb calls out instructions.

"Only red ones."

"Or maybe green."

"But nothing with sparkles."

"And definitely nothing with glitter."

"I'm *not* buying that. Put it back now."

Funny how in such a short time, his cool-factor has worn off. Now, I find him as annoying as a greasy-haired kid in kindergarten who insists on poking me in the side and showing me his latest scab. I drag myself to a standing position and glare up at him. I'm pretty sure a loose price tag is stuck in my hair, but I don't stop to remove it.

"Has anyone ever told you that you're a pain in the butt?"

"Only every day." At the first sign of a grin, I realize he's been doing this on purpose. It doesn't make it any less maddening. If he thinks I'll find it adorable, he's wrong.

"Well, they're right. Christmas shopping with you is now on my list of things I never want to do again. My first time doing it, and you've managed to ruin the whole thing."

If I thought he might be hurt, I thought wrong. His grin only widens. It looks…adorable. "What did you expect for an intervention? For me to go easy on you?"

I don't say that, yes, that's exactly what I expected. Stupid me. Before I have time to reflect on my idiocy, he reaches toward my ear and plucks off the offending tag. My breath catches when he brushes it against my cheek. "Huh." He frowns, glancing at the tag. "You seem worth more than nine dollars and ninety-nine cents. A *lot* more. Millions, even."

He flicks the tag to the floor, and my traitorous heart seems to fall in search of it. But first it flips once, bangs into my pulse, jumps into my throat, then collapses somewhere around my feet. That was the nicest thing anyone has said to me in years. I catch his eye, and neither one of us looks away.

"See something you want?" His voice sounds thick. Tense. He clears his throat and nods to my hand. "For me, I mean. Is that the one you like?"

At first I'm unsure what he's referring to, and then I look down. I'm holding a gaudy pink Christmas stocking shaped like a slipper, complete with sparkles, glitter, and everything he just finished lecturing me against. I shrug, deciding right then to just go for it. "Yes. This is it. And don't even think about putting it back. After everything I've just gone through, it would totally hurt my feelings."

To my surprise, he reaches for it. "A stocking fit for a princess. I wouldn't dream of putting it back." He tucks it under his arm and turns to walk away, leaving me staring after him like the infatuated servant girl I apparently am. Give me a mop and bucket, and I'd probably drop to the floor and start singing about my prince arriving while blue birds gather at my feet and field mice stitch me a dress.

"You coming, Princess?"

I find myself nodding, following after him. Of course I am.

Like the famous saying goes, the third time *is* the charm. He bought me a present. An intervention present. I've never had a Christmas gift before, and it doesn't even matter that it's a bag of sour Gummy Worms. I suck the sugar off my fourth one and dig out one for Caleb.

"Want one?"

"I can't believe of all the things in that store, this is what you picked out for your gift," he says. "These barely even qualify as a stocking stuffer, let alone a first-time intervention gift." He makes a face, but reaches for the worm anyway and pops it in his mouth. The Christmas tree is stuffed in the back of his truck and we're almost back to my apartment. I have no idea what happens when we get there, but I'm sure of one thing. I don't want this day to end.

"Don't criticize my taste in gifts. I never got to eat these as a kid, and when I saw your wallet open and ready, well… My only regret is that I didn't make you buy me two bags." I lick my fingers, more than aware that if my mother could see me now, she'd probably faint. Maybe that adds to the appeal of the worms, maybe not. I love my mother, but sometimes she's too focused on the sour to enjoy the sweet.

These worms are definitely sweet.

At least until we pull into the parking space in front of my apartment, and then everything turns bitter. Lucy is at the front door, struggling to make her key turn in the lock. She pulls it out and whacks it a few times, then promptly drops it into a planter filled with last summer's now-dead fern. Watching her drop to her knees is more entertaining that I should admit. Seeing dirt fly as she digs through the planter makes me want to grab popcorn and kick back in my seat. If I wasn't harboring any leftover resentment toward her for leaving me at the bar with a psychopath, I might jump out to help. As it is, I let her fumble, consoled by the knowledge that she likely has the world's worst hangover wrapped in a treacherous headache.

"Looks like your roommate made it home," Caleb says, with a hint of amusement in his voice. I turn to look at him, glad to see that he's finding the situation as entertaining as I am.

"Looks like it."

"Think we should get out to help her?" Lucy stands and jabs the key into the lock again. Her hair looks like a tangled mass of cobwebs, she's wearing one shoe, and her sweater is on backwards. I wonder if she even knows how awful she looks.

"Probably. But I'm not going to," I say.

"Good answer. Because I'm not going to either." He smiles, but then seems to think better of it. "Not that I'm not a gentleman, because I really do believe in helping women out and—"

"If you set one foot out of the car to give her a hand, I'll kill you."

He laughs and runs a hand across the steering wheel. "I'll admit my life could be better, but it's the only one I've got, so I think I'll sit here for a while."

"Good decision."

We sit in silence, which isn't uncomfortable as long as we have Lucy to entertain us. But then she walks into the apartment and closes the door, and the reality that we're completely alone descends inside the car like a wild-eyed monster. Suddenly, I can't think of a thing to say, even though my mind is shooting off ideas like a ranger blasting silver bullets. *Talk about the weather. What about the stock market? Ask him if he likes football.* But I hate football, so what would I follow it up with? Frantic and frustrated, I move on to the benefits of wearing sunscreen, my doubts about Global Warming, the outrageous price of milk. *The price of milk?* It's at this point that I'm fairly sure I'm insane. I've been with this guy for—I check my watch—nearly four hours now, and I choose *this moment* to get nervous.

"Are you finished freaking out over there? Because I swear I won't bite. Not even a little," Caleb says.

I look at him, trying my best to appear clueless. "I don't know what you mean. I'm certainly not freaking out."

He shifts in his seat to get a better look at me. "In the short time we've known each other, I've managed to pick up a couple of things about you. First, you're a terrible liar."

I open my mouth to protest, but Caleb silences me with a look. "Your aunt has cancer? Give me a break." I promptly close it as he continues to point out my shortcomings.

"Second, you're a germ freak."

"I am not!" At the exact same time, we both eye a package of wet wipes not-so-discreetly hanging out of my purse. Without a word, I slip it back inside.

"Third, you have awful taste in Christmas trees."

I can't let that one go. "Who doesn't like fake snow? That's the dumbest thing I've ever heard." But he doesn't listen, just keeps talking.

"Fourth—"

"This is more than a couple."

"…and I'm not sure you're even aware of this," he continues, ignoring me, "when you're working out something in your head, you use your fingers to count off the options."

"I do not!" Still, I look down at my hands, wondering if it's true.

"A minute ago, you held up all five, one at a time. I might be wrong, but I'm pretty sure you were trying to come up with conversation starters." He gives me a slow wink. "Am I right?"

I close my eyes and swallow, so embarrassed that I'm that transparent. Why can't I be one of those mysterious girls that make guys crazy with curiosity? Like Lucy with her eager string of one-night-stands. Like every other female on the freaking planet. "So what if I was? It's kind of hard to think of things to say now that we're not eating or shopping. It's not like you were doing any better, leaving me over here sweating and unable to come up with anything—"

"Then have dinner with me."

"What?" It's so abrupt, I'm not sure I heard him right. But I find myself really hoping I did.

"Tonight." His mouth tilts in a lazy—yet hopeful—smile. "Have dinner with me. Sit across from me at a table for a couple hours in a nicer place than Cracker Barrel, and maybe we can come up with a few more things to talk about."

"Tonight?" I immediately chastise myself for sounding so uncertain. Of course I'm not uncertain. I'm flying inside.

For the first time, Caleb looks worried. "Unless you have something else to do…"

"No!" I practically shout the word, then try to recover by picking a piece of invisible lint off my yoga pants. "I mean, I have some home-work, and I need to do laundry, but I suppose it can wait until tomorrow." Something tells me I didn't quite pull off the aloofness I was going for.

When Caleb grins at me, I'm certain of it. "If you're sure the dirty t-shirts can handle lying there another day." He fiddles with a knob on his stereo. "Pick you up at seven?"

Flying. Soaring. So high in the air I feel lightheaded. I manage to shrug. "Seven sounds okay." There. *That* sounded aloof. I open the door and climb out of his truck before a thought occurs to me. "What should I wear?"

"Anything is fine. I'm pretty sure no matter what you wear, you'll still look like a princess." And with that, he drives away.

Leaving me standing in the parking lot, wishing for a fairy god-mother.

11

Caleb

"Learning To Breathe"
—Switchfoot

I never knew my father. Not even his name.

The story goes that he spent every day in the hospital with me when I was born, checking my heart monitor, asking to hold me. I was premature by two months. Two months of medical bills added up to a whole lot of debt. I guess the money got to him. After a while, he stopped coming. Why should a man be expected to pay so much for a kid he doesn't even know?

By the time I was released, he'd made his decision to leave. No one knew, not even my mother. He picked us up, smiled for a couple of pictures, wheeled us out to the car, stuffed balloons and flowers in the trunk, and drove us home. After an hour, he left to pick up dinner. He never came back.

When my mother checked his closet later that night, it was empty. All his clothes, gone. All his shoes, gone. All his money, gone. What was left of it, anyway. Most of it had been spent on me.

Turns out the saying is true; history does sometimes repeat itself.

The end of our relationship was premature, too.

Dinner with Kate turned into lunch the next day, followed by a movie later that night. And even though I know I should've played it cool the way I've always done in the past, something hasn't let me. Of course, it

71

didn't help when she emerged from her apartment that first night in a pair of tight jeans, brown leather riding boots, and an oversized cream-colored sweater looking more like a Greek goddess than a princess. With those golden locks and bright eyes, a crown of glory hovered over her the whole evening.

I straighten in my leather seat, gripping one edge of the steering wheel. This girl has latched onto my mind, my soul, my body—and worst of all, a big part of my heart, too. I still haven't kissed her, but not for lack of wanting to. It's pretty much all I think about when I'm not wondering how these feelings could consume so much of me in three short days.

Who falls this hard for a girl in three days?

It's precisely why I'm telling myself to back off now. It's time for another reality check. A lowering of expectations. A big, fat dose of Kathryn withdrawal. My cell phone sits in the cup holder and screams at me to pick it up and dial her number like I did yesterday, but I won't. I ignore the way it jumps up at me, practically convulses its way across the gearshift toward my lap, and so far I'm doing a pretty good job of snubbing it. After all, I've lived twenty-four years without letting a girl under my skin—the last five not even letting one into my bed. There's no way I'm going to do an about-face on that now and give up everything I've worked for. I reach for the phone and toss it into the backseat. There. Done. It has no power over me.

Easy to say. Easy to believe.

Still, it's what I tell myself as I drive to work Monday morning. It isn't until I exit Interstate 35 onto highway 77 that I realize I've been humming "Bibbidi Bobbidi Boo" for the last five minutes, thinking of Cinderella and Snow White and a dozen other beautiful Disney characters I remember from my early childhood. In that moment, it hits me that I've officially morphed into the world's biggest pansy. Even the frilly pink robe can't top this.

And that's where the trouble lies, because I'm not sure I want it to.

It might have looked stupid on me, but I sure liked the heck out of that robe.

"You want to tell me why you're not answering your phone? I've only called you a dozen times in the last hour." Scott walks into my office and plops down into the chair across from me, propping his feet up on my desk. It occurs to me to slap them off, but it won't do any good. It never does.

"I guess I left it in the car by accident," I lie. Three days. Only three days, and I've leapt backward to a time when lies rolled off my tongue like lime juice after a tequila shot. I don't like this new side of me. "Scratch that. I tossed it in the backseat of my car. Don't ask me to go find it."

"Why?"

"Because I don't feel like digging around to—"

"No." Scott studies me with a wary expression. "Why did you toss it in the backseat? Usually that thing is glued to you like an extra appendage. What gives?" He reaches into my candy dish for a peppermint and pops it into his mouth. My candy dish is supplied by my secretary and refilled nightly by the cleaning lady. It doesn't cost me anything. I reach for one and unwrap it, too.

"Because I don't want to hear it ring." It isn't the ringing that bothers me; it's the person who might be doing the calling. I'm not stupid. One look at Kate's name—which I've saved into my address book as 'Princess' because I'm already a whipped idiot—and I'll cave. This isn't the time for caving. This is the time for playing it cool.

"That doesn't make any sense." Scott frowns. "You've never had an aversion to—oh my gosh. It's the girl." He stares at me like he just solved the world's hardest crossword puzzle, which for Scott isn't a stretch, because he's a nerd and actually *masters* them. "You like her. You took her home the other night, and now by some way only you can manage, you wound up liking her." He stretches his hands behind is head like a smug Mob boss and smirks at me. He just needs a fedora and a cigar to complete the look. "What'd you do, ask her out?"

My gaze darts to the side before I can stop it, the clear sign of a lie. I learned that on *20/20* when I was a teenager. How can you tell if someone's lying to you? Watch their eyes. They dart to the left? Lies. All lies.

"We had breakfast."

"Just breakfast?" Scott asks.

This time I look straight at his face. I might as well confront the stupid truth. "And dinner. And lunch the next day. Followed by a movie…" By this point, I want to laugh at my own self. But why bother when Scott is doing such a swell job for me? He throws back his head and howls.

"Oh man, what has happened to you? You rescue a damsel in distress and appoint yourself her knight in shining armor. Caleb Stiles with a girlfriend. Who would've thought?"

"She's not my girlfriend. Don't say it like that. It sounds ridiculous."

He pulls his feet off the table and sits forward. "It is kind of ridiculous. Although I can't say I blame you. That girl was hot. Even passed out cold that much was obvious."

"Hot? Did you say hot?" It's my turn to laugh. "I've never heard you say that word before unless you were talking about the weather or Mrs. O'Hare's flashes."

Scott's face turns serious. "That woman won't shut up about her personal issues, and for some reason, I'm the one she's chosen to describe them to. Just last night, she was telling me about the bunion on her left foot. I'm twenty-two! I don't want to hear about bunions!"

Mrs. O'Hare is my secretary and the only woman in the human race born without an internal filter. Some people give daily weather reports. She gives updates on bunions, warts, sinus infections, and leaky appendages. But only to Scott. Lucky guy.

I hear the intimate details about her husband. Unlucky me.

"Well, I hate to break it to you, but our lawyer has called twice. So you're gonna need to find that phone of yours and call him back. The news isn't good…"

That isn't what I wanted to hear. I eye him for a few moments, trying to settle my thoughts. "There's nothing we can do?"

"He has a couple of ideas, but he didn't give me any specifics. Said he needed to talk to you before proceeding with any of them." He sighs long and slow. Neither of us saw this coming, but one of us has to deal with it, and fast. Two days. That's all the time we've got. And it looks like the responsibility has fallen on me.

"All of this because of a donkey and some hay? Is this what the world has come to?" I tent my fingers and peer over at Scott. Unbelievable. That's the only way to describe the mess we've landed in. And all because we dared to—

"It's a little more than that, I guess," he says. "But, yes. That description pretty much sums it up. Don't spend too much time stressing about it. We'll find a way through this, even if it takes a while." He pauses for a moment before that stupid grin reappears.

"What?" I ask, knowing what's coming.

"Just thinking about the girl. I'm just so proud to see that my little boy is finally growing up."

While a growl, I push back my chair and stand. "Shut up. I'm two years older than you, and mind your own business."

At that, Scott laughs. "This time next month you'll probably be buying rings."

I can't let that one go and spin to face him. "I don't do commitment. Or rings. You know that." I'll never do commitment. A person can only take so much abandonment before they decide enough is enough.

Scott's smile slips a little. "I was kidding. But now that you've brought it up, one of these days you're going to figure out that you can't spend your life alone. Never mind this girl—maybe she's just some random face that you'll never see again. But eventually, I hope you can get over your past and decide the future is worth taking a chance on. Otherwise, you'll be facing a long, lonely life."

For a long moment, I just stare at him. I don't point out that Scott isn't dating anyone either. Or that he's hardly qualified to dole out relationship advice. Or that his family is pretty much perfect and he has absolutely nothing in his closet resembling my history. Or that if I wanted his counsel I'd ask for it. I just stare. And get mad. Not at Scott, but at myself.

Because something tells me Kate isn't just a random face.

And that freaks me out more than Scott's words ever could.

"Thanks for the advice, Dr. Phil. Next time I want it, I'll write you a letter."

Scott's smile returns. Thank goodness, because I can't stand when the guy gets serious on me. In the five years I've known him, it hasn't happened often. I pull my car keys from my pocket and head out of the office. Scott follows me, but gets stopped by Mrs. O'Hare.

"Scotty, can you come over here and look at this bump on my elbow..."

Serves him right. I hear Scott sigh and pick up my pace like the crap-head friend I am. It's survival of the fittest in this office, and if it's between the two of us, I have no problem letting him die. Figuratively speaking, of course.

My phone is already ringing when I open the car door. I lunge for it and then silently curse the disappointment I didn't expect to feel when I discover that it's just a stupid telemarketer. Eight-hundred numbers should be outlawed, especially because I've paid my bills. I don't owe anyone anything, so they should leave me the heck alone. I let the call go to voice mail and stare at the screen. The disappointment was real, so now I'm faced with a dilemma.

Before I can chop them off or talk some sense into them or whatever you're supposed to do with fingers that have a mind of their own, they start dialing. Kate picks up on the third ring.

Ten minutes later, we have plans for tonight. It's Monday, and I'm mentally calculating which restaurants we should go to that won't make the wrong impression, though I'm not sure how to make the right impression, either. Something unpretentious, but definitely not cheap.

After a few seconds I give myself my own personal eye-roll. This girl makes me stupid. Or so freaking excited that my mind goes on rapid scramble mode. Either way, my brain isn't working the way it's supposed to.

I give up on it and punch in a few numbers. This time the line rings twice.

I spend the next hour talking to my lawyer.

"Vanilla," she says.

"Vanilla isn't even a real flavor. That's like saying your favorite color is white. Boring. Bland. A cop-out answer if I ever heard one. Come up with something different."

"I know what I like, and I like vanilla." She licks her cone and goes for more, leaving a little milky swirl at the corners of her mouth. I open my mouth to point it out, but decide she looks too cute and say nothing. "Besides, you can add stuff like chocolate syrup and peanut butter and Snickers bars and have yourself a whole big sundae."

"Snickers bars?"

"Don't knock it until you try it."

"Wouldn't dream of it." And then that's all I want right then, a Snickers bar. Forget the bananas; this opens a whole new world of sundaes in my mind. And that's the way my brain works. It gets on a tangent and has trouble realigning. So I force it into submission with my next question, something I've thought about ever since we ate breakfast together that very first morning. Only three days ago, but I feel like I've known Kate forever.

"So this term paper you're supposed to write. Found a subject yet?"

She sighs and stares into her ice cream like it's the saddest sight in the world. "No. Like I said, I'm not sure how to approach it. I don't know who to ask or even where to start looking."

That's what I hoped she would say. Because I'm a sick, sick individual who will use things like children and unfortunate circumstances just for an excuse to keep seeing her again. So much for playing it cool and backing off.

"Turns out that I think I can help you, if you want it." I take a bite of my cookies and cream like the entire plan I've spent three days thinking up won't kill me depending on her answer.

Pathetic: that's one word to describe me. Loser: that's another.

"How?" She looks over at me skeptically, as if wondering why I didn't mention this earlier. Why indeed? Because scheming and plotting take time, that's why.

"I'm a Big Brother to a foster kid, and I visit him every week." I leave out the rest of it. One thing at a time. "I'm going to see him in the morning. If you want to, you could come along with me and talk with him. He's a great kid, and I don't think he would mind."

I crinkle up the wrapper from my vanished cone and drop it in a wastebasket outside the ice cream shop, then shove my hand in my pocket and turn to face her just in time to see her using her tongue to catch a drop of melted vanilla sliding down her chin. I quickly focus on the OPEN sign hanging to the right of the door. I can't watch her that way. I'm a guy, after all. A guy whose mind just took a dip in the gutter and went for a swim.

I clear my throat. "So, what do you think? Interested?"

A look of pure exasperation crosses her face. "Of course I'm interested. Why didn't you say something sooner?" She tosses her own wrapper into the trash and looks at me.

"I guess I just thought of it," I lie.

"Well, I guess someone has a really bad memory. What other secrets are you keeping in that closet of yours?"

"No secrets, and definitely no closets," I say. Another lie. With every second that ticks on the clock, I'm growing more jumbled up and crazy because of this girl I barely know. But when she smiles and moves in beside me, something inside me settles.

Before I can question the wisdom of it, I reach for her hand. When she responds by linking her fingers through mine, I feel like I can breathe.

And that's when I realize it.

I haven't breathed in years.

12

Kate

"Say It Isn't So"
—Hall & Oats

For someone going to visit a foster kid, I've spent an embarrassing amount of time getting ready. My make-up is done, my teeth have been brushed, I've rinsed with mouthwash twice—rationalizing that good hygiene is crucial. And now it's time for clothes. Reaching for a red sweater, I try to tell myself that I want to make a good impression. That I don't want to come across as stuffy or unfriendly. That I'm overly concerned with making sure the foster kid likes me.

All of this is true.

Except I'm not thinking about the kid. I'm thinking about Caleb.

I shove my arms through the sweater sleeves and pull it over my head, then check my reflection in the mirror. My hair has developed an odd part, so I run my fingers through it to smooth out the top. Sometimes I think about cutting it—the ringlets make me look a little like a darker-headed Taylor Swift on a bad hair day—but I haven't found the guts to do it. Plus, my roommates have threatened to kill me if I try, so I guess it looks okay. To everyone but me.

The red sweater might be too much. I'm eyeing a safe brown one balled up on a shelf in my closet when Lucy barges in and plops on my bed. Her feet hang off the end, and she swings them back and forth as she looks at me.

"Now, you know this guy could be dangerous."

"He's not dangerous." I pull on my cleanest pair of jeans and spray them with perfume, just in case they're not so clean after all.

"He could be a serial killer…."

"He brought me home from the bar and never once touched me."

"…or an animal abuser."

"He bought me Gummy Worms. Pretty sure he likes animals."

"That might be the dumbest thing you've ever said."

She's right; I roll my eyes. But we've had a hundred different versions of this same conversation since Lucy's hangover faded a few days ago. All the questions might be touching if I wasn't ninety-nine percent sure her guilt was spurring them on. I've lost count of how many times she's apologized since Saturday morning, but she's long since been forgiven. By me. Not sure she's gotten that far with herself.

"What does he do for a living?"

"He's a—" I start to say, but then I realize I have no idea. I frown at my own stupidity for not asking. The guy probably thinks I'm not at all interested, something I will have to remedy at the first opportunity today. "He sponsors foster kids." It's all I can come up with.

"And that pays the bills, how?" Lucy is so sarcastic sometimes. It's usually the reason we get along so well. Right now, I want to kick her out of my room.

I shrug instead. "I have no idea. I'll ask him and get back to you."

"Not if I ask him first. He'll be here in ten minutes. Better go jot down my interview questions."

She uncurls her ridiculously long legs from the bed and swings her perfect chestnut hair that falls in a graceful cascade down her back. At that moment I remember once again all the reasons I hate her. She bounces out the door, her bare feet slapping against the tile in the hallway. I can hear the opening and closing of drawers in the kitchen, which tells me she wasn't kidding. The click of a pen. The swish of notebook paper. When it comes to Lucy, poor Caleb doesn't stand a chance.

"Your roommate's kind of crazy," Caleb says as he opens the car door and climbs out. "Wait there." I sit in the passenger seat and watch him walk around the front of the truck. He's wearing worn, low-slung jeans and a tight black sweater that shows not only his ridiculous biceps, but also that lone eagle wing tattoo that insists on peeking out of his neckline. That wing has kept me distracted the entire drive here. My door opens.

"One hundred percent certifiable." I look up at him.

"Do I like dogs? I can't say that I've ever been asked that question before by a girl I've just met. Felt like I was being sized up as a serial killer or something." Or something. Boyfriend eligibility, actually, but I can't say that. Yet.

I shrug. "She's an animal lover. And don't forget—"

"Crazy," we finish together. I look at the small brown building in front of me. "This is the center? It looks different than I thought it would."

He looks down at me with a grin and holds out a hand to help me out of the car. "I parked around back. We'll be less likely to be bombarded by rug rats if we sneak in this way."

"Wait—can you do that?"

He shrugs. "You can if you work here." He seems slightly embarrassed, but the news both surprises and thrills me. Caleb doesn't look like the kid-loving type. "Anyway, what did you expect it to look like?"

"I don't know. A little less…flat?" He laughs at this, which does all sorts of warm and mushy things to my insides. I tell myself to shake it off—I don't *do* warm and mushy—and go to move around him, but he stays still. Looking at me. Blocking my way. The sight is both exhilarating and scary, and there it is again.

I guess warm and mushy is my new thing.

A slow grin tilts the side of Caleb's mouth, the kind of grin that makes you wonder what he's thinking even though it's *obvious* what he's thinking.

AMY MATAYO

"What?" I say, hearing the nervous tremble in my voice. Of course I'm nervous. He's going to kiss me. I know he's going to kiss me. He's going to kiss me, and I don't know what to do. He's going to kiss me, and every part of me is tingling with anticipation.

I think about closing my eyes. I think about leaning forward. I think about touching that eagle wing. I think about a lot of things. Until I realize it's unnecessary.

"After this, how about we see a movie?" he says, chucking me on the chin. My teeth actually tap together. Then he steps back, leaving me wondering what the heck just happened. Seriously, what just happened? And why didn't he kiss me? The car door closes and my face turns pink and I follow him into that beige building, and all I can think is that I should have worn that brown sweater so that I could blend in with the bricks.

"And so when you met Caleb, how old were you?" I have to shout to be heard, because this place is *loud*, but two hours later, I have three pages of notes, we've snapped a few pictures, and this is the most adorable kid I've ever had the pleasure of being around. Caleb hasn't only helped me by introducing me to Ben, he's practically written my term paper's entire opening.

"Ten, I guess." Ben shrugs his ebony shoulder, bare from a game of pick-up basketball. Sweat glistens from his forehead, matching the same ring that shines from Caleb's. The two are clearly fond of each other. I saw the elation on Ben's face as Caleb walked through the front door, elation he quickly covered with a cool, detached expression. You can't hide the eyes, though. His are still shining. "I've known him for a year. Usually we meet here, but sometimes he brings me to his—"

Caleb chooses that moment to slap the basketball out of Ben's hands, and just like that the interview is over. The game is back in full swing, and I have a suspicion that Ben is finished answering my boring questions. Necessary for my paper, but mind-numbingly exhausting for

82

him. I was eleven once, too. I know what it's like to be forced into interviews. I've been sitting for them for years now thanks to my parents and their—

I gasp. Lunge for my purse. Yank out the unopened invitation out and rip into the envelope. Studying the card and my father's handwritten note at the bottom, I want to die. Death by my own hand would be so much better than him killing me. I check the clock on my cell phone. Fifteen minutes. I have fifteen minutes to get there or my butt will be in a sling held tight by my father's firm fist. It occurs to me that there's something pathetic about a twenty-one-year-old still desperately trying to win her parent's approval. Maybe when I'm thirty I'll be over it, but it isn't likely. When you've been the spokesperson for a nationwide crusade your whole life, there's not much hope of your face being replaced. Unless maybe my children take over one day.

There is no way my children will take over, ever.

I shove my notebook into my bag and stand, nervous and fidgety but trying not to appear that way. I need to leave. Because of my inability to think ahead and open a freaking envelope on time, I need Caleb to drive me. But he's still playing ball, immersed in having fun with a kid who really needs the attention. I feel like a diva for pulling him away, like a prima donna only concerned about herself. It's a common struggle, one I've dealt with many times. Dropping everything for my parent's rallies has become a way of life, including friend's birthday parties, graduations, and one halfway enjoyable date I wasn't ready to end. The guy never called me again.

Panic starts to rise and grip me in its vise. Caleb sees it. Of course he sees it. The ball bounces from his hand and settles in a series of flat bounces as he studies my face.

"What's wrong?" he calls from across the room.

"Um...Uh..." I say, just so embarrassed. I sigh and shift positions, but there's no way to avoid it. "My parents have a thing..." I wince because it sounds so lame. "I forgot about it and I'm supposed to be there right now and I need to leave." My lip slides between my teeth in my usual nervous gesture. "I can walk if you want to stay here. It's not that far...I think. But they're going to kill me if I don't get there soon..." I let that last part trail off, just because it sounds so humiliating when I say it out loud.

But Caleb just grins in his adorable way and uses his sleeve to wipe the ring of sweat from his forehead. "Don't be silly. I'll drive you."

The relief I feel is irrational, and I know it. I shouldn't be this anxious about something involving my parents, but I've been late once before—back when I was fourteen and didn't want to leave a dance recital. The national news covered my father's reaction for days, analyzing whether or not his behavior teetered on child abuse. It didn't. My father can get angry, but he loves me. I've never doubted it for a second.

"Thank you." I breathe an audible sigh. I want to hug him, but stop myself and just look at him for a second instead. I can't decide if it's his easygoing attitude, the way he embraces the downtrodden, or the way he's so quick with a smile as though he doesn't have a care in the world. I know that last one isn't true. I'm certain he has a story that isn't all that pretty. All I know is that I really like that smile.

He winks at me before turning to Ben. "So what do you think of Kate? Think you can handle more of her questions if I bring her back here next week?"

Ben dribbles the ball a few times before resting it on his hip. A female worker in navy blue scrubs walks through a door and announces lunch. A dozen kids go running, but Ben stays back. He flips the ball onto a fingertip and begins to twirl it.

"I think I can take her, as long as she doesn't get pushy. Besides," he shrugs, "she pretty. I'll do anything for a pretty girl." Ben offers a smile my way that could light this room, but even that doesn't break his concentration. The ball continues to spin.

Caleb laughs when I blush. "So would I, dude. So would I." He gives Ben the kind of fist-bump that only a couple of testosterone-filled guys can give. "That she is. We'll be back next Monday." He looks at me for approval, and I nod. Of course I nod. And smile like a stupid teenager. I'll come back tomorrow and the next day and the day after that if he'll just bring me. With or without a paper to write.

Two minutes later we're in the parking lot behind the building, and he's tossing my bag in the backseat. I reach for the passenger door handle, but Caleb blocks me with his hand pressed to the glass. I haven't noticed the scar that runs from his thumb to the base of his ring finger until now.

"I thought I told you to let me open it," he says. In theory, the words might seem harsh. In reality, his soft tone sends all kinds of shivers down my spine.

I give him my best glare anyway, even though it feels weak. "Excuse me, drill sergeant. I didn't realize opening my own door was a crime." I step back, secretly happy at his open display of chivalry even though I'm single-handedly setting the women's movement back decades. But who cares about the women's movement? Not me. Definitely not me.

"From now on, if you're with me, it is a crime."

I start to protest with some stupid sarcastic comment about never riding with him again, but when I look up he's watching me with a look that borders on fascination and I like it. I more than like it. And it's that one small difference that begins to make me nervous.

"You were good with Ben, Princess. He liked you a lot."

"I liked him too. Are you sure you don't mind me coming back here with you? I don't want to get in the way." Not that I'll let it stop me. He can tell me yes, no, or start babbling in Pig Latin, but I'm showing up next week if I have to walk backwards the whole way to get here.

"Of course I don't mind." That look hasn't left his face, and I feel myself swallow. "He's right, you know," Caleb says. His left hand settles on the hood of the car, the other rests in his pocket. But then he pulls it out and reaches up to tuck my hair behind an ear...to frame my face with his fingertips. "You are pretty. So pretty I can barely think straight." His eyes ask a question, and then he leans in. I feel his breath on my face just before he brushes his lips with mine. It's a soft kiss. A sweet kiss. Different in the way he touches first my top lip, then the bottom, then covers both in a move that leaves me breathless. It doesn't last long. Not nearly long enough. He pulls back and I'm staring into the bluest eyes I've ever seen. Blue like the ocean. Blue like heaven.

"You taste good, too." His slow grin settles around me, warming me, enveloping me like the softest blanket. "Maybe I should try that again." I close my eyes and lean toward him, not waiting for him to take the lead this time. I feel vulnerable, left wondering how a boy could make me this happy in only a few days, thinking that none of it makes sense, but all of it does. This time, as his mouth covers mine, the kiss isn't as gentle. It's filled with an urgency that surprises…and excites me. A longing builds in me that I've never felt before, and I press myself closer. My hands find his hair at the same time his arms wrap around my waist and pull me in. He kisses me, and it's all I can do not to melt into him, but he pulls back a little before I have the chance. Not far; his mouth stays close to mine.

"Wow," he whispers. "It gets better each time. Maybe we should go for a third…"

I laugh, but barely, unable to manage more than a strange sound. My mind and legs have turned to liquid. Caleb seems to sense my struggle, and he smiles.

"Princess?"

I sigh and look up at him, a fog clouding my brain. "Hmmm?"

With a killer grin that does all kinds of weird things to my insides, Caleb fumbles around me and cracks open the door. "We'd better get going. I'd hate to make you late."

Late for what? And then I remember.

"Okay." I don't want to leave, but somehow I manage to make it into the seat anyway. My seatbelt goes on. Caleb slides in beside me. His hand finds mine.

It isn't until we back out of the lot that I remember we need to hurry.

"What's the address?" Caleb pulls the car in drive moves out onto the road. He twirls a figure eight over the top of my hand. It makes me feel secure, appreciated. Safe in a way I've never felt before.

I produce the paper and read it aloud. But instead of speeding up like I expect him to do, Caleb slows the car down and pulls to the side of the street, then studies me. He looks confused, puzzled. Like out of all the things I've said over the last five days, this one thing makes the least sense.

With a frown, he pulls the paper from my hand and reads it. "That can't be right. This is…" His words trail off and he reads the entire paper. From top to bottom, taking in every word. I know this in the way his eyes travel up and down and up and down, as though he can't take it all in with one pass and has to make another.

And then he looks at me. Really looks at me.

He's motionless, transfixed on something I can't see, like he's trying to process something. I know the feeling, because I'm doing the same thing. We need to get moving, and suddenly I'm not sure I want Caleb to come with me. It's not exactly that I'm ashamed of my parents, but this whole display tends to get a little embarrassing.

This display. Crap. I glance down at my sweater—my *red* sweater—and feel panic rise once again. My parents aren't going to like it that I'm not wearing my signature pink. I open my purse to look for a scarf, a pair of earrings, a pin to fasten next to my heart. There's nothing. My gaze drifts to the window. Nothing at all.

I take a deep breath before I ask the question. "Is there any chance you have something pink that I could throw on real quick? Like a glove? Or a hat?" It's stupid and I can't look at him while I ask it, so I stare straight ahead. Trees, flowers, and sterile concrete buildings sit idyll in front of me as though they haven't a care in the world. I'm jealous of them.

I expect his laughter. I don't expect his nonresponse. I glance over at him, but he's still staring at me.

I frown. "Why are you looking at me like that?" He doesn't answer; with his eyes locked on mine, he rolls the window down. The hum of distant conversation fills the car at the same time the color drains from his face. Still, he runs a hand through his hair and answers me.

"Check the glove box." His voice is hoarse. "There might be a wristband that my friend Scott left behind one afternoon after we played basketball at the center. Don't ask me why he chose that color. One of the many mysteries of being friends with that guy."

I try to smile at his words, but there's no humor in his voice. The wristband turns out to be red, the color mocking me once again. I close the hatch and lean back in my seat. It takes some work, but eventually I convince myself not to worry. I have more important things to think about than what color I'm wearing, like how Caleb will feel about this circus that is sometimes my life.

Much to my relief, he pulls the car forward again. My relief vanishes when—instead of accelerating—he turns into a parking space. I watch him lean forward, grip the steering wheel, and look at the crowd gathering in front of us. A faint alarm bell begins to ring in my head, but I have no idea why.

"Where's my phone?" he asks. "Can you please hand it to me? They showed up a day early." This time, his voice is lifeless.

Who showed up a day early? I have no idea what he's talking about, but I locate his phone on the ground under my seat—it's fallen from the cup holder—and hand it to him. My heart nearly jumps out of my chest when I see the look on his face. His emotionless face hardens as he looks at his phone, punches a button, brings it to his ear, and stares out the window. I process all of this, yet I process nothing. He's parked here, but I can't figure out why. Before I have time to mull it over, he's talking into the receiver.

"Man, don't kill me...left it on vibrate in my car...yeah, I see them...maybe three, four dozen...yes, camera crews...anything we can do?" He tunnels a hand through his hair and it's all I can do not to smooth it down for him. I just want him to smile again. "What did our lawyer say?"

At those words I forget about his hair as a sick feeling rolls through my gut...a feeling I don't like but can't begin to explain. He reaches for my hand and the figure eight starts again, almost desperate, the caress a reflection of his anxious demeanor. His look softens when he meets my eye. Somehow he manages to grin at me, a sad smile that clears away the frown lines between his eyebrows but does nothing to settle my racing heart. The car door opens and he climbs out, pausing in front of the truck to finish his conversation. Only thirty seconds or so pass before he hangs up and walks around to open my door.

Why is he opening my door?

With a quick glance around, I stand up to meet him and realize at that moment exactly how much I like this guy. He's kind. He's sweet. He's the best looking man I've ever laid eyes on. And for a moment, that great-looking man's gaze is locked on mine. I could swim in those eyes. Maybe even die in them.

Caleb kisses my forehead, then speaks against my skin. "We're here."

Maybe he notices the confusion in my eyes or the way I look toward the group of people gathering at the far edge of the parking lot. Maybe he doesn't. But for whatever reason I may never know the answer to, he steps back. He looks at me, really looks at me. He looks at me and his face looks tired and I'm sick for sure this time.

"What do you mean we're here?"

"This is the address you gave me. The center. This place."

In my confusion, I can't speak. Things might be better if he wouldn't either.

"Kate."

He says nothing else. He turns and picks up a flier that has fallen to the ground and blown toward us. A pink flier with my face at the top like every other flier that's ever been printed in my lifetime. His face falls as he looks at it. With wary eyes, he looks at me. And he knows.

And, oh dear God I think I know too.

"Kate, we're here." It isn't a statement this time. It's a match over gasoline.

I just stare at him, feeling my spine begin to tremble with no way to stop it. But I need a second. Just one second to figure out what in the world is going on. But there's no figuring it out, because it's obvious, even though none of this makes sense. My head starts shaking, back and forth, back and forth.

"Caleb, this can't be the right place." My parents…the invitation…this rally. There's no explaining it. I'm grasping at everything and nothing. And then I ask the question that I've wanted to ask for two minutes even though my voice is shaking almost too much to form the words. "Your foster center?"

I look across the parking lot at the crowd that's still growing by the minute, at the foster center behind me, at the church across the street, at the cameras set around the perimeter like they always are, because my parents aren't just controversial, they demand attention. Local, national, all of it. I pick out Jim in the crowd, his wife Shirley and their daughter whose name I can never remember even though I should know it by heart because they're always here. Every single time, they've always been here along with almost everyone else in attendance. I don't know if my parents pay everyone to show up or if they come because they believe in the cause my parents are fighting for. It's never occurred to me to ask.

And then I see the nativity scene. The nativity scene that I didn't see when we arrived two hours ago because we parked in the back. In the back, away from the controversy.

In the back, away from the offense.

I swallow as I study it, then turn away to focus on the flier still dangling from Caleb's hand, the "Good Without God" words at the top that have never mattered before but now matter more than anything. My parents are here to protest this place like so many other places before it because of that nativity scene, a nativity scene that will ultimately harm—no, brainwash—innocent kids. Specifically foster kids, if I remember right. Foster kids who attend a church-run center funded by taxpayer money that needs to be shut down once and for all because God and government shouldn't mix and this place is too stubborn to separate the two.

Oh, God.

Foster kids.

Caleb's foster kids.

This has happened so many times. This is just a normal way of life for my parents. For me. And every single time—whether at five or ten or twelve or twenty—my image has smiled from the top of that pink flier. Still, I have to grasp for something.

"You were in a bar." It's all I can say. All I can think.

He folds the flyer in half. "Kate, I was at the bar because I heard some of my kids were planning to show up there. A few of them have nowhere else to go. I can't just leave them on the street."

Of course he can't. He's too good of a person for that. But it still doesn't explain why we're here.

I'm frantically trying to figure it out as Caleb leans against the truck, paces the sidewalk, scrubs a hand over his face, taps his head against the door. And then he stops moving and looks at me. Really looks at me. And then he speaks. More than anything in the world, I want him to stop talking.

"Your parents are Don and Michelle Hawkins?"

I can hear the last thread of hope he's holding onto, hope that he's wrong, hope that I'll say no. But I can't say no…can't breathe as I watch this nightmare crash around me. Of course he knows my parents. *Everyone* knows my parents. They're only the most famous American atheists since Madeline Murray O'Hare.

A mix of anger and despair roll through me at the same time, and I barely manage a nod. He closes his eyes before slowly opening them again. Still, I'm not prepared for his next words.

"Kate, I work at this center, because it's owned by that church." He points to the steeple directly across the street and looks me in the eye.

"I work at that church because *I'm a pastor.*"

13

Caleb

"Blindsided"

—Bon Iver

My life stopped the day I turned seven. If you do the math, that means that for the past sixteen years, nine months, and eleven days, I haven't been living.

My life started again four days ago when God introduced me to a princess.

If I had known I was going to die again so soon, I might have remembered to beg for more time.

It takes two seconds for everything to shift. Two seconds to understand why Kate doesn't do Christmas. Two seconds to realize the girl I was beginning to fall for was the absolute wrong person for me. Two seconds for the one of the best days in recent memory to turn into the worst, as though catastrophe didn't have time to consult me or was just too bored to take a few extra minutes. Because what am I? Just a guy whose entire life has gone to crap in every single way except one, but right now I feel too sucker-punched to care about that One Thing. I look up to heaven for a second in a question, but a bull-horn blast behind me rips away the answer I hoped for.

"The rally will start in five minutes," a man yells across the crowd.

I ignore his words as the girl in front of me begins to sway. She reaches for the door to steady herself. "Caleb…" Kate struggles to grab a full breath. I know the freaking feeling. "I had no idea…not for one second did I think…"

"Neither did I." The words escape on a bite, but there's no way to make them gentle. If I believed in things like the Universe, I would say it is laughing hysterically at both of us right now. But I believe in God. I've believed in God for five years. This is the first time it gives me no comfort.

"So you're Kathy Hawkins." I'm resigned to the reality. I knew she looked familiar and…her driver's license. Why didn't I read her driver's license that night in the parking lot? I just let Scott spout off her home address and filed it in my memory in the same place I've filed everything since my seventh birthday so that I don't forget. I don't forget anything anymore. Not names, faces, destinations, or useless facts, like how many miles it is to the moon. I can't afford to forget things. All my memories might be gone tomorrow, and I'm the only who can keep them alive.

But I forgot where I'd seen her. Even the name Kathryn didn't spur a memory. The brief realization that Scott didn't remember it either doesn't make things better. It just makes it clearer that we both suck.

"I'm Kate," she says, bringing me back to the moment. "I hate the name Kathy. And I can't believe you're a pastor."

She says it like a curse. Like I have some third-world disease that she doesn't want to catch. I bristle, but I don't say that I can't believe she doesn't believe in God. Because who doesn't believe in God? Okay, tons of people, but whatever. I also don't tell her that I hate her name, too. Not *her*, but the notoriety of her. The willingness of her parents to bulldoze over everything good I've tried to build in the last five years.

My parents have this thing…they'll kill me if I don't get there soon.

She was born into this. She doesn't have a choice. In this one way, we're the same. I didn't have a choice either.

"Kathy! Kathy!" We both turn at the sound like two kids getting caught stealing candy before dinner. Her mother is waving her over.

Her smile is wide, but even from here I can see it's strained. The rally was supposed to start at eleven o'clock—twenty four hours from now, but I guess that's the element of surprise you often hear about but rarely experience, lucky me—which gives her only one minute to pull it together and get onstage. It's a scene I've watched played out on the news. Kathy goes up, says a few words about protecting precious minds, innocent minds that should be allowed to form and develop without the constraints of religious brainwashing. She rationalizes that it worked for her, and she's all the better for it. Happier than most kids, even. Then Kathy steps to the right of stage, giving her parents the limelight while she smiles and claps at all the right parts.

I can't breathe as I study her. Really, really study her. At the conflict building in her eyes. At the lower lip that's currently being chewed into submission. At the frustration sizzling underneath her skin. At the way she looks at her mother, then looks at me. Hesitant. Torn. Breaths become uneven as she silently implores me to understand. I don't, and then in a hundred ways that I can't quite grasp, I do.

Kate doesn't know what to do. Kate isn't happy.

That makes two of us.

But here's the difference: all hell's about to break loose and I'm the one getting burned.

My heart nearly cracked in half when she walked onto that stage two hours ago. For her entire speech I didn't move from the side of my truck, even though I had a speech of my own prepared and tucked inside a folder on my desk. The folder I planned to take home tonight and study after my date with Kate. Yet another reason for the universe to laugh. In my lifetime, I've given it plenty.

But even watching with a half-cracked heart was nothing like the pain I felt when she opened her mouth to speak, giving instance after instance of the negative effect religion has on children. Of all the ways God can be equated with Santa Claus—of the cruelty of allowing children to believe in something wholeheartedly only to have that belief ripped away and replaced with the cold reality of nothingness. Because according to Kathy, religion and God and faith are nothing. A childhood dream based on fantasy, perpetrated by blinded adults seeking modern ways to perform centuries-old mind control.

And nativity scenes on public display are just another form of brainwashing. Nativity scenes. At Christmastime. With donkeys. And cows. And dudes wearing crowns. And *babies*. According to Kathy, the display is the epitome of everything wrong in the world today.

She looked right at me the whole time. I looked right back, daring her to label me with every accusation she dropped. She couldn't. I knew she couldn't. Because even though her delivery was clear, I could sense the uncertainty behind it. I could hear the monotone in her voice. I could see the nervousness that continued to come through in the way she bit her lip.

So could her father. He cut her off mid-sentence and took over the microphone, unhappy with her lackluster performance.

Once he started talking, I'd had enough. Punishment may have taken a bigger chunk of my life than reward ever has, but even I can only take so much. I kept to the rally's outside perimeter and ignored her father as I made my way inside the building. Despite my best effort, a few words managed to make it to my ears, one worse than all the others.

Lawsuit.

As I walked, I felt Kate's eyes on me the whole way, but I didn't look at her. Not once.

Had I known what would face me inside, I might have reconsidered my decision. I lean back in my seat and snatch up a pen, tapping out a nervous rhythm with the silver cap as Scott waits for me to answer his question.

"Of course I didn't know," I say. "It never came up." Scott can't seem to understand how I could have spent three days and one night—technically speaking—with this girl without putting two and two together. The guy is exceptionally smart, but on this one issue, he has the ignorance of a crumpled piece of paper. I grab a fresh sheet and begin to drawl circles.

"How did it never come up? You didn't talk about your jobs? Your families? Anything other than the weather?" His sarcasm is getting on my nerves. The phone rings again. I send it to voice mail.

"You're not going to answer any more calls?" Scott asks.

"They can get their information from someone else for a few minutes."

"Caleb, you run the center, and you have a job to do. If you ignore this—if you're not careful—public opinion will begin to sway in favor of the Hawkins. I can't believe you didn't know who she was."

I've never been the most gracious person under pressure. Now is no exception. "First of all and in case you don't remember, I don't give a crap about public opinion. If I did, I wouldn't be a pastor right now, would I? A thousand bucks says I wouldn't even be a Christian." I seared him with a look. "A million guarantees you and I wouldn't be friends." Scott squirms in his seat. Round one to me. "Second of all, I'm not going to ignore it. You know me better than to think I'd walk away from a fight. Third, you read her driver's license and didn't recognize her either. Between the two of us, you're the only one who knew her last name." Scott's eyes dart to the side. End of round two. "Here's my question; when you looked for her address, did you read her name or just look at the numbers?"

Scott just stares at me, and I think I've found my answer. When he stands to pace the room, I'm certain of it. A knockout punch. I set the pen down and focus on my desk, feeling not at all victorious. Something occurs to me then, something I should have figured out when I saw all those missed calls. Something that makes me feel even dumber than I already do. My shoulders sag on a sigh.

"When did you realize it was her?"

"When a press release came through the fax machine about thirty minutes before they arrived." And I left my phone in the car like an idiot. "Her photo was at the top of the page. I freaked out and started calling you. I'm sorry, man. I read her name on the driver's license but never put it together. I think I was more focused on Kimball's puke and that dress she was wearing to think much of anything else."

"I think we both were. It's alright, seriously." I tent my fingers and lean my chin on them while fixing my stare on the desk, trying to come up with a solution to this but coming up with jack crap. Slapping my palms on my face and rubbing them up and down doesn't help, it only increases my headache. I drop my hands and look at Scott.

"What are we facing with this? In legal terms, I mean. What happens now?" I'm relatively new to this Christian stuff, and practically an infant at being in charge. My technical title is Youth Pastor. My actual responsibilities involve running the Chapman Center—an after school program named after the church's founding pastor designed specifically for underprivileged children, the majority of whom come from single-parent and foster families. But the program doesn't just run until the standard five o'clock after-work pick-up time so common in other programs like it. Ours runs into the evening—as late as seven, eight o'clock—for parents who work the late shift.

We make dinner for those who need it, and we help with homework so the older kids don't fall behind in school. In the direst circumstances, we have beds for kids who need a warm place to stay the night. The church provides safe, caring, capable people who've been background checked, fingerprinted, and practically full-body scanned to take care of them. In the two years I've been in charge, we've never gone a single week without at least one bed occupied. So far, the oldest child was sixteen. The youngest was two.

But we pray before dinner, we pray before bedtime, and there's a six-by-six silver plaque engraved with John 3:16 hanging on the wall to the left of the front door. And, of course, a plastic nativity scene on our front lawn that some parent didn't like and complained about, never mind that we've fed her kid—and have continued to feed her kid—for months now because we're sweet like that.

But for that sweetness, she contacted a lawyer who contacted the press who alerted the Hawkins' and now we've been slapped with a lawsuit. For that, a few needy kids with no place to go might be looking for another place to sleep.

"According to Senator Richter, in the best case scenario we'll have to pay money to the state and take down the nativity scene, then repay the taxpayers who, according to initial public opinion, couldn't care less about any of this. We don't exactly live in the most anti-religious state in the country. Most people pray at dinner and ballgames and have nativity scenes in their own yards." Scott looks at me and then looks away like he would rather end the conversation right now. But I'm not done and he knows it.

"And worst case scenario?" I wonder if my voice sounds as mad as I think it does, because I already know his answer.

"We run out of money, and we're forced to close our doors."

Close our doors. The doors of the only good thing I've ever done. The door that God Himself opened up after so many others had slammed in my face.

The tension crackles in the room like a firework just before detonation.

"And kick fifteen kids to the curb, just like that," I finally say. All because we dare to thank God for pizza before we eat it and stick a Virgin Mary in the grass. This is the most moronic thing I've ever heard of, but holy crap if the Hawkins' movement hasn't gathered steam. At least among the media, and even an idiot like me knows they have the last word on everything.

"Just like that." Scott nods while I sit there with my mouth hanging open like the defenseless little boy I used to be. But eventually I close it, because I'm not that helpless kid anymore. I ditched that "Poor Me" act a long time ago, back before Scott and his dad found me and gave me the first two people in years I could depend on. The feeling had been so foreign back then, frightening and unwelcome. When you've been left to your own devices for over ten years, leaning on another person makes about as much sense as swallowing your own excrement. It's unnatural. The last thing you ever expect to find yourself doing.

It took a long time for me to trust either of them, but eventually I learned to lean on other people and ask for help when I couldn't figure things out on my own.

This time, I'm not asking. This time, I'm taking matters into my own hands.

I grab the folder off my desk that holds the speech I never gave and push back my chair to stand. Scott's face grows alarmed when he sees the determined look on mine—the one that says "Screw The World," the one he's seen a million times before that I should have known he would recognize now. He jumps up to stop me.

"Caleb, think before you do anything. You've come too far to go off half-cocked, and we can't afford the negative publicity." He latches onto my arm, but I shrug it off and try to appear calm.

"I'm not going to do anything stupid."

"Says the man who threw a temper tantrum and gave the head pastor of this church a broken nose."

"It healed perfectly and your father got over it. You need to get over it, too." I take a step toward the door, but Scott moves faster and blocks it. If he wasn't my best friend, I would laugh in his face. With his red hair and five-foot-nine frame, I could obliterate his bones with one blow to the middle. I've done it to others before and barely missed a breath from the effort. But I don't. Because Scott is Scott and the guy has guts. I slam a hand on my hip and glare at him.

"I won't do anything to give us a bad name."

"Swear it." He might have guts, but he's also a pain in the butt.

"I swear."

"Hold up your fingers."

"Oh, for the love of—seriously, dude? Now?"

"Hold them up."

With a menacing stare that used to intimidate police officers but now actually manages to make Scott look bored, I slap the folder against my thigh and hold up two fingers—the same two-fingered Boy Scout salute we make the kids use when they get caught fighting or complaining or refusing to do their homework. This is stupid. I'll never make them do it again.

"I swear not to cause any more problems," Scott prompts me. "Now say it."

My jaw pops and I itch to punch something. "I swear not to cause any more problems." My arm falls. "Can I go now?"

"Sure." Scott wanders over to my chair and sits down, propping his feet on my desk. "But remember, if you wind up in jail again, neither me nor my father is coming to bail you out this time."

"Fine. Good thing I like bunk beds and open-view toilets."

"And roommates who could have a lot of fun with a guy as pretty as you, don't forget about that!" Scott's laughter follows me through the doorway, and despite my anger and outrage and all the other emotions that have managed to tick me off today, I find myself smiling.

It isn't until I throw open the door of my truck that it really hits me.

She's gone.

I look up toward the parking lot and notice the absence of cameras and people or even a single pink flier littering the sidewalk. It's all gone, as if none of it were here in the first place. There won't be a movie with Kate. Or dinner. Or a hundred other days that I wasn't aware I even wanted but now want with a longing so strong it nearly flattens me.

I want to go back to this morning and ask her stay, to skip the interview with Ben and her parent's event and anything else that doesn't involve just her, me, another kiss, and a long drawn-out conversation. But I can't, because that chance is over.

And now, like everyone else I've ever allowed myself to care about, Kate is gone.

I don't go straight home. Instead, as if the car has a mind of its own, I find myself in the next town, driving mindlessly. Doing figure eights around my problems as I replay the day, the week, the last seventeen years of my life as though a riddle might be solved somewhere between the mile markers. Even the folder—along with my resolve to do something—are momentarily forgotten.

In the end, I solve something, at least. Something I already know. Something that should have dawned on me sooner but doesn't until I exit off the highway toward my neighborhood.

It's Tuesday.

My mother…nine-eleven…Johnny Cash …Kate's revelation.

More proof I didn't need that nothing good happens on a Tuesday.

And when it comes to me, it's becoming more and more clear that nothing good happens ever.

14

Kate

"Speak Now, I'm Listening"
—Memphis May Fire

Two days later I'm listening to the interviewer speak, but I can't hear much past the monotone drone of the woman's voice. The questions are always the same—whether asked by passersby on the street or a local news anchor or one of the hosts on *Good Morning America*. It's almost as if some anonymous writer composed a list of acceptable ones and offered them for sale on Amazon—*Top Ten Questions to Ask an Atheist*, buy it now for the low, low price of $9.99. Answering them is exhausting. Boring. As predictable as the sun rising next Thursday morning, whether or not I'm still around to see it.

But as boring as the questions are, this is the first time they've ever bothered me.

I attempt to shake off the feeling and sit straighter in my chair, hard to do since the chair and the cameras and the rows of overhead spotlights are planted right in front of the nativity scene at Caleb's foster center. I can almost feel the eyes of the Virgin Mary burning into my back.

Earlier this morning, I asked for a change in location—maybe a bookstore or a coffee shop or a Christmas tree farm somewhere nearby—but it seems everyone thought this spot would make for the best possible publicity. It will, but the attention is the last thing I want.

Especially now.

Because even though I've wished to see Caleb at least a thousand times in the past forty-eight hours, right now I'm hoping with every fiber in me that he won't show up here.

I force myself back in the moment and make eye contact with the woman across from me.

"Yes," I say, nodding for extra emphasis. "I fully support my parent's campaign. Church and foster centers—while both admirable in their own ways—need to stay separate if taxpayer money is involved." I've given some variation of this answer a thousand times, but something about the look on her face tells me I messed up this time.

The way she sends an uncomfortable glance toward my father confirms it. Next to me, he clears his throat as she shifts in her chair. I don't miss the impatient raise of her eyebrow or the condescending tone of her voice when she tries again, nor the way my father looks at me expectantly. I'm failing here, and we both know it.

"That's all well and good, Kathy, but I asked you about how you feel about church leaders using their position to indoctrinate innocent children. Take this church, for example. What would you say to one of their leaders if you had the opportunity?" She leafs through a few pages of notes as a slow chill creeps up my spine. I know what she's looking for. "Here it is." She faces me again. "Last month in St. Louis, you were quoted as saying, 'Church members in positions of authority need to stop using their power to convert children to their old-fashioned ways of thinking. Faith-driven pressures like these might be the single most detrimental issue facing our young people today, even more dangerous than unemployment and inner-city crime.'"

I blink, thinking of Caleb flipping through albums in my apartment. Of his tattoo. Of those studded biker boots.

Try as I might, I can't come up with anything old-fashioned about him.

I uncross and cross my legs, wishing I had worn pants instead of a skirt because suddenly my legs feel sweaty and sticky even though it's forty degrees outside. The heat lamps surrounding us are too hot. Too bright. Too focused on me.

"So what would you say to the leaders of this church?" the interviewer says, settling her papers back in her lap.

It feels like a giant ball of cotton is stuck in my throat as I try to swallow. The cameras are on me and her eyes are on me and I have to say *something.* "I guess I would say…um…that as far as this church goes…It's probably best if…um…" I take a deep breath, wondering what in the world is wrong with me. I've been doing this for years. It should come as naturally as breathing. Right now, even breathing is difficult.

"I think what Kathy is trying to say is—"

I stop him with a hand to his wrist. I love my father, but I can't let him speak for me. Those days are over, and besides—when it comes down to it—I want to sound professional. My image is at stake here, too. My chin goes up. I square my shoulders.

"I would say the same thing I've always said. Like any other church, this one has no place trying to interfere in the lives of children while using taxpayer money to do so. It doesn't matter if they use only a little. That nativity scene needs to come down, or their doors need to close."

My words sound confident, in control. And when I see my father smile, a sense of pride envelops me. Finally, I've done the right thing.

So why does a tiny part of me feel like I've just betrayed the one person I care about most?

With my headphones tucked inside my ear, I'm trying to stay on a path well-lit by streetlamps. Needing an outlet for my restlessness, I took off walking an hour ago. It's dark, not as black as it will be but well past sunset. And call me crazy, but I'd rather not be attacked by some psycho stranger, especially when very few people are out here to hear me scream. So I follow the lights, which sometimes leaves me with the feeling that I'm walking in circles.

I'm on my fourth time around when I see him.

Lit up by his own set of lampposts, Caleb is jogging toward me like a scene from a movie, where the object of the girl's affection appears at just the right time. Music swells. A reunion ensues. And they all live happily ever after.

Except I know the moment he sees me, and Caleb is anything but happy. His steps slow, and he's skewering me with his eyes, sizing me up and not liking what he finds.

"What are you doing here?" Sweat drips from his forehead. He doesn't even try to hide the accusation in his voice.

"Walking, same as you. Last time I checked, it's a public park."

"I'm running. Walking's for wimps." He's comparing our workout routines, and it's a dumb thing to say, and I have about a million different retorts hanging out on my tongue just waiting to be released, but I hold them in because he's trying to prove a point. I'm not sure what exactly the point is, but he's mad. Of course he's mad. Gone is the boy who pinned me against his car door only a few days ago and kissed me until my knees nearly buckled. Gone is the boy whose devilish grin set everything to rights in my world, even through the turmoil of drunkenness and rallies and term papers. Gone is the boy I was falling for, which sounds so stupid when I think about it now, because what kind of moron falls in love in three days? *With a pastor,* my rational side whispers to me.

But the emotional side of my brain won't listen to the rational side, because the emotional side can only remember his eyes…his gentleness…his lips…his tattoo. The emotional side is too busy staring at his sweaty, ridiculously chiseled chest.

The emotional side is still falling.

His next words yank me out of my descent.

"Don't you have an interview you need to get to?" he says. "You know, one where you sit on *my* lawn in front of *my* nativity scene and give me more unsolicited advice about how I need to close my doors and quit brainwashing kids?"

My eyes fly to his face, *so* over his chest. If he expects me to feel bad about that interview, he's sadly mistaken. "I wasn't aware the church property belonged to you. And as for nativity scenes, I didn't know I needed to ask your permission before sitting next to Jesus."

His eyes flash. "Well, from now on, you do." It's the wrong thing to say, and for a moment I see a flicker of guilt because, seriously, he's going to keep me away from baby Jesus? But just like me, Caleb is an expert at masking anything but a stubborn streak. As quickly as it comes, the guilt disappears. "Got it?"

My temper flares. "Why don't you just take the nativity down? Then we wouldn't be having this conversation."

"Oh, you'd like that, wouldn't you?" His gaze narrows. "Well since you're such a fan of the media, here's a news flash for you: I don't bow to pressure, not from your dad and definitely not from you."

"You might not say that once our lawyers get involved," I snap. I regret the words as soon as they slip out.

"Bring it, Kathy," he bites back, insulting me. I swallow the sting and engage in a stare down, two iron-clad wills fighting to come out on top. I'm breathing hard and he's breathing hard and then he seems to remember something. "Speaking of lawyers, according to mine, I shouldn't even be talking to you."

His words punch at me, deflating my indignation, because he's right. So much for a fight; just like that, I've lost. With a sigh, I tuck my headphones back inside my ears. "I'll make it easier for you, then." I turn to leave, suddenly wanting to flee this creepy, too-dark park and its watchful, painful eyes, especially with Caleb taking up all the space.

He doesn't stop me like I hoped. He says nothing at all, and a crushing weight of disappointment settles around me. Even though it makes no sense, I want him to come after me. To challenge me. To make a desperate attempt to pull me away from my parents and over to his side. It probably wouldn't work, but I still want him to try.

And I want, more than anything, for him to call my name and tell me we can work this out.

Instead, there's nothing but silence and the sound of my sneakers treading dejectedly on the pavement. Less than ten seconds in, and I can already tell it's going to be a long walk home. I press play on my iPod, counting on the slow strains of Janice Joplin to shatter the oppressive silence as I break into a jog. It's dark now, and though I would never admit it to anyone, I'm a little afraid to be out here alone.

Just when I've gotten a good rhythm going, someone pulls on my arm and jerks me around.

"Get your hands off me!" I scream, then rip my headphones off and attempt to land a good punch on the body of whatever freak is stalking me, but stop just before my fist makes contact.

Caleb. I should have known.

"What are you doing, scaring me like that?" I drop my arm and shove him in the chest.

"I yelled at you six times! Turn your volume down!" My push did nothing but make him angrier, and he's in my face again, looking down at me while I look up at him, only a few inches away. All of a sudden, my rapid breaths have nothing to do with jogging at all, because Caleb is so close and I just want to kiss him. I want *him* to kiss *me*. The thought comes from nowhere with a longing that surprises me. Caleb either senses it or feels it too, because with a quick glance at my mouth, he takes a step back and runs a hand over his face. The distance is minimal, but large enough to highlight that we're once again on two sides of what feels like an insurmountable fence.

Still, he's here. I'm here. Maybe, just maybe, we can figure out a way for each of us to take a step up.

"What do you want now, Caleb?" I sigh and look beyond him at the blackening night sky, thinking that step feels awfully high. "If you're just going to yell at me again, can we reschedule for tomorrow? I don't want to be out here much longer."

"Then I'll walk you home, because I have some questions and I think you owe me some answers." What might pass for a smirk tilts a corner of his mouth for the smallest second. "Afraid of the dark, are you?"

A tiny thrill shoots through me at the idea of spending more time with him, but I'm not about to let him know it. "No, just of being accosted by strange men who have nothing better to do than ask me questions." This time, his grin is genuine. It's small and doesn't last long, but I'll take it.

I pick up a penny lying on the sidewalk and tuck it inside my pocket. I'm not particularly superstitious, but right now I'll take all the help I can get, even if it means I'm forced to deal with a few germs. "What do you want to know?"

He doesn't hesitate. "Why pink?"

I feel myself frown. It's an unexpected question, one I've never been asked before, but hardly difficult to answer. Because despite the thought that goes behind some organizations and their colors—Gay Pride with the rainbows, Just Say No with red ribbons—my answer is simple.

"Because on my first appearance at a rally—when I wasn't quite a year old—I carried my blanket onto the stage. It was pink, and the media covered me and that blanket relentlessly for nearly a week. I guess my parents thought it brought good luck, and the next time, in addition to that blanket, I wore pink hair bows. Then pink shoes. Eventually, pink became my signature color, and consequently, the organizations." I sigh, hating the explanation. "It sounds stupid, but since that day, we've never had a dip in interest. With every rally, more people attend and more people buy into our cause. Media attention has been huge since then, and it's only growing."

"Obviously," he says with a humorless laugh. "And you're proud of all this attention?" Whether on accident or on purpose, hostility creeps into his voice. I try to ignore it and answer as best as I can.

"I've never thought about it as a pride issue. Honestly, I've never really given it much thought at all. It just…is. I don't think my parents are wrong, if that's what you're asking." I guess it's only fair that a bit of that hostility now finds its way into mine.

He doesn't like it. "How can you think they're right when—"

"I have a question for you." Two can play at this game. "Why were you really at the bar?"

It isn't that I don't believe his earlier explanation, but the idea of a pastor hanging out at a seedy tavern is about as foreign as the idea of me showing up to a tent revival. Completely ridiculous. Senseless no matter how many ways you analyze it, concern for his foster kids notwithstanding. I saw how those women were dressed that night. I smelled the alcohol dripping off everything that moved. Was it coming off Caleb, too? I pull the penny from my pocket and roll it in my hand. "Pastors aren't supposed to go to bars."

Now, I have no idea if this is true, but it should be. Because if Caleb had done his job the right way, we wouldn't be in this mess. It occurs to me that I might be in a bigger mess of lying in a coffin or filling out police reports or submitting to the harsh reality of pregnancy tests, but it's easier, at this moment, to deflect blame.

Caleb doesn't blink. In fact, his gaze grows distant. "Met a lot of pastors in your life, have you?" He rolls his eyes. "I guess that would be a yes, since you and your parents have built careers out of targeting churches like snipers target enemies. I'm surprised you haven't tried to kill me yet, or is that next up on the agenda?"

I toss the penny on the ground and remind myself that he was blindsided. We both were, but he's the only one being publically attacked, and that fact alone reminds me that I need to take everything he wants to throw at me. He has a right to be angry. If I were in his shoes, I would hate me, too. "This isn't my career by choice, Caleb. I don't know anything about your church—whether it's good, bad, or uses Voodoo dolls to perform healing rituals."

"We don't."

Only hostility exists in his voice now. I try hard to ignore it and keep talking, because if nothing else, at least we're in the same space, walking side by side. "That's not the point. I don't know anything about any of the churches except what my parents tell me, because frankly, I've never given them much thought." I cringe when the words come out, but they're true. I'm tired. I know my place. I analyze my situation about as much as the average person analyzes a wart on their finger. As long as it doesn't hurt, you just ignore it. "I've been dragged to these events since I first learned to crawl. Obviously you've done your research by now. My face is to my parent's movement what the Gerber Baby is to strained peas. One doesn't exist without the other. I don't think it ever will."

I hear his sigh. For the first time in several minutes, he seems more concerned than angry. "And you're okay with that? Being the poster girl for a long string of hurt, false accusations, and misplaced kids? It doesn't matter to you?"

He doesn't get it. Whether I'm okay with it or not, that's the way my life works. It's the way it is, and the way it will be. I tell him as much. He doesn't buy my excuse.

"Life is what you make it, Kate. Anything else is a cop-out and you know it."

"You know nothing about my life, Caleb. You can judge me and yell at me and give me a step-by-step plan to turn things around, but you don't know what it's like to live my life." And he doesn't. He can pretend—he can get self-righteous and indignant and tell me sob stories of little boys like Ben who will be tossed out onto the street with no one who cares about them if my parents have their way—but I've heard the stories a million times. I hate the stories. The stories are the main reason I stopped watching television years ago and learned to escape into music.

Besides, if my parents are right, those kids just might be better off.

We turn on my street, and a small part of me dies inside. This might be the last time I see him, and we're not ending on the greatest note. That step up has sunk into a crater. It's lowering by the minute.

"You're right," Caleb tells me, bringing me back into the moment. "I don't know anything about your life. But here's the hilarious part— you know nothing about mine, either. Yet according to your father, I'm a thief, a manipulator, a corruptor, and a danger to kids. According to him, I deserve to lose my job and have the doors closed on one of the most special things about my church all because of a nativity scene that no one is forcing you to look at. It's *Christmas,* for heaven's sake. And since you stood beside him and clapped at all the right parts—even threw in a few of your own uplifting words—I can only assume you agree with his assessment. So Kate, excuse me if I'm having trouble feeling sorry for you. Because for all your self-pitying statements about me not judging you, it seems to me that the only one playing Judge here is you." He stops in front of my apartment and looks at me long and hard, and all I want to do is disappear into the pavement. "You personally handed me a death sentence the other day and then again tonight on television. But you're right, Kate. It must suck to be you."

I say nothing because there's nothing to say. His words might infuriate me if I could really focus on them. Instead, I can't get past the fact that Caleb just called me out on the one crutch I've always allowed myself—that this is my parent's cause, not mine. That if anyone gets hurt, at least I'm not the one doing the wounding. It's never me. Never, ever me.

It's always been me. From the first time my cherub baby-face appeared on that first flier, it's been me. News stations might show clips of my father speaking or my mother clapping, but every stitch of material that's ever been stuffed in mailboxes and doorways and fax machines announcing brand new press releases has always had my face slapped at the top. New look as I grew older, but the smile stayed the same.

The delusion has been easy to keep up until now. Maybe it's awful that I never cared about any of it until I cared about one of the targets, but it's true. I care about Caleb. I care a lot.

"Caleb, I didn't mean to—"

"We're here, Kate."

The last time he spoke those words in the foster center parking lot, my life exploded into a million tiny fragments. Now, he's simply dismissing me, and it hurts. Hurts like my chest is being forced into a vise and squeezed until air and space and matter are eliminated and nothing is left but obliterated, powdery bones. I can't catch a breath, but my voice manages to make it out anyway.

"Okay. Thanks for walking me home." I nod and turn to leave. Before I can, he's speaking again.

"I was at the bar because I've been to about a hundred bars in my life," Caleb says in a low voice, stopping me. I almost forgot I asked the question. "Before I became a Christian, I used to go every weekend to get drunk, to pick up women, to start a fight. But never, in all the years I used to go, was I ever there just to talk. Sometimes I wanted to, just to unload my misery, but no one was ever interested in that." Caleb looks at me, really looks at me, for the first time since we started this walk. "Yes, I was at the bar in case one of my kids showed up. But I was also there that night to talk to people. To find out their stories and listen while they told me. Because sometimes people just need to know that someone cares. For some people, it's the only thing that keeps them from ending it all."

It occurs to me that I haven't taken a single breath since he started talking, so I exhale slowly and swallow around the lump in my throat. "So basically, you're a Good Samaritan," I whisper.

His brow furrows in the middle.

"What?" I say. "I'm not completely ignorant about Bible stories."

"That's nice to know." A ghost of a smile tilts his mouth, which isn't really a smile at all but a knee-jerk reaction to hide the sadness I know he's feeling. I saw it earlier, just for a second, when he first saw me walking toward him in the park. "I wouldn't call myself a Good Samaritan…"

"I would."

I hold his gaze until I no longer can, partly because it hurts to look at him when he's staring at me that way, but also because my eyes are suddenly all watery. This guy is good. Kind to children and strangers. A savior to naive women in trouble. Caring through and through. Despite whatever has happened in his past, Caleb saved me that night, and for three glorious days I nearly had a shot of making him mine. Those days passed too fast, and now it's just me. Alone again. The way I've been forever even when surrounded by strange guys in bars who wanted to take me home.

My watery vision grows blurry. I would blame it on allergies, but it's December and everything is dead.

For a second he looks like he wants to say something more. His mouth opens, his arm moves a little, but then seems to think better of it. Whatever might have happened is over.

"Goodbye, Kathryn. I'll wait here until you walk inside."

I nod, trying to look appreciative. But all I can think is…Kathryn. Not Kate. Not Princess. Not anything but goodbye.

The loss seeps through my pores as I walk into my apartment and slump against the door. My stupid eyes burn for a minute or two, but I squeeze them closed and lean my head back. For that space in time, the darkness is the only thing that seems real.

But then I stand, head for the kitchen, and grab a glass of water.

I don't cry.

I never, ever cry.

15

Caleb

"Love Bites"

—Def Leppard

I can still see my mother's face right before she died. I can see it, because only three inches of air and space and ripped flesh and massive amounts of blood separated hers from mine. Her body was split in half, the center gear shift of our Toyota Tercel acting as a tourniquet, keeping her alive long enough to beg me to listen. My mother, once so beautiful and perfect and angelic and kind, left this earth wearing a bone-chilling expression of fear. But not before giving me one last order.

Fight, Caleb. And don't fall asleep.

Those were her last words to me, the words I repeated like a mantra inside my head for the rest of the afternoon as I waited at the bottom of that ravine for someone to rescue me. I sang to myself, I cried to myself, I made wishes to myself over my mother's dead body until the chime of sirens blasted through my ears like a jet engine.

I was saved. And it was my birthday. Turns out that even without candles and cake, birthday wishes do come true.

Even my mother's last one.

I didn't sleep again for the next five years.

It's 2 a.m. and I'm wide awake.

It's been four hours, twelve minutes, and thirty seven—thirty-eight—seconds since I dropped Kate off at her doorstep and jogged toward my own apartment, and aside from a quick shower, I've

115

managed to do only one thing since.

One thing.

Like the stalker she accused me of being just a few hours ago. Like a man obsessed with torture and too far gone from the sick pleasure of it all to make himself stop.

One thing. And here I am, stuck inside a world of play and repeat.

I get to the end of the clip and start it once again for the last time, or at least that's what I tell myself. I've said the same thing at least a dozen times since I began watching, once even getting up to switch a load of laundry and brush my teeth in an effort to prove that I'd conquered the world of compulsive Kate-viewing. But then I found myself on my sofa once again, hitting play on a two-minute segment of television just to look at her one more time.

Even now—as she's skewering me and pastors and God in general on the most heavily watched news station in our four-state area—she's beautiful.

It's there, for the world to see. With her blonde hair flowing in ringlets down her pale pink sweater and the tentative smile that flashes onscreen every time she glances at her father, Kate is beautiful. And she was nearly mine just a few days ago. Even earlier tonight, the loss didn't escape me.

When I first caught sight of her walking toward me in the park, I was aware of two things. One, I wanted to strangle her for the things she'd said about me. And two, I wanted to kiss her, hard and fast, right then, right there on that secluded stretch of pavement. A classic description of a homicidal maniac maybe, but then most homicidal maniacs haven't met Kate Hawkins.

But I've met her, and I've never been so consumed with the thought of someone else in my life. Worse, she's the absolute wrong person for me. I know this. I've prayed about this. I've told myself this over and over the past three days, but it isn't getting easier. Not when I remember her smile, how it feels to hold her, how it rocked my world upside down and back again the first time I kissed her.

I press play again, recalling that kiss in my mind, listening while the sound of her voice eventually lulls me to sleep.

16

Kate

"I'd Hate To Be You On That Dreadful Day"

—Bob Dylan

The uncertainty of our situation is the worst part, especially because things haven't gotten better all weekend. Not at home. At school. Driving in my car. Thumbing through racks of albums at various indie record stores. I've always known what I wanted.

Now, I'm not so sure.

I try once again to pinpoint of the source of my restlessness, but come up empty. Still, it doesn't prevent a long list of scenarios from flashing through my mind.

Maybe it's the media attention. As usual, I've been called a dozen times from local and national reporters wanting more interviews to clarify my statements. A nice, juicy sound bite to add to their already scandal-laden story—a tale of supposed cheating the system and mind-control mixed together with a refresher course on the merits of separating church and state. One reporter even made suggestions of tax-evasion on Caleb's part and questioned how safe the children were with him anyway because of his teenage stint in jail.

Jail. I hadn't known about that. Not wanting to hear it from a tab-loid talk show, I shut off the television before any new bomb could be dropped.

Maybe it's the news outlets. The story has grabbed headlines all week as suspicion surrounding Caleb's church has grown. Without materializing a single foster child, stations have peppered news reports with words like supposed and allegedly—*alleged* abuse, *supposed* forced prayers, *alleged* withholding of food—to prop up my parent's viewpoint that God has no place in a government-involved foster center. This has always made me proud. Thrilled by the attention. Justified in my participation. Confident that I was doing the right thing. After all, these poor kids needed a voice—a fearless leader to protect them from cruel adults and the harsh arm of a made-up God—and we were the one's giving it to them.

Except Caleb doesn't have a cruel bone in his body.

And I've seen these kids firsthand. No matter what their lives are like in the outside world, at the center they're happy. Well taken-care-of and content. This makes every one of these news stories a lie.

Because of that, now I don't know what to think.

So I'm trying hard not to. Except Lucy won't let me.

She climbs into the bed beside me and curls into a pillow, her not-so-subtle way of hinting for me to make coffee to help shed her new hangover. I flip my head the other way and pretend to not to notice her. She spent the weekend away again with some random guy whose name she can't remember and whose number she already deleted from her phone. If she ever has a pregnancy scare, she'll have no idea who to call, even though she insists her memory is to her brain what 20/20 vision is to a person's eyeballs. Perfect. A perfect memory to recall a perfectly irresponsible partner who would make a perfectly awful baby-daddy. The whole thing screams of romance and happily-ever-after.

Lucy lets out another long-suffering sigh. It's the last straw, and I get up with a growl.

"You know, in the time it's taken you to beg for coffee, you could have made four pots by now and been on the road to recovery." I sail past her, bumping into the doorframe on my way out of the room. Instantly, my shoulder throbs and I can feel a bruise forming. "But no, it has to be me because apparently I'm the only one who knows how to work an appliance around here."

With my eye on the washing machine, currently spinning the load that *I* started earlier this morning, I snatch the carafe and slam it under the sink, watching as it slowly fills with water because of our lousy water pressure, which is non-existent when the neighbors above us are taking a shower. I can hear Mrs. Combs singing some song about being fifteen and walking the halls of high school in her off-key voice that would make even the world's most tone-deaf coyote howl.

I don't know Mrs. Comb's, but I've seen her a few times. The woman hasn't been to high school in three decades—two if she's one of those people whose hard life makes them age before their time, which is what I suspect because the male company she keeps when her husband isn't looking seems a whole lot younger than her.

Some days I find this whole routine funny, even her sordid—albeit gross—affairs. Today I'm not laughing.

"Could you please not talk so loud?" Lucy appears with a hand to her temple. "My head is killing me."

"Oh, I'm sorry," I say, with tons more volume than the small apartment requires. I bump the carafe against the counter on my way to return it to the machine, then accidently on purpose drop the unopened metal canister of coffee grounds. It clatters into the sink and I reach for it. At the last minute, I decide to forgo that brand and grab a whole-bean bag from Starbucks, then scoop out a handful and flip on the grinder. "Is this too loud for you too?" Maybe it's mean that I'm shouting over the obnoxious whirring sound, but whatever.

When Lucy grimaces in pain, I'm suddenly not proud of my cranky mood. Still, she's the only one around for me to take it out on, and I need the outlet.

I should have known she would see through me.

"Why don't you just call him? You're going to be miserable until you do, you know." She's trying to encourage me despite the obvious throbbing in her brain, and because of that the remnants of my hostility fizzle like cool water over flaming embers. I close my eyes for a second.

"Call him and say what? 'I know there's zero hope of working this out, but want to get together for tea anyway?' Something tells me he'll say no."

"Kate, you didn't know it was his center," she says quietly. "Besides, if he's really a man of faith, he'll forgive you and move on."

She's right; at least I think she is. But it isn't that simple, and both of us know it. "But is it really fair for me to ask? Besides, I think he has the 'moving on' part down pretty well." I flip off the faucet and reach for the overflowing carafe and pour out some water, then fill the coffee pot. "Lucy, you didn't see the look on his face when he realized who I was. It was, like…" I stare into the living room, searching for the words, hating it when I find them. "Like I punched him when he wasn't looking. He almost looked defeated. Like life could not possibly get worse. But at the same time, he seemed resigned. Like he expected it." I shake my head, aware that I'm not making sense. "Besides, how I'm I supposed to ask for forgiveness when I don't even support his kind?"

Without warning, a memory flashes across my mind like a short clip of a silent movie, but I shut it off. Usually it's easy to convince myself that what happened when I was six wasn't real. It's gotten harder to do this week.

"God and forgiveness aren't the same thing," Lucy says. For the first time ever, I'm suddenly not so sure.

"Do you need anything else?" I want to be done with this conversation. It's doing nothing but sending my mood in a downward spiral. "Because I'm going back to bed."

Lucy frowns. "It's ten-thirty. Don't you need to get ready for class?"

I fill my own coffee mug and head for my bedroom. "I'm cutting today."

"Kate, you cut every day last week. Your parents won't be happy when they find out you're failing."

"I'm not failing," I say as the door closes. "Yet." Actually, I have no idea, because I haven't bothered to check. One semester away from graduating, one semester that might flatten my grade-point average for the first time since I began my educational career, and I can't work up the ability to care.

A couple seconds later, I'm grasping for sleep while buried under a wall of blankets. It isn't until I'm suspended in that space between awareness and slumber that it finally hits me. I know why I'm so restless. It isn't the media attention or the news outlets or even the fact that I haven't heard from Caleb all weekend and likely never will.

It's that I don't like to hurt people. For twenty-one years, I've gone out of my way to make people comfortable, to speak gently, to never intentionally give another human being a reason to feel bad. Strangers in the grocery store, the down-and-out hanging out on Meridian Avenue, even the protesters that show without fail to my parent's rallies. I've never once heckled back or shouted obscenities, even during the times I've felt threatened. Few things bother me, but the idea that another person's pain could ever be directly attributed to me is more horrifying than just about anything.

But I've hurt Caleb.

Worse, since he won't take the silly nativity scene down, I'm not sure how to fix it.

I've never been one to sleep in, mainly because I haven't been allowed. As a child, at the first sign of sun, my mother would throw open my blinds and tell me to seize the day, to walk toward the light, to embrace another day or some other useless cliché I didn't want to hear. And if I didn't bound out of bed, she would force me up with a ringing bell or a cold glass of water poured straight onto my forehead. My mother: Waterboarding expert.

But she isn't here now. So why can't Lucy leave me the heck alone?

The door hinge stops squeaking, and she pops in for the fourth time today.

"Are you awake?" she whispers.

"No," I bark, groaning into my pillow. What I really want to do is cuss her out and tell her to leave, but my mother didn't raise an impolite child. Only, apparently, a grumpy one.

"You've been back here four hours."

"That means I have twenty more to go before the day is over, but thanks for the status update." I didn't realize it was this late, and I mentally try to calculate out how long I can lay in this bed without food or bathroom breaks. I figure I'm good for at least another hour. There's a little pressure on my bladder from the coffee I consumed this morning, but it should be a while before it hits the "I'm-about-to-burst" stage, so for now I decide to ignore it. Lucy sighs. Ignoring her is slightly more difficult. "Don't you have somewhere to be? Like, class? Or Wal-Mart?"

She sniffs, the first sign of irritation. "It's your turn to go to the store, so don't pass it off on me." The bed lowers on one side as Lucy sits next to me. Oddly, she's still whispering. Maybe it's her hangover. Against my better judgment, I crack an eye open and study her. Along with having an almost inhuman tolerance for cold, Lucy is also the most expressive person I know. One look at her face tells me it definitely isn't the hangover.

"What's wrong?"

She looks at me with what seems like the weirdest look of apology on her face. Or maybe it's dread. Then she glances at my door, and something in the way she does it causes me to grow alarmed. Almost like…

"Lucy, what's the matter?" I prop myself on an elbow to brace for the worst. But even my lyric-loving, imaginative mind couldn't have conjured up the next string of sentences that come out of her mouth.

"When I opened the door to go to class, someone was standing on the other side. You have company, Kate, so you might want to throw on some clothes." Before I can ask what she's talking about, she tells me.

"Caleb is waiting in the other room."

17

Caleb

"Second Chance"
—Shine Down

It takes the Department of Human services less than forty-eight hours to call up every living family member, every neighbor, every acquaintance, and every John Doe in the phone book with the last name Stiles to try to compile information. And when it becomes uncomfortably obvious that no one wants you, it takes another twelve hours or so to find a foster family willing to take you in. Twelve hours isn't much time. Not nearly enough time to get your bearings, glance around your old bedroom, and gather up a few possessions to take with you into your new life.

For me, that was a blanket my mother knitted me for my second birthday and a picture we took together at JC Penney during a hunt for bargain back-to-school clothes. I can still see the black Spider Man tee that I wore in the photo—a size too small, faded from too many washings, the ketchup stain near the rounded collar that my mother tried to cover up with her hands as she wrapped them around me and leaned close to my ear.

Smile, *the photographer said.*

I smiled wide. Wider than I'd ever smiled before.

I lost that photo somewhere between my third or fourth foster home. The move was so abrupt that there wasn't time to gather many belongings. My social worker told me she would retrieve them for me, promised to bring them with her to her next visit. She lied.

Her next visit never came. Another lady showed up instead, and all she brought was a Happy Meal. I'm not sure why I remember this, but I do.

I wish I could remember what my mother looked like.

The Bible talks a lot about having honor—about keeping your word, about your yes being a yes and your no being a no, about the power behind a man with strong convictions. I believe in the Bible. I believe it's God's word. And so I believe in things like honor and strength of character and firm principles and the Golden Rule. All four, I've been told, are the mark of a good man.

But right now I want to take that honor, shove it into a black box labeled "Do Not Open Under Penalty of Death," slap a stamp on it, and send it straight to hell where it can burn for all eternity. Good riddance. No love lost. Adios, sucker.

That's what I'm thinking as I stand staring at the sofa in Kate's living room, at the same time trying not to recall images of violent retching and lacy pink robes but having a tough time with it. Even tougher? The memories aren't nearly as unpleasant as they should be. I turn to look at Kate's bedroom door. Lucy disappeared through it five minutes ago, and judging by the look on her face when she saw me standing outside, I'm not entirely sure she's coming back. I'm not entirely sure I want her to.

What was I thinking coming here? When I woke up this morning, all I wanted to do was shoot some baskets with Ben. Maybe head to the mall to buy a couple new shirts because one of mine shrunk in the wash and another got ripped when I tried to change a flat tire yesterday. Maybe head to the office. My conscience had other ideas. *I'll bring her back next week.* That was the last thing I said to Ben, and even though my words usually have a way of coming back to bite me in the butt, darn if I'm going to be that guy who goes back on something he says. So I'll take her, let her do the interview, and bring her back to the apartment as fast as my car will drive. Duty fulfilled. Honor intact. Word kept. Done.

I just wish I wasn't so nervous about seeing Kate again. I *really* wish I wasn't so excited about it. In order to distract myself, I eye her record collection. If I squint just right, I can almost make out the titles on the spines of the albums again, but a couple are hard to see even though I think I know what they are. I walk closer and lean forward a little to be sure. *Carole King*. It's stupid, but I mentally high five the empty room for being right.

"Caleb?"

Of course I knew she would appear eventually, but I'm not prepared for the way her voice rips through my insides and turns them to shredded remnants of what used to be decently functioning organs. Right now, nothing is functioning, least of all my brain. And when I turn around and look at her...*Oh sweet Lord in heaven,* even in sweatpants and a ratty t-shirt, she's prettier than she was on television. It took two days, but I finally deleted that stupid news footage after a few dozen more viewings that I'm not proud of and will never admit to. Still, a big part of me had hoped the image of those gorgeous curls had been exaggerated in my mind. That in reality they were nothing more than stiff strands of dried-out hay—unattractive, bland, no resemblance whatsoever to spun gold.

So much for hoping. Everything in me aches to reach out and touch them.

"Hey," I say. Eloquence isn't my thing, especially when all I can think about is the only time I kissed her.

"Hey." At first she stares at me like I'm not real, but then all traces of awe evaporate and change into confusion, like she can't figure out what would possess me to show up here after we said goodbye the other night. That makes two of us. "What are you doing here?" she finally asks.

"I told you I would take you to see Ben today for your interview." I shrug and glance up at the ceiling, as though it's the most obvious answer in the world. As though I haven't spent the last forty-eight hours watching her repeat the same four sentences on television. Inside my head, a few brain cells explode from raw nerves. "So, are you ready to go?"

Kate blinks at me, then looks down at her rumpled pajamas and grasps onto her pants. "Do I look ready? Why didn't you call? I could have showered before you got here."

Her words sound stoic, but I can see the furrow of her brow, the way she looks toward to bedroom, as though summoning help. I look back at the row of albums, hoping for some as well. "You look fine. Let's go."

"I'm not going like this, Caleb. I look like a homeless person."

"Then you'll fit right in with the foster kids."

I immediately regret my words. She winces but doesn't respond, and the quiet settles in for a long moment, becoming so uncomfortably thick with tension that even I want to fill it and I'm the one who got us here in the first place. A few years ago I would have let her squirm and laughed about it. Today, because of all the forgiveness stuff that's infiltrated my head and heart like perfume in a guy's locker room, I start to backtrack. But Lucy walks into the room and looks at me, then gives the apartment a loud sigh and eye roll.

"Okay, I just have to say it. How are you a pastor? You look like you belong on a billboard advertising underwear, not like someone who advertises God." Her gaze rakes me up and down, slowly taking in my hiking boots, jeans, white t-shirt, tattoo, and then making another pass downward, stopping at the studded belt wrapped at my waist, where her eyes linger long enough to become embarrassing.

"Lucy! Stop looking at him like that!" Kate scolds her.

"Well, have you seen him? It's kind of hard not to since he puts it all out there."

I'm not sure what I'm putting 'out there', but of all the things she could have said, that was the worst. My face is turning red and it never turns red, not even when Mrs. O'Hare squeezes it and says I remind her of her husband, who for forty years has turned her on more ways than a flashlight in a power outage. The woman loves the Lord; she also loves mortifying me.

"Do I get to give you the same once-over?" I ask Lucy, because turnabout seems fair play. I don't smile, not even a little.

No immediate response to this. Lucy's bold behavior obviously doesn't work both ways. Her face turns crimson, making it clear that she can look her fill, but far be in from me to give her the same treatment. I might be ashamed of my question if I didn't find it necessary. Besides, Kate is standing there watching us, and I don't want her to think I'm flirting with her roommate. Because even though I should hate her, Kate's opinion matters. It matters a lot more than it should. Her eyes light up in the corners like she can't wait for Lucy's answer. When Lucy finally gives it, it's better than I could have imagined.

"Look all you want. You probably never get to see anything but old ladies and nuns in that church of yours. I feel sorry for you. Even Adam got to see a naked woman once in a while."

I smile at the logic, but can't resist pointing out the obvious. "I'm not Catholic. We don't have nuns at my church."

"A pity," Lucy shrugs and turns toward her bedroom. "Some might say there's nothing sexier than a lady wearing a long black robe."

"Personally, I prefer pink."

I want to kill myself when the words come out. Kate's eyes go wide, but I try to brush it off and instead watch Lucy leave, knowing that little exchange was verging on sacrilegious and definitely took a dip into crassness. Still, I have to admit that it's nice when people talk to me like a real person with real issues and not always like a spiritual leader. It hits me then that that's what I liked about Kate in the first place. She yelled at me. Told me to get out of her apartment. Looked me in the eye and lied to my face without blinking once. Right or wrong, that kind of honesty has appeal.

Everything would be near perfect if only she shared my faith.

But she doesn't, which is what snaps me back into a sobering reality. My faith is my life. There might be things I miss about the old me, but I wouldn't trade a minute to go back. Not when God has given me everything. And when you come from nothing, you know everything when you see it and dive in for all its worth. I shove a hand in my pocket and look at Kate.

"About that foster kid comment…that was a rude thing to say. I'm sorry."

She crosses her arms. "It was rude, and you should be." She doesn't meet my eyes for a long moment, which makes me think she's looking for a way out of this awkward situation. I almost wish she would find one and spare us both. But then she surprises me by walking over to her record collection, snatching up a forty-five, and handing it to me. Our fingers touch for the briefest moment, and heat rushes up my hand. From the way she looks at me before glancing quickly away, I can tell she felt it, too.

"Here, put this on. You can listen to it while I shower and change." She swallows. "But break it, and I'll kill you. It's one of my favorites." I think I see her smile, but then it's gone and it's easy to convince myself I imagined it. She moves past me and retreats into her room, leaving me in the living room alone again.

I flip the single over and take in the classic James Taylor title. A few seconds later, the scratchy strains of "You've Got a Friend" fills the apartment, and after a few moments, I realize something. Kate didn't just give me a song to play. In a roundabout way, she gave me an apology.

For now, it's enough.

"You know, no one would have blamed you if you hadn't come today," Kate says. "I certainly wouldn't have. It's isn't like you owe me anything."

I took the long way to the shelter, so we've been driving a while. It's the first time either of us has spoken.

"I gave you my word, and I intend to keep it. So in a sense, I owe you that much."

She seems to think on that for a while, growing so quiet that I start to wonder if she's fallen asleep. But then she turns her head to look at me, and I feel the words coming even before she says them.

"No one would blame you if you decided to back out now. Least of all, me."

I shrug. "Well, since my shoes are size eleven hiking boots with more scratches than a cat could have given them, I guess I don't have to worry about it."

A ghost of a smile crosses her lips, and I look away. That smile is one of the things I like about her the most, the thing that might make me toss aside everything I believe in just to see it every day. Thankfully, we pull in to the shelter parking lot and I don't have to consider the idea further. Ben's face presses against the door waiting for us. A basketball rests between his stomach and the glass and his nose is pressed flat, making him look smaller than his eleven-year-old self. A sense of pride fills me when I look at him, which is weird because I'm not his father or brother or anyone who has a claim to him, but this kid has changed over the last year, all of it for the better. A selfish part of me likes to think I had something to do with it.

I can't help but wonder how I might have turned out if I'd had someone to hang out with when I was his age. Someone to play basketball with and eat with and—as Kate will find out in a few short minutes whether she wants to or not—pray with. Sometimes even the smallest prayers make a difference, especially when it keeps the belief alive that someone actually cares.

And belief, I've discovered, is a precious commodity. One easier to obtain at a younger age, rather than a later one. Although later is better than never, as I can attest to.

If only Kate would discover it…

I stop that train of thought before it can fully play out. Because Kate isn't an unbeliever. No, Kate has beliefs…firm, rock-solid ones. She believes that everything I believe in is wrong.

It's a tough thing to keep in mind when I'm sitting so close to her, but I do it anyway. The reminders are necessary if we're going to spend any time together, and since me and my stupid mouth both have the IQ of a slow-learning four-year-old, it looks like we'll be hanging out every Monday for the next three months.

I open the door and step out of my truck. Kate doesn't move as I walk around to open her door. She's learned. In just three short days of getting to know me, at least she finally learned.

I don't allow myself to smile, even though I kind of want to.

18

Kate

"Stuck in the Moment"
—Justin Bieber

This was a bad idea. A really bad idea. We've been here an hour, and though I appreciate Caleb's willingness to keep his word and see me through this project, right now I wish he would just brand himself a liar and be done with it. Put us both out of our misery.

Everything about this trip is different than last time.

I've already gone through the list of questions I quickly prepared in my head on the drive here—twice—and I'm out of things to talk about. Ben looks bored with me. Caleb looks like he'd rather be anywhere but here. And once I'm done talking, the silence in the room is deafening. I close my notebook and shove it inside my bag, taking an inordinate amount of time arranging it next to the novel I've been reading, making sure that both spines are pointed down, that the corners line up, that both sides are perpendicular to the pens that also need to be organized—

I sigh. Lucy is right, I *am* OCD in the worst possible way.

Dreading the next five minutes or however long Caleb decides we need to stick around, I sit up and try to appear calm. It isn't easy, especially because I somehow feel like we're in the awkward, post-break-up stage, and we were never even in a relationship. I hate this whole situation, and I'm angry at all of it because I see no way out. The only thing I know for sure is that I was happier than I'd ever been during the last week with Caleb; now all hope of repeating those moments is gone. Considering our differences, I doubt we can even be friends anymore, and the loss feels so palpable it hurts.

"What's wrong with you guys?" Ben says, looking between the two of us. He might be eleven, but he's observant.

I open my mouth to say something even though I have no idea what, but Caleb rescues the situation.

"There's nothing wrong. We're both just tired, I think."

"Did you have a fight?" Ben asks. "Because you both look mad, especially you." He nods in Caleb's direction. "She keeps asking me the same questions over and over, and you haven't even offered to play basketball once, and we always play basketball, even that one time when you had the flu." He sets the basketball on his lap and rests his arm on top, looking up at Caleb with chocolate eyes. "You mad at her questions? Because they weren't that bad, even if they were a little dumb. Maybe next time she could ask me something different, something better, and then we could play ball. You want to play ball today, Caleb?"

Ben's little speech has given me whiplash because it covered so many topics. But the theme was the same in all of it: He gets one day a week one-on-one with Caleb, and I've just ruined it for him.

"We're not fighting." Caleb's words are so forceful, even I almost believe them. "Something just came up that we can't seem to agree on, so we're both in kind of a bad mood right now."

Ben's eyes light up. "Oh, well then just do what they tell us to do at school." He bounces in his seat a couple times and smiles, convinced he has the perfect answer. I would smile at him myself if I could only remember how.

Caleb glances at me. I look back at him and for a minute we just hold there, neither one of us able to look away.

Without taking his eyes off me, Caleb asks the question. "What's that, buddy? What do they tell you to do at school?"

I break eye contact first and connect with Ben's wide smile. He's sure this will work. I'm sure it won't.

"The teacher tells us to talk about it for a few minutes, and if we still can't agree, we have to hug each other anyway and learn to get along." He looks between us both, expectation and hope making his thoughts transparent. We need to talk. We need to hug. Like a strip of gauze secured across an ugly scrape, it's just what we need to make it all better. After all, his teacher said so, and teachers have all the answers.

Ben pushes on Caleb's arm. "Well, if you're not gonna say anything, at least hug her, man."

I look at Caleb and Caleb looks at me and we both take a tentative step forward. The minute his arms go around me, everything fades away except the scent of his cologne and the feel of his back muscles and the sound of his labored breaths that seem to stumble one over the other. But when I feel his lips brush my neck and hold there for the briefest second…that's when I melt. Turn into a puddle of want and longing and bittersweet sorrow right there in the middle of the gym floor. I'm not sure I'll be able to pull myself together.

But the second he lets go and only halfway looks at me, I do. Somehow, someway I'm pieced back together in two breaths. A few extra parts are broken that weren't before, but I'm together all the same.

The hug didn't make things better. The kiss only made things more difficult.

When I try to smile over at Ben, the hope on his face fades.

He knows his idea didn't work.

After Caleb drops me off, I forgo the apartment and head for my car instead. I can't face Lucy's questions right now, nor can I listen to any shallow talk of Caleb and his hotness. I *know* the guy is hot. The guy is practically perfect, and not only in the looks department. But my heart is two minutes away from breaking in half, and all my life, there's been only one person who knows, without fail, every good and perfect way to piece it back together. I pull into my parent's driveway. Right now, I want my mom.

My mother's car sits in the driveway next to mine. My father's Volvo is parked in the garage. Only then do I remember that today is Monday. My parent's day off, the day they spend resting and relaxing and rejuvenating for the busy week ahead. That day might be Sunday for most American families, but we're not like most people. For obvious reasons, Sunday is one of our busiest days of the week.

But I don't want to think about that now.

I walk through the front door and toss my purse on the bottom step of the iron staircase. An Oklahoma City Thunder game plays on the big-screen television, and my father sits on the corner of the sectional leather sofa with his feet propped up on the table in front of him and his hands behind his head. I feel a small amount of comfort from the familiar sight and take a minute to revel in the normalcy of the picture my childhood home makes. But then my father shoots forward and shouts at the television, effectively turning the nice moment into something that makes me cringe. Boys and their sports. No matter the age, they're all the same.

"Are we losing again?" I say, coming up behind him to give him a backwards hug. Surprised, he flips around to look over his shoulder at me.

"What are you doing here on a Monday afternoon? Shouldn't you be at school?"

"I didn't have a class today." Technically, it's true. I didn't have a class because I didn't *go* to one. The semantics of my words aren't important.

"Well, I'm glad to see you. We never got a chance to talk after that speech last week." He reaches for the remote and turns the volume down. His look grows concerned. "Was something wrong with you that day? You didn't seem like yourself."

For a moment, I pretend to think back on the day as though it's hard to recall. When an appropriate amount of time has passed, just like

Caleb did with Ben earlier, I make something up. Not exactly a lie, just an omission of the full truth.

"I just wasn't feeling well, I guess. Upset stomach." I don't add that it was spurred on by nervousness from my deep infatuation with the pastor of the foster center. Another thing he doesn't need to know. "Is Mom here?"

On cue, she calls from the kitchen. "Don, is Kate in there with you?" She walks out of the kitchen carrying a red mixing bowl, stirring something with a white plastic spoon, and a smile takes over her face when she sees me. Even at age forty-five my mother is beautiful, and it's easy to see why my father fell for her all those years ago. Since then, they've had the perfect love story—never a separation, rarely a fight, and no obstacles, large or small, to get in their way. Just the sight of the two of them in the room makes me feel a little better.

Most people say I look like my mother. I suppose I agree.

"What are you doing here on a Monday afternoon?" she asks, focusing once again on the bowl. "Don't you have a class?"

Unable to stomach another lie, not even a half-one, I brush off the question and chew on my thumbnail, forcing my voice to sound upbeat. "What are you making? It smells good." Despite her fit frame, food is my mother's passion, and like I hoped, in no time she's completely forgotten about school and my lack of making it a priority.

"I'm making a lemon cake for no other reason than I want one. And when I'm done, I just might eat the whole thing. Do you want to stay and—"

She stops. Frowns at me. I know that frown; I should have known my mother would see through me. Stupid thumbnail habit. I drop my arm.

Too late. She cocks her head to the side and rakes my face with her eyes, trying in the span of four seconds to locate the source of my damage and scramble for a way to fix me. When she comes up empty, she settles for the old standby. The one I came here hoping to find in the first place.

"Do you want to come in the kitchen and help me ice the cake?"

Ice the cake. It's our code word for *tell me your problems.* My mother used that phrase for the first time when Sarah Simmons pulled my dress up in front of my whole first grade class, and all the boys laughed at my Hello Kitty underwear with the tear up one side. I cried for two hours that afternoon, alternately licking mocha icing off an old wooden spoon and dipping it back into the bowl while I poured out my seven-year-old heartbreak. My mother never once scolded me for the saliva-laced frosting I applied all over the triple-layer chocolate cake she made for an upcoming dinner party. I think she knew I couldn't handle the lecture.

If only I could be that same little girl right now, whose biggest worry was public embarrassment in front of a few laughing friends rather than private heartbreak that could potentially involve the entire country.

If the whole country ever found out. Which it won't. Because there's no story to tell except a short one, which is really the most disappointing kind of story, because the words always run out before you can really begin to fall in love with the two main characters. As they say, art has a way of imitating life.

My mother hands me the bowl of lemon buttercream and reaches for a spoon. She waits until I've spread frosting on the first layer before she finally brings it up.

"Do you want to talk about what's bothering you?"

I don't. But I do it anyway.

"I think I might have a problem." And in the kitchen I grew up in, with the strains of a losing ballgame and my father's frustrated voice in the background, I tell her about everything, sparing no detail.

I'm not sure what I expect her to say—maybe delve into a lecture about why being seen with Caleb could effectively end my father's career and all he's worked for. Maybe express her disappointment that I would participate in something as controversial as Christmas without consulting with them. Or maybe just give me her signature disappointed look which worked really well when I was a kid and would probably still be effective today.

This is why it shakes me to the core when my mother says nothing and walks out of the room.

With silent tears falling from her eyes.

19

Caleb

"I Had Me a Girl"

—The Civil Wars

Nightmares are to me what sweet dreams are to normal people. A nightly occurrence. Sometimes even—if I'm lucky enough for a nap to claim me—a mid-day one. They're an unsettling inconvenience that even my faith in God hasn't taken away, no matter how many times I've prayed for it. And they're always, always the same.

Help me, Caleb. Stay awake, Caleb. *When the sound of the one voice you desperately want to hear suddenly whispers in your ear in the middle of the night, the only thing left to feel is turmoil. For that moment in time, faith is nothing but a distant memory.*

My mother…the most loving woman in the world.

My mother…the person who sometimes scares me more than anything.

In seventeen years, the nightmares haven't stopped. They almost did once, but that was before I met Kate. I've had them every night since. They show no sign of letting up, which worries me more than anything.

I slug back my fourth cup of coffee and wish for a fifth, but the canister is empty and I need to make a run to the store for more. It's a vice I wish I didn't rely on so heavily, but it's a necessary evil to get me through the day, because like always, I had a worthless night's sleep thanks to one bad dream after another, and I see no hope of a nap in my future. It would be a futile attempt anyway. My kind of naps never last more than ten minutes and usually leave me feeling worse than a tequila and whiskey-induced hangover.

It's a feeling you never forget, even if you haven't had one in years. *Help me, Caleb.*

I drop my mug into the sink and flip on the faucet, trying to drown out the persistent cry of my mother's voice that called to me from my bed. After all these years, it should be a long-forgotten sound, but it isn't. I guess when you're privy to that sort of anguish, the memory never truly fades, no matter how much you wish it would.

Instead of fading, the words get louder. *Don't go to sleep, Caleb. I'm sorry, Caleb.* Just when I think I might scream from the mantra that plays in my head every morning until something comes along to silence it—the phone rings. I've never been so happy to hear the sound.

"Hello?" I assume it's Scott because I'm already late for work, so it surprises me to hear Ben's voice on the other end of the line.

"Are you coming today, or what?"

It's Friday. He rarely calls me at all, but when he does, it's always first thing Monday morning to see if I remember. Of course I remember. No matter how messed up my mind sometimes gets, it's the one thing set in stone. The one thing I never forget.

He almost sounds annoyed. I bite back a smile at his words. "It's Friday, Ben. I never come on Friday. You know that."

There's a pause on the other end of the line. "Can you come anyway? I feel like playing basketball, and you totally skipped our game last time, you and that lady with her stupid questions. She might be pretty, but she sure knows how to ruin a fun time." His bravado is thick, but I hear the catch in his voice and I know why it's there.

"Do you need me to come today?" I ask the question slowly so that he'll hear my meaning. He hesitates, but eventually the tough-guy act fades. The voice of a frightened little kid takes over.

"Can you, please? I need to play basketball today."

I scrub a hand over my eyes in an attempt to keep my emotions in check. "I need to make a coffee run, and then I'll be there. Give me an hour."

"Don't be late if you know what's good for you," he says, his attitude firmly back in place. I grin and hang up, but just as quickly my smile fades.

A family wants to adopt Ben. After all this time in limbo—after shuffling from one foster home to another—a childless couple in their late forties has expressed an interest. More than an interest. They've scheduled regular visits with him, they've taken him on outings, and the "dating" period has morphed into a desire for a permanent relationship.

The couple is great. Married fifteen years, no criminal record, volunteers in the community. Even their mortgage is paid in full. Everything has lined up perfectly, except Ben is scared. Scared in the way I was scared. And since I know exactly how he feels, it's time to play some basketball. Because nothing cures a bout of frenetic nerves like a pick-up game of hoops.

I call Scott on my way out the door to let him know I'm not coming.

I'm walking across the damp Kroger parking lot with my bag of Folgers when I see her.

I know that coat. I hate that coat. Never mind that my pulse speeds up at the sight of it.

Kate is parked two spaces down from me, so there's no convenient way to ignore her. Besides, I don't want to ignore her, which makes my head pound and makes me long for that fifth cup of coffee right here, right now. I should have driven through Starbucks. I've got to learn to like that place.

"What are you doing?" I ask. She peers into the window of a lime green VW Beetle—not at all what I expected but why am I not surprised? My traitorous gaze rakes her up and down before I have a chance to stop it. I can imagine the outline of her hips even with that awful coat covering them up. When she turns around, I force myself to focus on her face. Another mistake since it rained this morning and sunshine is beginning to peek through the clouds. The rays are hitting directly on her head, circling it like a halo. Figures.

I glance toward heaven and give it an eye roll. She doesn't notice.

"I locked my keys in my car, and Pop-A-Lock won't be here for another hour." She spins around to look in the window again. "I can see them right there in the cup holder. So, so stupid."

I should be annoyed, but I'm not. "Move back and let me look." She takes a couple of steps away and I look inside, but just as quickly her face is pressed to the glass right next to me, a strand of her long hair brushing against my cheek. It's all I can do not to groan out loud. Focusing on the task at hand is next to impossible, but necessary. *Keys, simple press-button lock at the top of the door, her hair smells like strawberries...*

I give myself a mental flogging and eye the object dangling from her fingers. "How much do you love that umbrella?" I try to remind myself that I'm allergic to strawberries. It doesn't help.

Her eyebrows push together and she holds it up. She shrugs. "I have another one just like it in my trunk," she says.

"Good." Remembering that kiss at the center and careful not to touch her, I take it from her hands and pop out two thin metal rods and hook them together, then use my own keys to pry open her window a fraction of an inch. When a small slit materializes, I slide the metal rods inside and push them down, hit the lock, and—voila—the lock pops up and the alarm goes off. The whole process takes about ten seconds.

As she silences the loud noise, I open her door and hand her the remnants of her broken umbrella. "Sorry about that."

She just looks at me with raised eyebrows. "Do I even want to know how you knew to do that?" she says.

Biting back a grin, I look across the parking lot before leveling my gaze back at her. "Probably not. Scratch that, definitely not."

She blinks at me a couple of times before apparently deciding I'm not that threatening, and then gives me a little smile. My pulse trips over itself. "Thanks," she says. "Now move back so I can unload these groceries. My ice cream is probably melted already."

I grab two bags and walk them around to the other side of the car. "Healthy girl, I see. What kind?"

"Heath bar crunch and cookie dough," she says. "I couldn't make up my mind, so I bought them both."

"What happened to vanilla?"

She gives me a look. "I decided to be more adventurous."

"A girl after my own heart," I say without thinking. The girl doesn't believe in God, and I'm a pastor. Why do I keep forgetting this? Clearing my throat, I shut the back door and shove a hand in my pocket, wanting to be anywhere but here and nowhere else in the world at the same time. Finally, I give in and say what I've wanted to say since I saw her out here. "What are you up to today? Have any big plans?" All of a sudden I'm hoping she has none. I want to have a reason to ask her to join me in mine.

"I'm supposed to meet Lucy for lunch, and then I have a meeting with my advisor to discuss next semester's classes," she says. Not what I wanted to hear.

"Oh. Okay." I wish I wasn't facing her now, because I'm certain she can see the disappointment on my face. I twirl my keys and fist them in an attempt to shrug it off. "Then I'll see you around."

"Caleb?" I've taken a few steps toward my car, so I have to turn around to see her again.

"Yep?" Casual. Cool. Collected. Indifferent.

"What are you doing today?" The question takes some effort, and I can see the internal struggle in her eyes, probably wondering if hanging out with me is a good idea.

I stop twirling my keys. It isn't a good idea. "I'm on my way to see Ben."

She cocks her head. "On Friday? I thought you said you only saw him on Mondays."

I rub the back of my neck. "He's having a bit of a tough time right now, so I told him I'd come. In fact, he said that if I'm not there in fifteen minutes, he'll beat me up."

She smiles. I smile back at her. For the first time all week, I have a reason to. "I'd be scared if I were you," she says as her gaze drifts across the parking lot. She bites her bottom lip in thought. "Do you mind if I come with you?"

Casual. Cool. Collected. Indifferent. This time it's harder to pull off, because I'm elated at her question. "I guess that would be okay." I shrug, trying to make the act look convincing. "You'd better work on your questions, though, or he might ban you from coming back."

At that, she rolls her eyes. It's all I can do not to stare at them. "You let me worry about the questions, hot shot. You just worry about following me to my apartment." At my questioning look, she says, "I have ice cream to unload, in case you've already forgotten."

I had. So sue me.

Hot shot. I like the nickname.

She slams her door and starts the ignition, not even waiting to see if I'm following behind her.

She knows I will.

20

Kate

"All My Mistakes"

—The Avett Brothers

"**L**ooks will only get you so far, pretty lady. You might be beautiful, but eventually you're gonna need to learn to play basketball, or I'm telling Caleb not to bring you back, and I'll mean it this time," Ben says after we've wrapped an hour later. I've asked him my questions, this time not as boring according to him, snapped a few more photos, and waited an obscenely long amount of time while Ben visited the bathroom…time in which I used to tighten up my notes and lose a miserable game of HORSE to Caleb. I shot nothing but air balls and one direct slam to the rim, which is exactly the way I'm playing against Ben now, except his rules are much more bizarre than Caleb's were, especially for the athletically challenged who hate sweat unless it involves the occasional jog or lying on a beach towel close to a tropical body of water.

Like me.

My make-up is definitely running now. I swipe a sweat droplet off my eyebrow and try hard to maintain balance. All three of us are surprised I haven't fallen over yet.

"This game makes no sense," I snap. "I've never seen anyone in a real basketball game shoot a ball backwards with one leg hanging in the air. It's dumb. Not to mention a little degrading." I need to pee, and it doesn't help matters that Ben and Caleb are making me stand for so long with my thigh pressed to my stomach. And this is the third straight time. They both deserve zero points for creativity and a punch on the arm for cruelty.

Instead, they stare at each other like I'm the crazy one.

"Kate, Kate, Kate," Caleb says on a sigh as he slaps the ball from my hand. My stomach flutters a little at the way he says my name, but I mentally command it to settle. We're as different as sun and rain. Besides, that combination usually creates a summer storm, and I've never gotten over my fear of thunder. "The first rule in HORSE is that there are no rules," he continues, giving the ball a bounce. "The second rule is that anyone who complains has to do twenty sit-ups." He nods once to the floor. "On the ground, now."

My breath rushes inward. "That isn't a rule! You made that up! Besides, Ben hasn't done any sit-ups today, and neither have you." And considering my current predicament, sit-ups are the last thing I need. I shift my weight from one foot to the other as a sharp pang of pressure hits my bladder, but I really don't want to mention my need to go. Caleb gave Ben the hardest time when he finally returned from his trip that lasted forever. I just can't subject myself to the same fate. Sometimes my need for self-preservation trumps all things logical. I'm a girl. Whatever.

"That's because we haven't complained one time."

"You have no reason to complain when you control the whole game!" I protest.

Caleb and Ben eye one another, sharing a wicked gleam that I don't like. I can sense an ambush, and this is definitely going to result in one. But that's the thing they don't know about me—I'm nothing if not prepared.

"I think it's my turn to make some rules," I say, with much more bravado than I feel.

"Okay," Caleb nods, unable to hide a smirk. "Now you're in charge. So tell us, Michael Jordan, how are we going to play?" He tosses the ball at me. I breathe a sigh of relief when I actually catch it.

"It's about time you let me call the shots." I raise an eyebrow and bounce the ball, cringing when it hits my foot and shoots sideways. Retrieving it, I try my own smirk that really doesn't work under the circumstances as I sidle up against the three-point line. "See if you can do this." Thinking I need to learn to keep my mouth shut, I sail the ball in a hook-shot over my head.

Ben and Caleb both laugh as though they rehearsed it. "Now," Caleb says, retrieving the ball, "are we supposed to air ball it into the water cooler like you did, or should we actually try to make it into the basket?"

"Shut up, Caleb." I eye the cooler, checking for a leak or some other sign that it's broken. Seeing nothing but a slight tilt to the side that wasn't there before, I ignore it and turn to watch him, and then Ben, hook-shot the ball straight into the net. It's like I was cursed with an inability to be superior, even in my attempt to play a dumb game.

I say this out loud, and two minutes later, I have all five letters, and I've griped my way through eleven sit-ups. It's on the twelfth that I can't take it anymore and get up to run, the sound of more obnoxious laughter following me the whole way down the hall.

A few minutes later and feeling a whole lot better, I emerge from the bathroom, only to find an empty and silent gym. No sign of Caleb, Ben, or any of the other kids that had been so loud only a few minutes ago. A woman walks out of the kitchen and glances at me with what I interpret as displeasure, although it could be my guilt creeping up for hitting that water cooler. She walks away, and since she's the only one of us who seems to know what she's doing, I follow her around a corner. And that's when I see it.

Everyone is congregated around three long tables preparing to eat dinner. What had been only moments before a very rambunctious group has morphed into a roomful of silent and respectful observers, each listening to a man at the front of the room give what I'm pretty sure is a talk about acceptance. There's no microphone, so it's hard to hear from the back of the room.

For the first time—since a gymnasium scattered with children doesn't allow for the best perspective—I see the children in light of their varying circumstances. To my right sits a gathering of a half-dozen teenagers in contrasting degrees of cleanliness. Two of them text on old flip phones while three others talk in less than quiet whispers. A few empty spaces over, a group of elementary-aged kids sit with their hands in their laps, listening as best they can with the pleasant aroma of grilling hamburgers hovering over the room.

On cue, my stomach growls. I quickly try to absorb the sound with my hand just as my gaze lands on the lone toddler in the room, a three-year-old boy with skin the color of warm cocoa wearing an ill-fitting t-shirt and diaper, legs swinging back and forth from his perch on a man's lap. Everything stops except my heart, which speeds up to twice its normal rhythm.

Caleb is holding the boy. I watch as he tweaks the toddler on the chin and whispers something in his ear. A lump forms in my throat when the little boy rewards Caleb with a wide smile—the cutest smile I've ever seen. From his spot next to Caleb, Ben laughs. Caleb grins and holds up a finger to quiet him, then steals an arm around Ben's shoulder and pulls him gently to his side. Ben settles in as though he belongs there, and I wish with a longing deep in my chest that I could take his place—that I could be the one to lean into Caleb's side. But I don't belong there.

I don't belong here, either.

Feeling suddenly self-conscious, I turn my gaze to the speaker.

The man looks to be in his late forties, maybe early fifties, with the trim build of a man who still keeps up a regular workout regimen. His auburn hair is parted on the side in the clean-cut style most politician's wear, but it's thick. Age has served him well. Something about him looks familiar, but I can't place where I've seen him. I take a cautious step forward to get a better look, but just as things start to click into place inside my brain, he goes silent.

For a horrifying second I think he's looking straight at me, and I want to turn and run away. I'm caught. Outed. Identified as the imposter in the room. But I don't run fast enough.

He bows his head.

All around the room, one-by-one, everyone else bows, too.

Even Caleb.

And that's when everything inside me explodes—even though every muscle inside my body goes rigid, even my lungs, because I was raised to believe that God doesn't exist. As far as my parents are concerned, I've never prayed in my life.

Except for one time that I never, ever talk about.

I can't breathe, because I'm not supposed to absorb this. I can't focus, because I'm not supposed to see this. I can't think, because I'm not supposed to know this. I can't listen, because I'm not supposed to hear this.

The man with the athletic build prays.

And then it clicks. This is the man whose picture hangs on my parent's refrigerator—has for four weeks now. The man I see every time I visit and want a glass of milk, a slice of cheese, a scoop of ice cream that my lactose-intolerant body isn't able to tolerate but craves anyway. He doesn't look like a threat. He doesn't sound like one either.

Dear Lord, thank you for this food and every one of the children repre-sented here. Bless them, bless what we're about to eat, and bless the remainder of our time together. Amen.

Everyone opens their eyes, and just like that, the silence in the room detonates, replaced by the sound of three dozen overly-excited voices as dinner is served. Fellowship and laughter rings everywhere, and from his spot two tables over, Caleb catches my eye and waves me over. I force myself to walk towards him, and when I'm halfway there, he tosses me a roll that I somehow catch even though I don't recall my hands moving. Score one for me. Needing something to settle my nervous stomach, I sit down next to him and take a bite. He situates the toddler between us and looks up at me.

"Where've you been, Princess?"

Princess. The nickname is back. I wish joy was the first emotion I felt upon hearing it, but it isn't. Any trace of joy that might've been inside me disappeared a few minutes ago during that prayer. The woman I followed in here places a plate on the table in front of me and I pick up my fork. Hamburgers after all—my favorite—but I can only manage to pick at it. Even the thought of eating makes my stomach churn.

"Princess?"

I'm saved from having to answer when the man who gave the speech saunters up and stops in front of our table. My pulse sputters, but I take a deep breath and focus on the man's features to calm myself down. Up close, he's even more handsome than he appeared from across the room, though his nose has a slight bend to it that probably came from a break. A high school fistfight? A run-in with a door? His thick auburn hair shows signs of gray at the sideburns, but his face is surprisingly free from lines except along the sides of his eyes. This is a man who likes to smile. He smiles at me. I work to return it, hard to do when I want to throw up.

Caleb studies me. "Kate, this is Scott's father, Chris Jenkins. I'm not sure if you remember Scott…"

"I remember Scott," I say with very little inflection in my voice. I hate the way it sounds and I only vaguely remember him, but it's enough. Scott has red hair. Scott sat next to Caleb at the bar.

I blink up at Mr. Jenkins. He and his son resemble each other. When I don't give the customary "Nice to meet you," which I should say but can't right now because my brain is still on pause from the man's earlier speech, Caleb clears his throat.

"Chris is the head pastor at my church. We've been friends for a few years now." The way he says it implies there's more to the *friends* story, but he doesn't elaborate. I don't ask him to. Some things are better left unsaid.

"Oh, really?" It's all I can manage, all I can think as the man looks questioningly at me, then recovers his frown with a smile that seems more genuine than forced. My reciprocating smile is obliging by contrast, but it's the best I can do. The most I can feel.

I feel fake.

I am ripped apart.

Caleb's eyes stay on me as Mr. Jenkins says goodbye and walks away, but I don't look at him. I look at my plate. Only my plate. Everything blurs into one mass of muted red as my mind tries to process the only thing I've been able to think about since Caleb's pastor—his supposedly evil, overbearing, threatening pastor, because isn't that what pastors are—said *Amen*.

He told the children they were accepted here.

He prayed for the food.

He blessed them and the workers busily buzzing around us now who are clearing plates, refilling my water, volunteering their time to make sure a bunch of orphans, foster kids, and one underdressed toddler are taken care of.

And for that, my parents are punishing them.

For that, I'm punishing them.

For that, a nationwide organization that makes my parents, me, and my big fat trust fund a ton of money is punishing them.

Unable to breathe, I jump up from the chair and take off, retracing my earlier steps and barely making it before panic sets in. I lean over the sink and force air into my lungs, but my mind stays in the same place. The place that I don't want to visit, but am being forced to visit anyway. Chris Jenkins never once yelled. Chris Jenkins never once threatened. Chris Jenkins didn't look evil. Chris Jenkins looked…kind.

I straighten and unroll a strip of paper, using it to wipe the anxiety from my mouth. Wild eyes stare back at me in the mirror, eyes that look nothing like mine. Then again, I'm not the same girl I was just a few minutes ago.

You're okay with that? Being the poster girl for a long string of hurt, false accusations, and misplaced kids? It doesn't matter to you? Caleb's words from last week come back in a rush, but the difference is now I'm not. I'm not okay with it. For as long as I can remember, I've punished so many people with a great big smile on my face.

But how many? And how often?

And how many times has it happened because a church leader just like Caleb dared to tell a kid he cared about them? And, heaven forbid, pray for a plate of food?

How many times?

21

Caleb

"Looking for a Reason"
—Little Big Town

*M*y first foster family couldn't handle the crying, said I kept them awake at night. The second family thought I talked too much. The father was a writer and needed the quiet to think. The third thought I should smile more, interpreting my lack of enthusiasm as a buried violent streak that might rear its head unprovoked on their ten-year-old daughter. I liked their ten-year-old daughter—Abby was her name, I think—and I was only eight. I'm not sure what he thought I might do, but Abby and I used to climb the sweet gum tree and look for the bubble gum inside those weird, spikey balls that fell from the branches. We never found any, but then again I only stayed with them two weeks. Two more and who knows? We might have discovered some.

By the fourth foster home, I actually had a violent streak. I punched a hole in their garage wall when the new social worker fed me some lame line about my mother's memory lasting forever in my mind. That's what adults say to assuage their guilt when they do something stupid like try to replace irreplaceable mementos of your mother's face with a hamburger you don't even like.

Translation: She forgot the picture, so I took it out on the wall.

Because of my fist-to-drywall reaction, instead of the standard home visit she showed up for, she put me in her car and we went in search of *another home. That one—the fifth—finally stuck. It was the worst experience of my life aside from watching my mother die on the curve of my own bloody knee. At that home I learned not to cry or talk or frown or hit or even climb a tree. The one time I did, I fell. After I fell, I cried. While I cried, I got hit for making too much noise. Over and over and over.*

That's when I learned to stop talking.

I don't force anyone to talk, ever. If someone needs the silence, I'll join them in the middle of it. Even if that means I have to wait forever to hear the sound of another human voice.

She's been quiet for a long time, but I'm not sure why. One minute, we were playing a rather ridiculous game of HORSE, and the next thing I know she's gone. Gone where is anyone's guess, but it took her twenty minutes to come back, her eyes all downturned and worried. Kate can sometimes seem on edge, but underneath the layers of pink is a woman with a ton of strength. If she'd been mad about the game, I have no doubt she would have tossed the ball at my head. Her aim might be off for everything else, but she definitely would have made that target.

"You haven't said anything since we left the Chapman Center," she finally says, staring out the car window. I turn to look at her profile, mainly because I'm surprised she's finally spoken.

"I was kind of waiting for you to talk. Call me crazy, but it's never seemed like a good idea to interrupt a girl when she's in the middle of a mood swing. Kind of like pulling food away from an eating dog—you just might get snapped at." I swerve to avoid the shredded remnants of an old tire lying on the road.

The glare she levels my way makes me grin. Maybe it wasn't the nicest comparison, but it had the desired effect all the same. Her bad mood seems to lift a little. A good thing, because I hate to see a woman down. Too many memories come with the picture.

"You really should pay more attention when you're driving," she says. "This truck can't exactly corner like it's on rails, you know."

"Don't insult my truck. It's sensitive."

"Don't compare me to a rabid dog, because so am I."

"I didn't say rabid. I said hungry. There's a difference."

"But both have sharp teeth." She bumps my knee with her own. "All the better to bite you with, I suppose."

I want to make a crack at that, but my throat goes dry. I'm pretty sure she didn't mean it the way it sounded, but I find myself *liking* the way it sounded because it has me thinking about her lips on mine—which is wrong on every level, but I'm a guy so of course I'm thinking about that. I clear my throat and tell my sarcastic self to shut the heck up and move on.

"Why are you so quiet, Kate?" It probably isn't the best thing to ask, but the fact that I'm still thinking about her mouth on mine means it's time for a little redirecting. "What happened back there when you left the room?"

She stops and stares at me, obviously not expecting the question but also not retreating from it. She doesn't look away, doesn't even blink once or twice to give herself time to answer. Just stares, almost unseeing, like she's too unsure to formulate a response. But then she comes up with one, and by default shows me a little of that strength I knew she possessed.

"I didn't expect the prayer." She nods behind her, back in the direction we just came from. "I expected a speech and a whole bunch of indoctrination, but not the prayer."

I guide the car into the parking lot in front of her apartment and manage a shrug, not following her logic but trying to appear confident anyway. "I'm not sure what you mean about indoctrination—we don't believe in that sort of thing. But how could you not expect a prayer at a church-run foster center? We're Christians there, Kate. Of course we would pray."

"That's not what I mean. Of course I expected the *prayer*."

She doesn't elaborate, just grabs a penny from my cup holder because for some reason she seems to have an obsession with them, either that or it's the only thing she can think to do with her hands, but it doesn't matter which theory is right because both somehow manage to irritate me. So now I'm confused and annoyed and completely lost, so I slip the coin from her fingers and flip it back where it belongs, aware that I just threw a tiny fit over bubble gum money, but still.

"Those are covered in filth, just so you know."

"I'll scrub my hands and mouth with Clorox when I get home," she says. For the span to two breaths, the car is silent.

"So you're upset about a prayer," I finally say, "even though you knew a prayer would happen? Forgive me for saying it Kate, but isn't that the clinical definition of a schizo?"

"I'm not schizophrenic, and you're not paying attention."

Again, silence, and I'm about to break my self-imposed code never to interrupt it because this girl is acting crazy. And crazy deserves an exception to my rigid rule. But thankfully, Kate speaks first and I don't have to.

"Of course I expected a prayer, Caleb. My whole life, I've been told about your kind of prayers."

"My kind of—?" I force my jaw closed to keep from saying anything else, feeling my muscles tense and my defenses rise. It's all I can do to stay quiet, because I think I've just been insulted and even though the Bible says to turn the other cheek, I'd rather insult her right back because it would be a lot more satisfying.

But I won't, because I'm me and my stupid brain can't seem to grasp the fact that the two of us together are a terrible idea on the most important level. I won't insult her, because I still like her. I kissed her, and I'm still thinking about that kiss. I want to lean over and do it again right now, which makes me the biggest glutton for punishment who ever lived.

I sigh. "What do you mean, my kind of prayers?"

Kate runs a hand through her curls while I try not to stare. "The sort of prayers that make people feel guilty for having bad thoughts. The sort of prayers that remind people they're going to hell if they cuss or drink a beer or stay too late at a frat party. The sort of prayers that make you feel hopeless and worthless and completely lacking in—"

I stop her. "Now, have you actually heard someone pray these prayers you're talking about, or is this another one of your assumptions?" I eye her. "And for the record, infomercials don't count. You know, the ones where the supposed pastor tells you that bad things will happen if you don't send two-hundred bucks to his address in the next five minutes?" I shake my head. "Other than that, where have you heard someone pray a prayer like that? Because I, for one, never have."

"So you're saying you wouldn't go to hell if you have a beer?" Her tone sounds defensive, as if she issuing a challenge and daring me to deny it.

"Of course I wouldn't go to hell if I have a beer." I can't decide whether to be patient with her question or tell her how stupid it is. I relax my face and go for the former.

"So you've had a beer since you became a Christian?" She doesn't ask it like a question. She asks it like I'm related to Pinocchio and my nose is about to grow.

"A few times, but not lately. I don't drink anymore."

She nods and raises a smug eyebrow. "Because Christians can't drink. Because God will smite them, ruin them, punish them, and all the rest of that hell-fire and brimstone stuff."

If this is what she thinks, no wonder she isn't a fan of God. I take a breath and decide to lay it all out there, figuring her reaction about what I'm about to say is her problem, not mine. I dealt with it years ago and have almost forgotten it. Almost.

"No, I don't drink anymore because right after I became a Christian, I skipped church and met up with some old friends. One thing led to another and we wound up at a bar, I got drunk, and before the night was over I wound up in jail for nearly killing a guy. Not a fun thing to explain to Scott's father, especially when he'd just given me a job at the center." I lean forward to look at her in the eyes. "And in case you're wondering, the charges were dropped. They conveniently left that part out of the news story last week when they ran that report about your parents' rally." I run my palm over the steering wheel. "So that, Kate, is why I don't drink anymore. And I can tell you with one hundred percent certainty that if I die tonight I will wind up in heaven, even if I get smashed out of my head on whiskey. Which I won't. Because, like I said, I don't do that anymore."

She doesn't speak for a while, which isn't all that unexpected I guess, but then I look over at her and she's got her hand wrapped around another of those darn pennies and I didn't even see her reach for it. Her lips are parted and she's rolling the coin across her bottom one, and then she looks at me. She looks at me with that penny stuck to her lip and I see fear. Fear and uncertainty, and neither are attractive on her, especially because both seem directed at me.

"You sound so sure," she almost whispers.

I reach up to pluck the penny from her mouth, then run my thumb across her lower lip. "Like I said, one-hundred percent."

She exhales, long and slow. "I've never been that certain about anything."

"Well, maybe it's time you look for something different to believe in." I let that sentence hang, thinking that she can draw her own conclusions. I've never been one to force my beliefs on another person or beat them over the head with spiritual lingo, but I have been one to pray. And now I start. Kate needs prayer. Kate needs hope. Kate needs God, but I keep that to myself. For now.

Again she gets quiet. I don't know what to do and I don't want to leave, but I need to get to work. I was supposed to be there ten minutes ago. Not that I'm on a strict schedule, but I said I'd be back at noon and my word is generally important to me. But Kate isn't finished talking.

"What you said earlier…" She turns toward me, and I expect a bunch of questions about my time as a convict, but she doesn't go there. In the weirdest way, it's like she didn't even give it a second thought. Like my criminal past—a past that hardly justified my imprisonment in the first place—doesn't even matter. "I've never heard those kinds of prayers, Caleb. The judgmental kind, I mean. My father has told me about them, cautioned me against them, but I've never actually heard them." Her hand falls to her lap and her voice sounds far away and in awe, the way a person might sound after recovering from a long bout of amnesia and all of a sudden remembering their forgotten family members. "Caleb, I've never actually heard them. I just assumed…"

Her words roll around in my mind, and I respond in the only way I know how. "Assumptions aren't usually pretty, and they're hardly ever right. Kind of like thinking a girl is shallow just because she likes the color pink."

She catches her smile, but not before I see her mouth twitch at the corners. "I'm the unshallowist person you'll ever meet."

"With the worst grammar. Pretty sure that wasn't a word." A smile forces its way across my mouth. And then we're just looking at each other. Sitting there side by side in front of her apartment, with neither of us able to look away. I'm staring at her and she's staring at me and all I can think about is the girl I met just two weeks ago. The girl with the cool record collection and the gorgeous hair. The girl who deals with drinking and being drugged in the nastiest way possible. The girl who's as competitive as I am, even when playing a kid's peg game. The girl I still happen to like, way more than I should. And it's like we're back at that place—in the middle of the easy familiarity I felt when we shopped for Christmas trees and bought the ugliest pink princess stocking that's now hanging from my bedroom doorway.

Christmas. It's only two weeks away.

Maybe it's nostalgia messing with my mind. Maybe it's the thought of new beginnings and the opportunity that comes along once a year to start over. Maybe it's the random snowflake that lands on the windshield, putting me in a brighter mood. Maybe it's the fact that work will be there tomorrow, but she might not be. Or maybe it's just that Kate is Kate, and I'm just not ready to let go of her.

So I kiss her. Lean across the seat before I can talk myself out of it, and kiss her, the feel of her soft lips underneath mine nearly undoing me for the brief seconds it lasts. When she moans into my mouth and my pulse skyrockets and plummets at the same time, I pull away. There are only so many things I can take without completely losing my mind, and right now that isn't one of them.

But I can't leave her, of that I'm certain. Forgetting my earlier vow to keep my distance, to take her home right away, I open my mouth and say this.

"You interested in spending the afternoon together, or do you have someplace you need to be?"

22

Kate

"I'm Only Me When I'm With You"
—Taylor Swift

I have fourteen places I'm supposed to be right now, and standing in a vintage record store in downtown Oklahoma City isn't one of them. Yet with one invitation from Caleb, with one *kiss* from Caleb, I'm flipping through musty-smelling vinyl at two o'clock in the afternoon without a care in the world.

School fell by the wayside again, but sometimes life works that way.

"This one?" he asks, holding one up.

"Yep. For my eighteenth birthday from my cousin." It's the fifth one he's asked about, and so far I own them all.

He gives me a look. "Your cousin bought you a two-hundred dollar James Taylor record for your birthday?"

I shrug like it's no big deal even though I know exactly how stupid it sounds. "She knew I didn't have it, so...yes. I think she found it in Dallas, though it might have been Houston. I can't remember." Her family lived in Dallas for two years before they moved to Houston, where they still live, but I can't remember if the move happened before or after my birthday. It might have been before, because—

"Well, la di da," Caleb says before dropping the record back into place and making a face at me like a kid who's just been told he can't have candy before dinner. I blink at him, because the fact that he said it is cute. *Really* cute. But not a phrase a twenty-four-year-old guy who looks like him should ever utter out loud.

"You did not just say that. What are you, a four-year-old girl?"

His eyes narrow. "I got a thirteen dollar iPod case from Scott for my last birthday. So yes, I did just say that. And no," he looks down and gestures to himself, "pretty sure I'm not a girl." I blush. Darn right he's not a girl. Not in those faded-just-right jeans and fitted white tee that shows just enough of his tattoo to make me think bad thoughts. If Caleb notices my red face, he says nothing about it. "You, on the other hand, are a spoiled rich girl, and I'm not sure we should hang out anymore. Not with your expensive taste in music and who knows what else. I can't afford you. Next thing I know, you'll be telling me you only buy three-hundred dollars jeans and fly to New York City to get your hair cut."

"Only once a month," I say with a straight face. "And I think we both know these jeans cost more than three hundred dollars. I mean, look at them. They've got upscale written on the back pocket." I look down at the old Levi's I pulled on in my rush to get dressed this morning and shrug. I don't look great, but I won't apologize for it. It's not my fault Caleb helped me with my car in the rain and then decided to forgive me.

I'm still in awe that he's here talking to me.

I still can't get over that kiss.

"I'm surprised they're not pink."

"You're not going to let go of that are you? One pink coat—"

"And robe. And comforter. And—"

"I get your point. As soon as I get home, I'm burning all of it."

He laughs. "Don't do that. Everyone knows princesses wear pink." And just like that, he's back to looking at albums, flipping through them like he didn't just make my heart leap three feet in the air and land in my stomach. Other guys have given me nicknames. My father called me Sugar Bear the day I was born, and the name has stuck through skinned knees, a particularly painful molar extraction two days before my twelfth birthday, and my first broken heart. My first boyfriend called me Katie-pie even though I repeatedly told him not to and broke up with him just to get away from the sickening moniker. My date for senior prom called me baby after midnight when I told him payment for the wrist corsage he bought wouldn't come in the form of sex in the back seat of his Fiat, or any other place he had in mind, even if he were the last man on Earth, and for heaven sakes get your groping hands off me.

Funny how Princess is a whole lot sweeter than Katie-pie, but Caleb could christen me with it a hundred times a day and I doubt I'll ever get sick of hearing it.

"Take a look at this." He gives a little laugh and scans the cover of an album closely before flipping it over to read the back, and I gasp so fast that something catches in my throat and I cough. The sound is obnoxious and I can't seem to quit, but I don't care because if I'm seeing it right, Caleb has just stumbled across the one album that I've tried to find for three years with zero success. And he's gone and found it in a record store with green shag carpet and a broken light bulb on 5th and Lewis. I dart around to his side of the isle and inch in close to his side. He pats my back as I strain on tiptoe to read the album's title over his shoulder. I would swat his hand away because I'm not a baby who needs help to quit choking, but I like the way it feels there.

I like it even more when I stop coughing and he makes no move to drop his arm. I lean in a little closer.

"I can't believe you found it." The words come out on a squeal and I'm almost certain a tear or two might fall if I don't pull myself together, but Caleb has just found *my Precious* and I need a moment to come to grips with it. I sniff and press shaking fingertips to my lips, overcome with pent-up emotion.

But then Caleb has to ruin the moment because he's a guy, and that's what guys do.

"You can't be serious. This thing?" His arm falls and he's looking at me like I have two heads, but I ignore him and carefully take the album from his hands. It's the most beautiful thing I've ever seen—even prettier than the pink cashmere scarf my mother bought me last month that I'm sure as heck never going to tell Caleb about.

"That is the most ridiculous album I've ever seen in my life," he says.

"It is not!"

"Donny and Marie's Osmond's greatest hits? You're crying over Donny and Marie's greatest hits, sung by what is quite possibly the cheesiest act in musical history? The fact that you're the only person I've ever met who owns Dylan's *Freewheelin'* doesn't even make up for the shame you ought to feel for wanting this."

"You wouldn't understand. My grandfather bought me this album when I was a kid, but I lost it when we moved. He died of cancer three years ago and I guess I thought if I could just get my hands on one—"

"Oh, cut the crap. Are you going to use that fake cancer excuse for every dumb decision you make? I suppose you're going to tell me he died of breast cancer like your aunt?"

I suck in some air, and a tear finally slips down my cheek. He has to be the most insensitive person in the entire world. I clutch the album to my chest and breathe deeply, telling myself to remain calm. After all, he's not *trying* to be a jerk.

He looks at me, and his whole face falls. "Hey, Kate, I didn't mean—I thought you were kidding. That you were just making up an excuse for your bad taste in music." I think it's supposed to be an apology, albeit a bad one. He makes up for it when he gently slides the record from my hands and tucks it under his arm. With his other hand, he pulls me to him and folds me into his chest. He smells so good, like mint soap and leather, like musk and man and everything right in the world. I close my eyes and inhale, and quite possibly bury myself a little deeper into him. "I have an idea," he whispers into my hair, "It isn't that expensive, so I'll buy the album for you. That way, you'll have something to remember him by. Is that okay?"

I nod without raising my head, and nearly die when his lips brush against my forehead. He holds them there for a moment and the feeling is heaven, but then he breaks away and exhales long and slow, like he can't decide if all this kissing is a good idea or not. I'm not sure, either, but I want it to happen again and again. Of course that's when I start to feel guilty, and because fate has a way of kicking me in the teeth, when he finally releases me and I swipe under my eyes and turn away to scan the racks and racks of vinyl, it happens. I'm an idiot, and it happens. And if I'd waited one second longer, I might have been home free.

"Did you just smile?" Caleb asks.

Forcing my face into a neutral expression, I turn back around blink up at him. "Excuse me?"

His eyes narrow. "You smiled. I saw you."

I feel my stupid lip twitch, which doesn't help me at all. "Well—I mean, you *did* kind of kiss me and—um…it *was* kind of nice, and…well…" I run my finger along a row of forty-fives and think about whistling, but decide it might not be the best move.

He shakes his head. "You are the biggest con artist I've ever met in my life, and I spent forty-eight hours in jail. Cancer, my butt. You probably don't even have a grandfather. Buy your own stupid album." In one swift movement, Donny and Marie land back in my hands.

"Are you seriously accusing me of lying just to cover my embarrassment over this?" I hug the record and try to muster up some genuine outrage. All that materializes is fake outrage, but that'll work, too. "I do too have a grandfather!"

A hand goes on his hip. "Did he die of cancer?"

"Not technically, but—"

"Is he dead at all?"

I tilt my head. "Dead in what sense?"

"Dead in the dead sense." He rolls his eyes. "Donny and Marie. What a joke." He snatches the album back from me and begins to read the titles out loud. *I'm A Little Bit Country, 'A' My Name is Alice*—is that actually a song? That's the dumbest title in the entire world. Now, let's see—" Okay, now I'm a little embarrassed and I grab it from him before he can shout out anything else.

"Stop it! There's nothing wrong with wanting this record. Just because you're an album snob—"

"Says the woman who has a forty thousand dollar one tucked away inside a cheap Wal-Mart bookcase at home."

"I'm buying the album, Caleb. Because despite what you might think, I did have it as a kid and I did lose it in a move." I head for the register, secretly hoping he'll follow. He does. "I've been trying to find it for three years, but funny enough no one seems to have it—"

"Because they were all wisely destroyed in a church album burning," he interrupts.

That stops me cold, and I wheel on him. "Churches do that?" The idea is preposterous. Outrageous. Wrong on every level. What if something was burned that I don't have yet?

"Not since the eighties, and not mine. Not one I personally know of, in fact. I was just making a point."

I roll my eyes and plunk my purse on the counter. "A stupid point. I'll take this," I say to the heavily pierced guy behind the counter, wanting to ask if the barbell running through his top lip hurts, but keeping the question to myself because the guy looks scary and I wouldn't want to make him angry, even with Caleb here to protect me. Which I suddenly doubt he would do since he thinks I have horrible taste in music. I dig out my wallet and pull out two bills.

"Dude, you're buying this?" pierced guy says. "I didn't think this would ever sell. Couldn't see the point of carrying it in the first place since it's so incredibly lame and only someone with rotten taste would—"

"Please just tell me how much is costs." Men. Is there really a point to their existence? And why is he calling me a dude?

"Seventeen ninety eight. But are you sure you want—"

"I'm sure." I plant two tens on the counter and storm toward the door, forgetting about the change, not caring about a bag, hearing Caleb high five pierced guy and chuckle softly as he trails behind me.

"You don't have to get so mad," he says as the door closes behind him.

I'm not mad—how could I be when I still haven't wrapped my mind around the fact that Caleb doesn't hate me—but then again he's still laughing, so all of a sudden I am, in fact, slightly ticked off. It's like a whiplash of emotions around him. Surprise. Fear. Regret. Sorrow. Embarrassment. Attraction. I've run the gamut today, and the sun hasn't even made a full pass across the sky.

I toss a half-hearted glare over my shoulder. "You're a pain." A childish thing to say, even if it's true. I clutch my new album to my chest like a favorite teddy bear, thinking about how excited I am to listen to it when I get home, because despite what Caleb says, 'A' My Name is Alice is a brilliant song, one I'm currently humming in my head as we walk. He opens the truck door for me and I climb in.

"What's that you're humming?" Caleb asks as he slides in beside me.

So apparently it wasn't just in my head. "Nothing."

He starts the car and slides me a wink. "That isn't nothing. It sounds pretty upbeat, a little on the silly side, almost like—"

"It's nothing. Not anything you would know. Definitely not a Donny and Marie song. Shut up."

He laughs harder and shifts the truck into reverse.

Five minutes later, he's no longer laughing. Neither am I. In fact, the whole mood inside his car has changed, and not for the better. Just as we pulled onto the highway, Caleb got a phone call from Scott, one that lasted less than a minute but was filled with more tension than a two hour horror film, and he hasn't said a word since. Not to me, not even to himself. I wish he would scream. I wish he would yell. I wish he would pound the steering wheel and call me a hundred different names whether I deserve them or not, except I'm pretty sure I do. I heard the call. I heard Caleb's responses.

It doesn't matter that he only said four words. I know what Cease and Desist and Defunded means.

The lawsuit was filed. Caleb's job…the kids…his reputation…

Everything he's worked for is in jeopardy, and I have no idea what to do.

I only know that every time our relationship takes a small step forward, something comes along to drag us right back into disaster.

23

Caleb

"A Church, a Courtroom, and Then a Goodbye"
—Patsy Cline

*T*he best way to guard against unnecessary emotion is to surround yourself with a barrier, an invisible fence so intricately constructed it's impenetrable by even the most well-meaning of souls. That worked for me for years, but it's hard to hold a fence together when outside forces are constantly pushing against it.

The first chink in the fence fell the day Scott Jenkins walked up to me at a Boys and Girls Club and asked me point blank how long I planned on carrying around that crate-sized chip on my shoulder. Like most other days, I was high at the time—don't remember on what—but I do remember that he came there often, tried to talk to me often. I made fun of him for it. The guy was scrawny, practically a waif. I was twice his size.

Turned out he wasn't intimidated by me in the least.

I wanted to punch him for his question.

So I did. Right above the jaw on that spot where the lower lip meets the chin bone. Instead of the cowering I expected, Scott stood up from the dirty gym floor and fought back. The pitiful effort earned a laugh from me until his stupid high school class ring cut a three-inch gash in my left hand. Despite the wound and my failed attempt at not squealing like a girl, it earned both of us an exit from the place. Not sure anyone has ever been evicted from a Boys and Girls Club before or since. We hold the distinction.

We became friends that day. He's my best one now.

The second chink in the fence appeared when I got arrested and Scott's father bailed me out of jail. The third when Chris Jenkins, at Scott's insistence, brought me into his home and gave me a place to stay because his son wouldn't give up on me. I had no idea why back then; now I know it was his belief that anyone as stubborn as me could be just as tenacious about God if harassed enough to actually develop a relationship with Him. The fifth and sixth and seventh chink unraveled without my noticing, but I guess that's what happens when you find yourself living among a group of people who eagerly make you part of their family.

I hadn't been part of a family in forever. I'd almost forgotten what it felt like.

The fence fell in a heap the day I finally found God. For the first time in years, I was free.

I can feel the fence going up again. Choking me. Binding me. Snagging me in its grip.

Link by link by link.

I want to stop it, but I'm not sure how. Even prayer doesn't seem to work.

I've never prayed so hard in my life.

It's been exactly eight days since I dropped Kate off at her apartment without saying goodbye. I know this because I've thought about it six hundred and ninety-one thousand times since then, once for every second that's ticked by. I'm not proud—of my thoughts or my behavior toward her—but sometimes life is just life, and I can't change what happened.

I can change my clothes, though. I'm going for a run.

By the time I've made it to the bedroom, I've slipped off my shirt and both shoes, my whole body on edge, ready to take out some pent-up frustration on the pavement. I normally run every morning before work, but in between reporters calling and appeals being filed and nerves being soothed, everyone involved at the church is jittery. I haven't run all week. My muscles are tight, gripped in an iron fist of protest, screaming for release.

If I have to run twenty miles in one direction, I'm going to give it to them.

It takes me no time to drag a t-shirt over my head and replace my dress pants with a pair of black running shorts. I pull on my running shoes without untying the laces, because I found just the right combination of loose and tight a couple of weeks ago and haven't messed with them since. Finally, even though I'm burning up, I pull a hoodie over my head because it's December and if Mrs. Jenkins sees me wearing nothing but a thin shirt she'll give me a lecture about catching my death or the flu or any other disease that might be catchable nine days before Christmas.

It's nine days before Christmas. I'm not any more excited about it than about the way things finished with Kate. One week has messed up my outlook on everything.

I lock the apartment door and jog down the steps, then stop short when I see Scott pull into the driveway. I live in an apartment above the Jenkins' detached garage—have for a while. Somehow along the road called my life, I was blessed enough to find a family that fit, and I haven't been eager to let them go just yet. I was eager to move out of the main house, however, because Scott is a pain in the butt to share a bathroom with, so a couple of years ago, I moved into the apartment. Seeing Scott in the driveway is a normal daily occurrence.

The look on his face is not.

"What's wrong?" It's the kind of question people ask to be polite, not because they really want to know the answer. I don't. I want to run. And based on the incredibly crappy week we've had so far, the news is bound to be bad.

Scott loosens his tie and raises an eyebrow. "Are you going for a jog dressed like that? Do you realize it's freezing out here? It's almost Christmas, Caleb." He says it to be funny, knowing those kind of comments get under my skin. The difference this time: Scott doesn't smile at all.

"Don't be your mom. Now, what's wrong? Whatever it is, the shock of it is written all over your face, so you might as well tell me."

In eight short days, we've been through orders to cease and desist, an order by a merciful judge blocking the original order, countless interviews by the press who've made us sound both sympathetic and like heartless fools who only care about money. We've had offers of representation by well-known attorneys who charge exorbitant fees we can't pay, and offers from attorneys to represent us for free who have no winning records to speak of. We've been shut down and reopened, funded and de-funded. We've been picketed and protested, cussed at and prayed for. We've been accused of being too Christian and not Christian enough. We've sent out press releases, granted interviews, and answered phone calls from local television stations to *The Today Show*, but every time we issue a statement, the game changes.

A new order is given. A new opinion is granted. A new judgment is issued. Public opinion is swayed.

But through it all, Scott has stayed upbeat. Hopeful. Surprisingly faith-filled where my faith has been shaken. Old habits have settled in with me, habits I'm hoping to break tonight, even if I have to pound them out of me.

But the look on Scott's face has me doubting that will happen.

"They've been granted an emergency injunction." It sounds bad, but I'm not about to admit I'm not entirely sure what that word means.

"Who has? And what's the emergency?"

"The Hawkins's. Their organization. Kate. Whoever you want to put the blame on. And apparently, the emergency is us. We're a threat to small children, a threat so dire that our funding has been stopped. As of this moment—until we appeal and even then only if we actually win it—the only way we'll be able to operate is through private donations. And since that barely adds up to enough money to pay the light bill…" Scott sounds bitter. Scott never sounds bitter, and that bothers me more than anything.

Except for the part about Kate. That pretty much has me seeing red.

"How can the ruling go into effect so fast? Shouldn't they give us thirty days or something? Isn't that the law?" I have no idea if it's the law; I just know that it should be. Funny how you never pay that much attention to things likes rulings and laws and injunctions and politics in general until you're standing in the middle of political chaos. Now, I'd give anything to be a lawmaker so I could tell these local judges to stick it up their—

"Not when it's classified as an emergency. In that case, a ruling is immediate."

Scott and I just stare at each other, both lost for wisdom, direction, and words. Eventually I find some. "So what does that mean for us? More importantly, what does it mean for the kids?" I pull the drawstring on my hoodie, toying with the idea of burying myself inside the fleece lining. "Twenty of them are going to show up tomorrow, and what are we supposed to tell them? The older ones have been kicked out of school and we're their only option. The younger ones…" I grip the back of my neck and turn toward street, determined to get ahold of my emotions. Scott has never seen me cry. Never. His father has twice, but that's about as far as I'm prepared to take the family bonding. Once I get control of myself, I face him again. "The younger ones. For a couple of them, we're the safest place they've got."

I'm in the bottom of a ravine again, holding on to my mother's lifeless neck. I'm alone, scared, cold, without anyone to rescue me. And maybe that's why I relate so fiercely to these kids, because as neglected as they might be, I've been there, too.

"I don't know, Caleb. I really…" He scrubs a hand over his face, a move I've seen from his father a hundred times before but never once from him. Scott is composed. Scott is unruffled. Scott is glee club and ironed slacks and perfectly starched shirts. But for maybe the first time ever, Scott looks as frazzled and messy as me, and it's beginning to show up on the outside. "I don't know. All I know is that we need to trust and pray and hope that—wow." His eyebrows shoot up and he looks at me. "I haven't seen that face in a while."

I study him, only now aware that my arms are crossed. "What face? I'm not making a face." A rock is at my feet and it's bugging me all of a sudden, so I kick it down the driveway. It's hard to miss the way Scott rolls his eyes, especially when he adds a well-placed sigh just to annoy me more.

"You're definitely making that face. The one that says '*Quit talking to me about God and trust and praying and crap and I won't talk about your inability to dress better.*'" I cringe, remembering the night I said those words verbatim after his father bailed me out of jail. Scott asked if he could pray with me. I ignored him, so he prayed anyway, out loud. I let him go on for a few minutes, tried not to listen as he finished up and began to ask me about my life, my childhood, my mom. And then I snapped.

Don't ever talk about my mother.

The way I figured, God had taken everything from me that mattered—my father, my mother, my home, even that stupid JC Penney picture. Obviously the Man hated me, so over time I learned to return the sentiment. I wanted nothing to do with God, even less to do with Scott and his Bible and his concern and his talks about faith. But like mold that sticks to cheese no matter how many times you cut it off, Scott wouldn't go away. Scott prayed for me all the time. At breakfast, in the car, in the freaking bathroom. I finally became a Christian just to shut him up.

Scott is living proof that prayer actually works.

"I wasn't making a face."

"Don't give me that line. I know that look when I see it. I've only been on the receiving end of it about a thousand times from you alone."

Now I'm cold. I zip my jacket and blow into my hands. "I swear I wasn't—"

"Caleb." The way he says my name shuts me up fast. "Don't let this mess up your faith. I know this situation stinks, but you've been through worse, and we'll get through this, too. Do you still believe that God is still God?"

Scott is two years younger than me, but in every way that counts, he could be my father. He has the wisdom of men twice his age, maybe more. I rub my hands together, uncomfortable with his question. Of course I believe that God is still God. That He loves me. That He can take care of everything, even this. Don't I?

"Yes." Even I can hear the doubt that turned that word into a question.

He doesn't believe me, I can tell by the way his left eye almost imperceptibly narrows, but he lets it slide. "Good. Those kids need a place to be, and I have no idea how, but we'll give them one. Somehow things will work out. They always do."

"Can I go now?" I'm not trying to brush him off. I just need to get out of here, be alone with my thoughts and take my anger out on the pavement. That's the strange thing about anger. No matter how hard I pray, and no matter how much I've changed, it's the one thing determined to hang on. Right now, it's gripping my chest in an iron fist, squeezing and churning until the air in my lungs feels heavy like blood.

"Sure. Go." I see the way Scott's shoulders slump but pretend not to. And with that, I take of running.

Five miles later, the blood in my lungs has changed to bubbling lava, and I can barely catch a breath. But I won't stop. I have no plans to stop unless I fall over or run out of air, whichever comes first. It might make for a long walk home, but I don't care. The last thing I need is the four walls and one television waiting for me inside my garage apartment. Walls tend to close in, and television almost always delivers bad news. If I never hear another piece of bad news in my lifetime, I'll still have heard more than most people.

I've run past neighborhoods and stoplights and a drive-in movie theater that closed down years ago. I've passed a middle school and three churches—two Baptist, one Latter-Day-Saints. I've run uphill and downhill, through twists and turns and one Do Not Enter sign with a Detour pointing right. I ignored it and took my chances, jumping over a three-foot crater in the pavement without breaking stride. Laws haven't stopped me before, especially ones as meaningless as that.

My adrenaline has pumped so hard that a whirring began in my ears a while ago and hasn't let up. I like the noise, I just wish it were louder. Then it might drown out the sound of Scott's earlier question. *Do you believe that God is still God?*

It isn't the first time I've been asked that question. It's the first time I don't have an honest answer.

Of course I believe He made the world. That He died for me. That He lives in heaven, and all the other stuff most kids learned in Sunday school but I didn't learn until a few years ago. Those things are easy. But God wasn't there when my father left. When my mother died. When my foster father hit me. When I wound up in jail. God seems great at performing the big things—making animals, trees, humans out of nothing but dirt. It's the little things He doesn't seem to care much about.

How am I supposed to believe He'll take an interest in this?

I'm depressed and no closer to an answer when I find myself in front of my church. My feet carried me here of their own accord, without thought or consideration whether I wanted to be here or not. At least that's what I tell myself. I don't want to be here. It's the last place I feel like visiting now. As I look at the gleaming white and red building, I'm resentful and pressured and angry all over again, because suddenly I hate the sight of this place. With its steeple and cross and great, big welcome sign. I hate it.

At least that's what I tell myself.

For a minute.

And another.

Until I remember.

Until my breathing slows and I stare at the cross—really stare at it and all it represents—and I know it in my gut all over again. Until I'm certain that I'll never walk away, never, no matter how angry I get. God waited around for me; the least I can do is return the favor.

This place is home. This place is me. This place is my life and my soul and where I found meaning a few years ago. This place is the kids and the elderly and the addicts and all the other lost souls who need the same grace I was offered back when I didn't want it.

This place is God and friends and family who made me their own. It took blood and lava and sweat and screaming muscles to rediscover the thing I already knew but tried for a week not to believe.

God is still God. God cares about everything. Somehow this will get fixed. With God's help, somehow *I'll* fix it. Even if I have to climb through lawsuits and accusations and look up the definition of injunction to do it.

Apparently the definition of injunction doesn't include a detailed description of why an opponent in a lawsuit who keeps making ridiculous nativity demands should stay the heck off your property, because if it does, a certain pink-wearing, record-loving blonde is ignoring it for all it's worth. She sits in front of Joseph—*Joseph*, like she owns him or something—with a thin black bag leaning against her leg, looking as out of place as a stripper at a tent revival. Except Kate looks beautiful as usual. Perfect and gorgeous and angelic.

Just like that, lava burns in my lungs once again, dripping a little of its hot sting into my heart as well. Because I don't want to think about Kate being beautiful. Or angelic.

I want to think of her as the enemy. The instigator. The devil amongst the holy family in this little scene. It's worked for me all week, and she's on the verge of blowing that image just by sitting uninvited on a pile of hay.

Maybe someday I'll get control of this anger issue. Maybe someday I'll get control of how much I like her. Someday isn't now.

"What are you doing here?" I say, aware that the bite I intentionally forced into my voice sounds even harsher than I meant it to.

She looks up at me, grimacing a little but not at all intimidated. I'm sweaty, winded, and tired—not exactly making my best case to appear threatening.

"Wow," she says. "I thought churches were supposed to welcome people, not yell at them to get off their lawn."

"I didn't yell, and you're sitting in my nativity. Get out of it, or I might scream loud enough for the whole town to hear."

Surprising me, she stands and picks up her bag, walks slowly across the yard, making sure each step is extra firm, and sits down in the grass right at the edge of the dead flower bed. The ground is frozen and I'm certain she's cold, but instead of jumping up, she sears me with a look and picks up a landscaping stone. She tosses it in the yard, and then tosses another.

"I bet you feel like screaming now."

She's mad. This keeps going until stone number seven, when I tell her to stop. She's made her point. She thinks I'm a jerk. A jerk who kissed her last week and left without a word. Maybe so, but I'm also a jerk who doesn't feel like transferring stones from the grass back to the flower bed all evening.

"Get up," I say. "I'm not going to yell at you. Just tell me what you're doing here."

She stands, but she has to think about it first. The girl is as stubborn as I am. "I came to see you."

"And you just assumed I would be here? I do have a life, you know. I don't spend all of it at church." I don't know why I feel the need to say this. Sure, I have a life. But almost all of it *is* spent here. I like it that way.

"Well, I stopped by the bar first but didn't see any fistfights breaking out in the parking lot, so I left. Thought I'd give this a try."

Smart mouth.

"Cute. Now, you want to enlighten me so that I can run back home before midnight?"

Her bravado slips, and for the first time she looks nervous. She chews on her lower lip and clutches her bag to her chest. "I don't know why you won't just take this thing down," she gestures behind her to the nativity. "But I don't want the foster center to close, Caleb."

It isn't what I expect her to say, but this girl has surprised me a dozen times in the three weeks I've known her. Still, it doesn't matter what she wants. She waited too late to decide.

"Even if I took it down—which I won't because it's Christmas and I don't bow to that kind of pressure—it doesn't matter. Because without funding we'll have to close our doors eventually. It costs a lot to feed these kids, and short of a miracle, we just don't have the resources. It's too bad you didn't have a change of heart *before* you decided to sue."

"I'm not the one who decided to sue. Last night, I begged my parents to drop the lawsuit. I told them about you and about everything I've seen on the days that you took me to the center. About Ben and your pastor and his speech..." She stares into the yard, her gaze following a leaf that releases itself from a branch and drifts to the ground. She stays focused on that leaf for the longest time, and when she looks up at me, her eyes have changed. They've lost their fierceness. Now, they just look sad. "My parents have done this sort of things for years. They're driven, determined, and it's never bothered me before." She blinks up at me in a look I can only describe as haunted. "Now it does. I don't want you to lose your money. I don't want the center to close."

My heart twists inside me. One, because I think she means it. And two, because the ruling has already been made. We're out. Broke. It's too little, too late.

"There's nothing I can do about it now." Using the hem of my sweatshirt, I mop up the trail of sweat sliding down my forehead. "Until the appeal is filed, until a ruling is made, our hands are tied. Right or wrong, we rely on public funds to keep this place running. Without them, we can barely afford to keep the kids fed, never mind the tutors and counselors and the electricity needed to keep the building warm at night."

When it comes down to it, I don't know why she's here. It's great that she's changed her mind, but I might be more appreciative if she'd decided before now that I wasn't the bad guy her parents have portrayed me to be on every news outlet that would run their story.

"What if I can help? Would you let me?"

"Why should I?" I'm acting like a child, but I don't care. Besides, short of personally demanding the judge reverse his decision—an impossible action—there's nothing Kate can do.

"Because I can. Help, I mean."

I breathe a humorless laugh. "Kate, you've helped enough already. How exactly do you think you can help now?" It's a mean thing to say, but I'm running low on nice.

Without skipping a beat, she hands me the bag she's been clutching to her chest the whole time we've been standing here. In the time it takes to pass from her hands to mine, it hits me. She's right. I'm a jerk. I'm an idiot. I'm clueless. And she's an angel.

All I can do is stare at the thin piece of cardboard as the bag burns in my hands. It hurts to look at her, hurts in every single part of me. Because hurt is all you feel when your heart's about to explode.

I can't believe what she's done.

24

Kate

"A Hard Rain's a-Gonna Fall"
—Bob Dylan

H e closes the bag slowly and tries to hand it back to me, his face two shades paler.

"I can't take this. You're crazy."

My arms stay wrapped in front of me. I knew he would react this way, so I'm prepared with an answer. "No, what's crazy is saying that you can't take it. What's crazy is thinking that this," I nod toward the bag still dangling from his fingertips, "is more important than a foster center that feeds and shelters kids."

His arm falls, but he hasn't dropped the bag yet. "Kate..."

"I have a lot more, you know. Probably enough to keep the place running indefinitely. And if I need to give each of them to you one by one, I will."

For the longest time he just looks at me, shock, disbelief, awe, relief and about million different emotions crossing his features. Then I see something that looks a lot like—

I can't afford to process that one.

"Kate..."

"I think we've established that you know my name. Just take it, Caleb. Please. If I could get the cash, I would, but I can't until my twenty-fifth birthday without my parent's permission. This is the next best thing. I can't live with myself if the center shuts down because of me."

"I can't live with myself knowing that you gave this away. You need to keep it."

"Why? So it can sit in a frame on a cheap Wal-Mart shelf? There's no value in that."

"*The Freewheelin'* costs forty thousand dollars. There's a heck of a lot of value in it, if you ask me."

"I didn't ask. I asked you to take it. So will you please stop arguing with me and just do it for heaven's sake?" I try to sound tough, like I'm not hurting inside. Not because of the record or the money or the fact that my parents are going to be seriously angry with me if they find out what I've done, but because of Caleb. It's been a long eight days, and I miss him. I miss talking with him. I miss laughing with him and eating with him and picking out Christmas trees.

Last week I bought a tiny, pre-lit artificial one—one covered in fake snow and everything—and put it beside my bed. My very first tree. Every night I plug it in and stare as the blinking lights lull me to sleep. No one knows this. Not even Lucy. Caleb won't know either. Because after today, I'm not sure I'll ever see him again. Right now, I'm giving him my last reason to need me.

He's still staring at the bag. I sigh. "Caleb, you need money. I've done my research. If you lose public money—which you already have, if the news stories are correct—" I raise an eyebrow and wait. He gives a single nod. "So, your funding is gone. Will that make up the difference?" I indicate the package he's still barely hanging on to.

"Yes, but—"

"It's an old record. I'm not offering you a kidney, though the way I feel right now, I'd probably give you that, too." I look away, the first pricks of tears beginning to sting my eyes. I've made such a mess of things. Ignorance isn't an excuse. "It's a record. And it's yours. Besides, I don't want it anymore. It takes up too much space. So if you don't take it, I'll probably put it in a garage sale or something."

Finally, he looks at me, the faintest trace of a smile behind his eyes. Then his expression turns serious and he searches my face. He searches my face and I'm not sure what to think. And then I can't think at all and my breathing turns shallow because he zips his hoodie to cover his damp shirt and takes a step forward and does the one thing I never thought he would do again—no matter how much I wished for it. He pulls me to him, and I don't even care that he's sweaty and sour and smells like the outdoors. There's no place I want to be, not now or not ever. I wrap my arms around his waist, and he presses his lips to my forehead and leaves them there. I grasp the sides of his jacket and sink a little. And sink a little more. Hours go by and seconds go by, and before I've found enough time to fall completely, he releases me. I wish he wouldn't. Falling is nice.

"The kids...you have no idea—" He clears his throat, rough with emotion. "No idea." He looks at me. "Are you sure?"

I nod. "I'm sure."

"Then I'll take it, and I'll use it, but I want you to do something for me first."

Maybe alarm bells should chime in my head, but they don't.

Instead, all I hear is music.

Under the cover of nightfall, it's easy to relax, easy to forget about cameras and lawsuits and reporters and public perception, even when public perception is everything in a business like the one my parents are involved with. Then again, Caleb could have asked me to fly with him to the moon and back, and I would have gone without thought to consequence or safety or responsibility.

When Caleb said he wanted me to do something for him, I expected him to request a condition I couldn't meet, a statement I wouldn't possibly make. Instead, he asked for this. I haven't seen nearly as much of the guy as I want to in the past few weeks, but still he surprises me.

We're in his office. Inside his church. Halfway through *A Hard Rain's-a-Gonna Fall*. Facing each other on the blue-carpeted floor while Caleb listens with his eyes closed. He's been this way since the album started playing, and if I didn't know better, I'd think he was praying. As it is, I'm pretty sure he's trying to memorize this moment. I know he is, because I've had this exact same moment myself. It's been five years, but I'll never forget the first time I heard this particular album. There's something inherently pure about the sound of a needle on vinyl—the crackle, the static, the rich undertones of music playing in its most basic, unprocessed form—especially rare vinyl that only a handful of people own.

Once upon a time, I might have described the experience as spiritual. Now, for a reason I can't even fathom, I'm no longer comfortable with the label.

I look down at my hands, at the stubby fingernails and torn cuticles that are screaming for a manicure I will never give them because I can think of a hundred better ways to spend my money. My mind drifts to Caleb just as it has every single second of the last five weeks.

His collection of records surprises me. Haphazardly stacked a foot high behind his desk, his is an assortment of genres—blues, country, folk, gospel, and hard rock. It's the hard rock that amazes me most. I didn't know you could have Alice in Chains, or KISS, for that matter, inside a church.

When it comes to Caleb, I'm quickly finding out that I don't know much. I'm also discovering that every one of my pre-conceived notions about Christians are as laughable as the idea of me inside a place of worship.

Yet even that doesn't seem so far-fetched all of a sudden.

I swallow and close my eyes, disturbed by that last thought. I barely recognize myself anymore. At the same time, I find myself liking the old me less and less. This new version of me seems much more pleasant. A lot less suspicious. And not nearly as closed-off.

The song ends and another one begins, but I keep my eyes shut. If

Caleb gets to hide inside himself, so do I. At least that's what I try to do for a few seconds, until he speaks.

"Dance with me."

My eyes fly open and I gape at him. "Dance? In *here*?"

"No, on top of the roof," he says without skipping a beat. "Of course in here."

"But we're inside a church. Don't they have rules against that?"

Caleb has the gall to look amused. "Only that we can't use a disco ball. Not that I would want to, considering that I hate bell-bottoms and I wouldn't be caught dead in—"

"Caleb," I stop him. "I am not dancing with you inside your church. What if we get caught?"

He stands up and brushes off his shorts. "Then I suppose we'll be hauled off to jail, but the sentence isn't nearly as long as you might think. Not since the president loosened up restrictions last year." I can feel my eyes go wide as he pulls me to my feet.

He laughs as one arm snakes around my waist. With the other, he pulls me to him, locking our hands together and bringing them to his chest. My half-hearted attempt at resisting melts at the feel of him so near. He seems happy. Like this is the best idea he's had all day and I'm certainly not going to spoil it for him. Ignoring the doubts that assault my mind, I tuck my head into his neck and let him sway us back and forth as the song ends and another one begins.

"So I take it you were kidding about us going to jail," I say against his skin.

He laughs over my head. "You're so cute."

"Gullible, you mean. Stupid and gullible." His laughter fades, and I smile. An intense quietness invades the room for several seconds even as the music continues to play. Not an uncomfortable silence, not the kind where awkwardness settles in and no one knows what to say. This silence is different. There's an expectation to it, a lingering. Like neither one of us wants to leave and we both have a million things to say and absolutely no idea where to start. This is where my training should kick in, but it doesn't. I've made dozens of speeches over my lifetime—all written for me, all designed to rail against God and caution multitudes of youngsters my age not to fall for religious brainwashing. But here, with Caleb, I'm completely lost for words. Ashamed and lost, the most heartbreaking combination. Maybe someday I'll quit feeling so intimidated. I doubt I'll ever get over the regret.

I realize then, with a generous amount of defeat, that I'm hoping for a someday. With Caleb, I don't see a way for someday to come. We're too different, on opposite sides of a very wide fence, even though my patch of grass seems to get smaller every day.

As we dance, I think back to a few minutes ago when Caleb first brought me inside this church. I was scared, felt like a trespasser with the spotlight of a thousand sins shining directly on my head. But this church isn't what I expected. First of all, there's no finger-pointing Jesus that I've come to associate with Christianity—the kind of Jesus that says "I Want You" with a stern expression on His face, Uncle Sam-style. I have no idea if this Jesus exists somewhere or if I made Him up, but He definitely isn't in this building. In fact, I haven't seen a picture of Jesus at all, only a few Bible verses framed against the wall that speak of loving your brother and doing unto others, and a rough cross mounted behind a make-shift stage in the auditorium. It's weird—but with its blue cushioned chairs and airy, glass-encased walls, this place almost seems normal. Like a mall. Or a museum. Definitely not a building with something to hide.

Second of all, I don't smell bleach. Maybe that's crazy, but the one time I do remember entering a church—sometime during my ninth year and only because protesters backed me into a doorway—the overpowering scent of bleach is the only thing I recall. When I asked my parents about it later, they explained that churches are cleaned daily to scrub the smell of sin from the air. I was young, so I believed them. I've believed them this whole time, but something tells me now that it might not have been the truth.

It seems I no longer know what's true anymore.

"Do you want to keep moving like this, or should I turn the album over?" Caleb says over my head.

I blink up to look at him, having gotten so accustomed to the quiet and my own thoughts that I didn't hear the album stop playing. I feel stupid knowing we were dancing without music all because I chose this moment to space out, but Caleb doesn't laugh. He doesn't even smile. Instead, he's looking straight at me in a way that makes me think he can peer into my soul. I have things inside me that I don't want him to see, so I look away before he can.

"Sorry. I didn't hear it stop." My arms fall to my sides and I step back. "How long has it been over?"

"A couple of minutes, but you seemed to be thinking pretty hard about something so I didn't want to interrupt you. Do you want to hear the other side, or…" He lets the sentence hang, an open invitation.

I want to. Stay, I mean. If I could have anything in the world, I would stay here all night. With him. Doing nothing but sitting knee to knee on this outdated carpeted floor as we finished this album and moved onto another. I haven't listened to Alice in Chains in years.

But I can't. It's time to go. Anything else is just prolonging the inevitable, and for Caleb and me, the only inevitable thing is goodbye. Because even if I decided to drop it all and join him on his side, my background wouldn't make things that simple. My family is too sensational. Our cause is too.

I can't do that to him. I can't do it to me.

"I should go. I have class tomorrow and…other stuff to do." I pick up my purse and hang it over my arm, fully aware that the excuse is a flimsy one at best. But when your heart is breaking, sometimes a lie works like a Band-Aid; it patches you up just long enough to make a getaway before everything falls apart. I'm two seconds away from bleeding everywhere.

He looks at me a long moment as though waiting for me to change my mind. I don't.

"Okay. I'll walk you out." With a sigh, Caleb takes the album off the turntable and returns it to the sleeve, then pauses with it in his hand. "You're sure about this?" He raises an eyebrow, giving me another chance to reconsider. About the album or about leaving, I can't be certain. But it doesn't matter, because both require the same answer.

"Completely sure."

He opens a desk drawer and slides the album inside, then quietly follows me out of his office. We walk in an awkward, wordless silence toward the exit, neither of us sure about what to do, me feeling the sadness of yet another goodbye. But just as I reach for the front door handle, he suddenly stops me, pressing his hand firmly against the mahogany wood. His arm is planted against my shoulder, pinning me in place. I don't have to see his face to know he's battling with himself. I'm fighting the same thing.

"Stay," he says in a low voice. I feel his breath on my neck, surprising me. Unable to stop myself, I turn and see that we're close, too close, but everything about it feels right. I can't force myself to move. My pulse throbs in my throat.

"Don't leave. Stay here with me a little longer." Caleb scans my face, my throat, my mouth. The look in his eyes is the same look he wore before he kissed me last week, full of conflict. Hesitant, but determined.

"Caleb, I—" It's all I can manage, because right now all my reasons for leaving have left my mind, and before I can come up with one, he exhales and his lips are on mine. His fingers thread through my hair, trace my jawline, run down my back and meet in the middle, pressing me to him. Our first kiss was gentle and soft, our second was sweet. This one is laced with a definite hunger, and I return his kiss with the same feverish urge. I run my hands through his hair and settle my back against the door again, pushing away the screams inside my head that tell me to stop. He positions himself against me, and that's all it takes for me to lose it completely.

But then his lips break away and he moves backward. "I'm sorry. I don't know what came over me, but we can't do this—not here. It's not—this isn't—" He squeezes his eyes shut and looks at the ceiling, and maybe I shouldn't, but I go to him again. I reach out with a shaking hand to touch his arm, and that's all it takes before he's against me again, backing me against the door, lined up with me from mouth to hip to knee to feet, kissing me with more intensity than before. My mind turns to liquid as his hands reach around me, his fingertips caressing the bare skin above the waistband of my jeans, behind my back, up my spine.

Just when I begin to contemplate how far to let this go, he's gone.

He practically jolts away like he's been electrocuted. He turns around, both hands behind his head as he faces the hallway. I can almost hear the internal chastising he's giving himself, a warning to back off and get control. He's breathing hard; his chest rises up and down.

"I'm sorry," I say. My legs feel weak and I fumble behind me for the doorknob for support, trying to catch my breath but having a hard time. I've never been kissed like that, I'm unsure if I ever will be again, and I want it more than anything. But I can't have it. "I won't say anything to anyone, ever. No one will know that you kissed me, Caleb. I mean it."

He spins to face me. "You think I'm worried about you talking? You think I'm ashamed of you?" He shakes his head, lines deepening in his forehead. "If I had it my way, the entire world would know that I've fallen for you, Kate. But I can't tell them, because no one will take it well. It would be a media nightmare. You'd be raked over the coals, and we both know it."

I can't breathe at his words, my mind stuck on the first part. He's fallen for me. Caleb has fallen for me. But he's right; no one in my world—probably not his either—would understand. The pastor and the atheist—perfect fodder for late-night television. Yet a big part of my heart soars anyway, because I've fallen for him too. He's perfect and gentle and tough and big-hearted and so good looking and everything I've ever wanted in a guy, and knowing it makes me fly a little more.

"This can't happen again," Caleb says. "I mean it, Kate. It isn't good for either one of us. Most of all you."

Part of me knows he's trying to protect me, but with those words, I crash land back to earth, all at once angry and defensive and wounded. I'm a big girl. I can take care of myself.

"You're right. It won't happen again. I'll make sure of it." I feel my chin go up. Darn him and his stupid rules. His stupid morals. His stupid nativity scene that he won't take down. His stupid convictions that don't mean anything. If he would just throw them all away then we might have a chance. But he won't, because he's too stubborn. I turn toward the door again, and stop. Everything inside me folds in on itself, because I know.

It's those convictions that make him so attractive to me.

Even his faith in God. Even though I don't understand it.

Caleb is right. This can't happen again.

"You don't need to take me to see Ben tomorrow." The pain of a thousand needles stabs me behind the eyes. Mondays with Caleb are the best part of my week. "I'll find another way to write my paper, so please don't worry about it."

I hear him move behind me. I feel the soft flutter of my hair and know that his fingers are touching the ends of it, caressing it, before they drop away completely. He sighs, long and labored.

"I'll be there. Same time as last week."

"Caleb, don't—"

"I'll be there. Like I told you, I'll be there every week until you're finished. You've given everything to me, Princess. I'll try hard to return the favor."

I squeeze my eyes shut and try not to gasp from the heaviness crushing me, but I don't cry. Sometimes it's hard to remember not to. With a nod, I open the door. My shirt is twisted at the waist and my hair is mussed a bit from his hands, but I don't stop to fix either as I walk down the stairs. The sound of Caleb's keys jingle in the air as he locks the front door behind me.

"Kate, wait," he calls after me. "At least let me walk you to your car." I stop, but I don't turn around. There isn't anything left to say, and the longing is still there, stronger than ever. "Please don't be angry," he whispers when he catches up to me.

He's right; I shouldn't be. None of this is his fault; he didn't ask for it any more than I did. So when he steps up beside me and wraps an arm loosely around my shoulder, I lean into him. He slows our steps and pulls me closer. Unable to take it, both of my arms work their way around his waist, and it takes us much longer than it should to walk across the sidewalk.

Under the cover of nightfall, it's easy to relax, easy to forget about cameras and lawsuits and reporters and public perception, especially with Caleb's arm around me. Especially with my arms around him. Especially when I feel so comforted and so secure and never want to leave and hate that I'm doing that very thing now.

But then I hear it. He hears it, too, and my arms fall and his arm drops and he spins around to search the night. There's nothing but trees and blackness in front of us.

And a camera. Maybe two.

They click in our direction.

We can't see them, but they see us.

And I have a feeling. A sick, sick feeling, that the time I've spent with Caleb, the private time that has felt at moments like heaven itself…

Has just gone straight to the tabloids.

25

Caleb

"Back To Me Without You"
—The Band Perry

Judgment binds you up in chains, yet it's handed out so freely.

By well-wishers lacing concern for a seven-year-old with threads of "this poor kid doesn't stand a chance." By Christians asking for prayer, then listing out the intimate details of another person's life while convincing themselves it isn't gossip. By the news media passing out condemnation without knowing all the details.

Judgment hurts. Until now, I'd forgotten how much.

She wasn't at her apartment on Monday when I went to pick her up. She wasn't there Tuesday when I stopped back by to check on her. Reporters were, however, and they saw me. Shoved microphones in my face while I struggled to get to my car. Later that night, I was the lead in the six o'clock news. *Jesus Dates the Devil* was the headline they chose to use. Clever. Cute. It hurt like a cigarette burn.

If I'm torn up this much, there's no telling what's going through Kate's mind. In my world, it's just me. In Kate's, she's bound to have an entire sea of people ticked off at her.

I'd hate to be in her situation, but I'd trade places with her if I could.

I haven't seen Ben all week. I'll have to make it up to him somehow.

26

Kate

"You Are Not Alone"
—Michael Jackson

I'm scared and confused and lonely and worried. I've been accused of things and shouted at and threatened by many. I've alternated between the silent treatment and a dozen rounds of twenty questions from my disappointed parents. But it's my own fault, and I'll learn to live with the consequences, even if no one seems to care one way or another if I fall apart.

But what I can't live with, what I can't forget, is that I've felt this way before.

Once before. When I was little and afraid and lost inside a Target store, when a frightening man who didn't look right picked me up and told me to be quiet and proceeded to carry me to his car even though I cried and asked him not to. But the difference is that day, even though someone strange was carrying me and I was screaming and no one was around to help me, I didn't feel alone.

Because back then, I did the only thing a little girl knows how to do when she's scared.

When she feels threatened. When all she wants is someone to rescue her. When she hasn't yet lost her innocence. Or faith.

I prayed. And right then, I felt it. A Presence with me. And just as it came, another man was there. He walked towards us—the kindest face

I've ever seen before or since. *Don't be afraid,* he said before he told the stranger to put me down.

Just like that, the stranger did.

And right then, before I could say anything at all, my mother came outside. When I looked around to tell her about the nice man, he was gone.

I dreamed about the man last night, the only time I've revisited that day in my life. *Don't be afraid,* he said in my dream. As soon as the words left his mouth, I woke up covered in a sticky sweat.

It's becoming harder and harder to convince myself I don't believe in God.

But I'm trying.

So many people are counting on me to try.

With blood rushing in my ears, I shift in place and step toward the stage. My father just spoke the usual line, my cue to step beside him, to the same little pink X that's been taped there for years. It's time for me to deliver another speech. Another town, another school, another government building, another church. I've never been nervous before, but now I might faint.

Good Without God.

The motto I've lived by my whole life.

In four short weeks, I've grown to hate it more than my own name.

"Come up here, Kathy…" My dad does a double take, one so subtle I'm the only one who sees it. His eyes rake my face and he frowns, and then recovers with a smile as he turns toward the audience. The sound of applause is deafening as I walk towards my father, and on my way up to the microphone a small part of me dies inside.

27

Caleb

"Angel at My Door"
—NeedtoBreathe

I spend a lot of time thinking about my life, about how early circum-stances led to my own personal downward spiral—like a venomous snake that writhed and hissed its way into the threshold of hell itself before slithering, scalded and feverish, back up again. About how it took hitting rock bottom and a stint in jail to know I was sick of the poison and needed a change, a way out of the darkness that had become my existence. Motherless. Fatherless. Abused. Unloved. Alone. All of it led to meeting Chris Jenkins. He led me to God. I lost friends in the process. I made new friends on the other side.

I've rediscovered my friends this week. The close ones have stuck with me, the not-so-close have accused me of abandoning my faith. The ones who know me have called me a brother, the ones who don't have called for my resignation. I still have a job, but the future of it is shaky. Even with the promise of initial funding, nerves are rattled, and faith is thin. Even Scott's.

I've always thought his faith was rock-solid. Impenetrable. Like that invisible fence I built around myself years ago. It's strange how a fence that goes up because of a lawsuit comes right back down because of the same lawsuit, all in the course of one week. Then again, one week can change everything. God created the entire world in less time than that and still had a day to spare.

Kate was back onstage the other night, standing next to her father, calling for yet another church to close its doors. It surprised me, but then it didn't. This is her life, the only thing she's ever known. But this time she looked different, nothing like the girl I learned to care for. This Kate was scared. Unsure. Timid. Alone.

It didn't hit me until later that night.

Kate was wearing black. Her dress. Her boots. Her coat. Even her eyes. There wasn't a trace of pink on her anywhere.

For all the commotion surrounding us, my office is unusually quiet today. I've managed to get a little work done in spite of the screaming silence—if you call pulling up YouTube clips of Kate's latest speech and drawing penciled switchblades all over a scrap piece of paper in front of me work. There must be at least twenty, and I've wasted my whole morning. It's Monday again, two days before Christmas, and I'm sick of being depressed. I'm thinking about cutting myself with one of these pictures just for fun, but of course the effort would only garner me a pointless paper cut that barely bleeds but hurts like a wasp sting to the eye. Paper cuts are the worst.

The door opens and Scott walks in. He never knocks, so it doesn't surprise me when he's suddenly in front of my desk. But when he plants his hands on either side of my computer and stares hard, I'll admit to a little discomfort. The guy doesn't usually pull out his confrontational streak—he looks like a grown version of that kid on Andy Griffith, for heaven sakes—but today is different.

"What?" I don't look up. This particular knife is taking shape nicely, and I don't want to disturb the muse.

"Would you stop doodling and do something productive?"

"Don't insult me. This isn't doodling. It's art." The side of my pencil shades the blade to make it look more dangerous. Better to slice me with.

"I drew better pictures in first grade. Now get up."

This surprises me, and I glance at him. "What do you suggest I do?

Let's see...I can go hang with Mrs. O'Hare and hear another talk about the nauseating things her husband did to her last night—I'd rather you stab me in the ear with this." I hold up my paper. "Or I could walk outside and be accosted by reporters—equally as thrilling." I'm aware that I'm throwing the temper tantrum of a twelve-year-old girl, but I'm on a roll. "Or I could call up Kate and ask her how it's going, but something tells me I ought to avoid that conversation, seeing she's the devil and all..."

"No one called her the devil."

"Do you even watch the news? That's been the headline all week."

"Dude, she's an atheist. What did you expect?"

That attitude right there. It ticks me off. I slap my paper on the desk and glare up at him. "She's not an atheist." It's a dumb, untrue argument, but it's the only one I've got.

Scott sighs and pulls out the chair across from me, then sits down. He looks at me. Sometimes I hate it when he looks at me. "Unless something has changed that you haven't told me about, yes she is. From what I can tell, she's been one her whole life."

In a rush, my anger pours out of me. Scott's right, and I'm lost for what to do. Still, the desire to fight hasn't left me. "That doesn't make her the devil, so you can take your pompous attitude and shove it where—"

"Don't bite my ear off, Mike Tyson." I meet his hard stare, and we study each other for a moment, eye-to-eye, man-to-man. "You're right, it doesn't. It makes her someone who needs a little grace."

Those words settle me. Not much, but enough for now. "Yes, she does. It just seems like lately...like maybe, she's starting to question things...maybe..." I lean back in my chair and rub my eyes, knowing my words sound stupid but unable to explain myself better. Finally, I give up trying. "What am I supposed to do?"

Scott rubs an eyebrow. "You could spend some time praying. If you're right—if she's starting to wonder about God even a little—she needs your prayers more than ever. Do you pray anymore, Caleb?" His tone is laced with concern so I can't get angry. I try for a second anyway, but come up short.

"Of course I pray. You know I do. I think my faith is stronger now than it's ever been. I'm just tired of the labels, and even sicker of the accusations. How did we get tangled up in this mess? And why the heck do reporters keep calling me Jesus? It's stupid." I flip my pencil to the desk.

"I don't know. If they knew you like I do, they'd come up with a different comparison."

"Shut up." I close my eyes and lean back, locking my hands behind my head.

Scott leans back to stretch his legs in front of him. "All kidding aside, I really have no idea. One minute we're just going along, living life day-to-day…the next we're embroiled in a national battle. It's unreal." He shakes his head and disappears inside himself for a moment, staring unseeing, straight ahead. "It's a new world, and we've got to learn to navigate through it. First things first, we need to fund the center privately from now on."

Wait a minute. My eyes open and I give him a look.

"What about the nativity?" I say with an edge. "Are you going to cave and take it down?"

He makes a face. "A judge hasn't ordered us to, so no. Although even if we were, I'm sure you could figure out some way to keep it up that's mostly legal.

"Darn right I would," I say.

"But as far as funding goes…" Scott says, unwilling to give me time to elaborate on my supposed illegal ideas, "…right or wrong, we've relied on public funds since our doors opened. Only for food, but food is expensive, and like I said, it's a new world. Separation of church and state means a lot more than it used to, and we've got to deal with the changes or be prepared to fight battles like this for as long as we're open. I, for one, don't have the desire."

I just look at him. "I don't cry 'uncle.' You know that."

"I'm not saying uncle. I won't water down our message for anyone. But I won't let the doors close on this place, either, Caleb. If we have to, we'll find another way to get the funds we need. Too many kids depend on it."

I hear what he's saying, but defeat tries to claim me anyway.

"What are we supposed to do, ask Kate for more albums until she runs out? I don't have the slightest idea how to fundraise, and I can't do that to her. I won't. Besides, I haven't heard from her all week." My voice has a bite, but I'm not stupid enough to think Scott doesn't hear the disappointment behind it.

He just looks at me. "You like her more than you're letting on, don't you?"

I chew a thumbnail and shrug. "A lot more than I should." A lot more than I can even admit to myself. Yet another reason to keep drawing these knives. I pick up my pencil and get started on a new one. "Go ahead and call me an idiot."

"Jury's still out on that. But I've met her. And from what you say, she wasn't any more prepared for this than you were."

I sigh, remembering that kiss the other night, those tears, the heart that seemed torn in half for a few minutes until she hopped in the car and drove away. I swallow…recalling the disappointment the first day I discovered her identity, and again a few days ago while she delivered that speech dressed like a widow in mourning. I shift in my seat and don't look up.

"She wasn't." Knowing it's true doesn't help.

"I didn't think so." Scott clears his throat. "I can't lie and say I'm not worried about you, Caleb. Because I am. You've been through more than anyone your age should be. Just, please don't—"

I blow out some air. "I won't let it affect my faith. What do I have to do to prove it to you?"

Instead of getting defensive, Scott raises an eyebrow and laughs. "Well, there's one thing that becoming a Christian never changed about your personality. You still have the temper of a demon on fire." He scratches the back of his neck. "I wasn't going to question your faith. I was going to say *please don't forget* that I've got your back. No matter what anyone says, no matter what the media tries to portray, I'll personally rip the arms off anyone who gets too rough with you." He gestures to himself. "I might not look like much, but I've been known to pack a mean punch if anyone gets too close."

That earns a laugh from me, my first one all week, and it feels good. Except for the accidental cut he gave me a long time ago, Scott is full of crap and he knows it. I've seen him pick spiders up off the kitchen floor and set them free in the backyard more than a few times. And flies…don't get me started on the way he treats those nasty things.

"It wasn't that funny," Scott says.

"Yes it was. Hilarious, actually." I wipe at my eyes. "But thanks."

"You're welcome." He smiles at my still-shaking shoulders. "I'm serious, man. Anything you need…"

"Thank you. I mean it."

He stands up and pushes the chair back an inch. "And as for Kate, I'm praying for her, Caleb. If God wants things to work out for the two of you, He'll turn things around. Besides, she's hot. Incredibly hot. All we need to do is get her to side with us and you'll be the luckiest guy on the planet."

Geez, is that all? I ball up my paper of penciled switchblades and throw it at his head. "Keep your eyes off her if you know what's good for you. Or wait—maybe you want to wrestle for her. Show me some of that famous mean punch of yours."

"Be afraid, Caleb. Be very afraid."

I laugh harder this time, even though when it comes down to it, none of this is funny. Nothing at all. Kate and I are as different as black and white, as sunrise and sunset, and really… there's not much hope. Barring a miracle, we're doomed. We were from the start. I won't abandon my faith, and as deeply entrenched as she is in her parent's movement, I don't see her embracing the God I believe in. It's pointless. I stand up, too.

"You headed out?" Scott asks.

"Yep. I have a truckload of gifts to deliver to the center and Ben has already been waiting an hour. If I stand him up one more time, he might never speak to me again." I pocket my keys and shrug into my jacket.

"It's two days before Christmas, so you'd better show up. You're practically Santa Claus for those kids, you know. I don't know how you manage to buy so much for them on your salary."

I buy the gifts because I save all year. I buy them because there may not be another chance for these kids next year. I buy them because Christmas stalled for me for nearly eleven years while I was growing up and these kids will have a present each year we're open if I have to forgo eating and cable to afford it. As it stands, the only thing I've sacrificed so far is my gym membership, and running on the street works just as well.

"Need help delivering it?" Scott asks.

I shake my head. "Kimball rounded up a couple of guys. We're meeting in the parking lot in five minutes." I hold out my hand. Scott is like my brother, the best friend I've ever had. But sometimes thank you isn't enough, and I've never been one for hugs. "Thanks, man. I mean it."

He nods and shakes it. "I'll see you tonight."

I slap the doorframe on my way out. "Keep those prayers coming," I call behind me. "You never know what might happen."

It's a nice thought. As far as nice thoughts go.

I'm still trying to recover from Mrs. O'Hare's retelling of the ballroom dance lessons she and her husband took last night as I pull into the parking lot. I almost made it out the door undetected, but she caught me walking by on her way out of the bathroom and spent the next ten minutes giving me a detailed description of their evening. If she had stopped at the dance moves, I would have been fine, but the graphic details of her husband in skin tight black pants and jazz shoes has pretty much assured that lunch will be nothing more than a passing dream for me today. My stomach can't handle it. Not sure how to wipe the memory from my mind, however, since whiskey is no longer an option. Maybe aspirin? Maybe I could pay someone to whack me between the eyes with a two by four. I'd choose the pain over envisioning a seventy-year-old-woman wearing sequins and shaking her thing with an equally old man any day.

I climb out of the truck just as Ben flies out the door.

"It's a good thing you showed up," he says, stomping across the sidewalk like the pseudo-tough kid he thinks he is. "I'm still not speaking to you since you bailed on me last week, though. What's in the truck?"

"I can see that," I say. "The silent treatment you're giving me is just deafening." I open the back hatch, smiling at the sound of his loud gasp. "That, my friend, is what's in the truck."

"Christmas presents! That's more than you brought last year! Where'd you get the money for all them? You win the lottery and not tell me?" His jaw hangs slack, the width of his mouth matching his round-as-quarters eyes.

I pick up the largest package. "No to the lottery, and don't look a gift horse in the mouth. You ever heard that expression before?"

Ben just blinks. "What horse? There ain't a horse around here."

This makes me laugh. "I'm the horse. And it means, don't ask people about money unless you want everything returned to Wal-Mart. Grab a package, will you?"

"Yes sir." That's the great thing about Ben. He doesn't have to be asked twice. He practically lunges for the pile of gifts and snatches up three, steadying the stack with his chin. Kimball pulls into the parking space next to me and hops out of the car. Two ninth grade boys I recognize from youth group spill out of the back seat.

"Sorry we're late," Kimball says. "Give me some of those." I dump two large gifts in his arms and reach for more. "Looks like you went all out this year," he says. "I still can't figure out how you afford this stuff."

"I start saving for next year as soon as all the gifts are unwrapped. Trust me, it isn't a hardship." I turn to the other boys. "Thanks for helping. Grab what you can carry and set them under the tree. Has anyone checked to see if anyone fixed the lights? A couple strands were out when I came by last night and Scott was supposed to find someone to swap them out."

"Yes!" Ben bounces on his heels. "That dude with the blonde hair came by this morning and now they all work!" That dude was Matt, and I share a smile with Kimball at the way he shouts. The tough-kid demeanor has vanished in favor of a little boy as excited about the prospect of lights and gifts and toys as he should be. Christmas is for everyone, but there's a special part of it that I'm convinced God reserves just for kids.

It doesn't take long before we're joined by a few more children that match Ben's enthusiasm, squeal for ear-splitting squeal. In spite of the truckload I brought and the half-dozen packages Kimball splurged for and brought in his own vehicle—a gesture that would have made me cry if I were a lesser man because the guy makes pennies and doesn't have much extra to spend—we manage to unload everything in two trips.

I'm shoving the last package under the tree when I hear the front door open. The door to this place always opens—kids get picked up, workers come and go, Pastor Chris or one of the associate pastors like myself stop by for a visit. It's like a revolving door for the down, out, and socially needy all wanting to hang out in one place for a while, so I'm used to it.

But I'm not used to Ben getting so excited when it happens. Or the words that come out of his mouth when I'm completely unprepared. "Hey, pretty lady, what are you doing here?"

I freeze at the same time Ben taps my arm and Kimball sucks in a breath and Matt's eyes go wide. It's like Mt. Rushmore with a rumbling stomach and I'm wondering how long until the explosion. But there's nothing, nothing but silence for the longest time, so I do the only thing I can do…the thing I'm *dying* to do…and turn around.

Kate stands just inside the doorway holding an armload of packages.

28

Kate

"Cry a River"

—Amy Grant

I try to imagine everyone naked, because that's what people say helps to alleviate stage fright. It's worked in the past, in the early years of making speeches at my parent's rallies, back when it was no longer an option to merely stand onstage with my pink blanket and big hair bow and just look cute. For me, adorable ended at age six, when my father coaxed me with bubble gum and Tic-Tacs to say a few words. *I don't like God.* Those are the words I whispered into the microphone that day…the only words I could make myself say even with additional prompting from him and my mother. Even when she pulled out the orange kind, the Tic-Tacs that don't actually freshen your breath but taste like Pez in its best form, minus the fun dispenser. I sucked down candy for the rest of the rally, completely forgetting that I had two lines left to speak. But orange sugar dripped down my chin in a sticky trail, so I no longer cared.

I try to imagine everyone naked now, but of course all I conjure up is a naked Caleb in my mind and something tells me a church Christmas party isn't the appropriate place to be thinking about this. Suddenly my face feels hot and my mouth goes dry and my legs really really don't want to carry me away from the doorway.

"What are you doing here?" Caleb doesn't move from the tree.

207

Thank God he's wearing a sweater.

He doesn't sound angry, he sounds like...nothing. Numb without the anesthetic. Surprised without the gasp. Confused without the scrunched forehead. He continues to look like that, through my three awkward blinks that pass for an excuse-finder. Coming up with none, I tell the truth.

"I brought gifts." I shrug. A mistake when one package shifts position and falls from my grasp. It's just a Scrabble game anyway. Nothing broken. Nothing damaged. That honor still only belongs to me.

"For what?" He isn't going to make this easy, even though I'm fairly certain he isn't trying to make it hard.

"For Christmas. Hence the red and green wrapping paper." I'm hoping that sounded confident, but I'm pretty sure everyone in the room heard the way my voice wobbled on the last word.

"You don't do Christmas." That statement further isolates me from everyone, all the people clustered around the tree to share, laugh, and celebrate the holiday I don't *do*. I heard the excitement from the parking lot. I noticed the way it died at the exact moment I walked inside.

Caleb still hasn't moved from his spot in front of the tree. I think he's afraid.

I'm afraid, too, and press my back against the door. "I don't do trees either, but that didn't stop me from putting one up in my bedroom last week." That surprises him, and an eyebrow shoots up. He shifts from one leg to another, and there's a lot of distance between us so I can't be sure, but I'm almost positive I see his mouth twitch in unbelief. Just like that, defensive mode kicks in and my chin comes up. "I bought a stocking, too. And hung it in my doorway. I even put candy canes inside, just in case."

His mouth opens slightly and he takes a step toward me. "You're kidding me. You've just broken the cardinal rule of Christmas: 'Never fill up your own stocking.' It's like taking a baby bird from its nest and then trying to put it back. Santa won't touch your stocking now."

I nearly roll my eyes. "The bird thing is a myth, you know." Inch by hopeful inch and without actually moving at all, we're drifting back to where we were last week. I'm starting to wonder if we really left, or if we were just temporarily sidetracked. As if to echo my thoughts, he moves even closer. I try to swallow my nervousness. Speaking around it isn't easy. "Mother birds don't shun their babies just because human hands touch them. That's cruel. Birds aren't cruel."

Breathing is impossible when he keeps coming toward me. He's close. *Close* close. If I could take a step back I would, but this stupid door is in my way and I really don't feel like going back outside.

"Well, too bad for you that Santa is," he says.

"Hey!" Ben shouts, thankfully jolting us out of this semi-standoff. "Why are you sayin' Santa's mean? Santa's not mean!" He stares open-mouthed, outraged and unbelieving, like Caleb has destroyed every holiday vision the kid has ever had. I'm wondering how Caleb will dig himself out of this one.

"Not to you." He cuts his gaze to Ben. "It's just that Santa doesn't like people who don't believe in him, and Kate never has. Can you believe that? She's never even celebrated Christmas. What gives her the right to start now?"

He winks at me, and just like that I'm no longer the enemy. I can't even pretend to get mad anymore because I'm too relieved to try. It's all I can do not to break out in a huge smile. We may still be on opposite sides, but this is a start. One I can work with.

"Caleb…" Ben blinks up at him, all wide-eyed and serious. "Because it's Jesus' birthday. Everyone has the right to celebrate Jesus, birthday, even her. You should know this already. You're the one who told me."

Caleb has the decency to look chagrined. It's genuine, like he can't believe he's just been put in his place by an eleven-year-old. A little color creeps up his neck, and I almost feel sorry for him, except I'm too busy mentally high-fiving Ben for knocking him down a few notches.

"Yeah, Caleb. I have a right to celebrate too." That gives me the courage I need to push off from the door and make the long walk to the tree. I may only have a few board games a couple packages of play-dough in my hands, and they might be wrapped so elegantly that the kids are bound to be disappointed when they open them, but I have as much right to be here as anyone.

At least that's what I tell myself as everyone watches me. I refuse to let their stares affect my fragile confidence. Not when I lay the packages down. Not when I pretend to organize them. Not when I feel Caleb's stare like a hot branding iron on the back of my neck.

And definitely not when I see the little fist pump he gives himself when he thinks I'm not looking.

One hour later and all we've done is play a little basketball, drink some water, arrange a few chairs around the room, throw some tablecloths on tables, and stand around. Matt and Kimball—I finally learned their names—have already left, so it's just me, Ben, Caleb, and a few kids who haven't been picked up still left in the building. I discovered today that Ben is always the last to leave.

But the sun is going down, and we haven't opened a single gift, and I want to. I've never opened a Christmas present before. I've been given them—by my grandparents on my mother's side and by an aunt I've never been allowed to see who I think might be married to a pastor of some Mega-church in Toledo. I saw her once on television and asked my mother about her because they looked so much alike, and the lady had the same first name as my mother's sister. My mother went all rigid and wouldn't answer even though her eyes kept flashing to the screen until she turned the set off altogether. Bottom line: I've never been allowed to have the gifts. My parents always sent them back unopened. Even when I was little. Even when I cried.

I know nothing here is for me, but I want to watch the whole Christmas present-opening ceremony, just to see what all the hoopla is about. I've seen it on Hallmark commercials. I've heard about it in school. Finally, I can't take it anymore.

"What time do we open these?" I'm next to the tree looking down at the sea of gifts swirled across the ground in front of me, and I'm vaguely aware that I just did a couple knee bends like a toddler who's doing all she can to repress her excitement. But there must be fifty in all, and twinkling lights are hitting them in a way that makes them practically shine, and all I can envision is sparkling paper shredding and flying everywhere—like Mardi Gras in December. I can't stand the anticipation. Guilt follows right behind it because years of believing this is wrong won't go away overnight, but excitement is winning out so I shove the guilt down.

Ben drops the basketball he's bouncing and Caleb looks up from tying a little girl's shoes. Both look at me with open curiosity. Both look like they're laughing without sound or smiles.

"What?" I say.

"We don't open them until tomorrow night." Caleb answers me.

"Yeah. We gotta wait a whole 'nother twenty-four hours," Ben says with a slight whine.

They're kidding.

"What?" I say again, this time with force. "Tomorrow night?" I look around the room. "Then why are you setting out all these tables and chairs? Isn't everyone coming back for dinner? I smell food cooking."

Caleb suppresses a grin and pats the little girl on the foot, her permission to run and play. He stands up to stretch his legs. "Yes, everyone's coming back for dinner. And food is cooking. A beef tenderloin. For tomorrow night." He says it all like he has to explain it slowly so I'll get his meaning. I don't.

"But that's stupid. When I stopped by the church earlier, Scott said you were taking gifts for the kids to open later." I'm grasping at air, but my dream of an Oklahoma Mardi Gras—right here, right now—is fading. Plus, my courage to come here might be a one-time thing and I'm worried I won't find it again tomorrow. A door opens and two kids run to it. Caleb grabs a couple of backpacks, hands them off to a woman, says a few parting words, then locks the door behind them as they leave. He turns back to me.

"You stopped by the church?"

I give him a dismissive nod. "Yes, but what about the gifts?"

"Before you came here?"

I make a longsuffering sound. "Yes, Caleb, I went to the church before I came here. Big deal. Now what about the gifts? Why aren't we opening them tonight?"

But he fixes his eyes on mine, and it's obvious he isn't going to be deterred by talk of presents anytime soon. He stares for so long that I start to get uncomfortable, as if he sees inside me to the parts I don't want anyone to view. But Caleb is Caleb and I can't look away, and we stay that way so long that even I can no longer remember what we're talking about. Then his look changes into something like respect, and my discomfort vanishes. He could stare at me like that all day, and I doubt I would ever get sick of it.

"I'm proud of you."

"For what?" My voice sounds thick. Hopeful.

"For walking inside the church by yourself. For showing up the other night. For sitting in front of Joseph and throwing rocks at me and not running away. For being your own person no matter what your parents, or me, or anyone else thinks. But mainly for walking in here," he nods toward the front door, "without having a clue what to expect. We could have thrown ornaments at you, yelled at you, or told you to leave. Yet you still showed up with gifts."

He does this a lot. Compliments me for things he should hate. I've met a lot of people in my life—thousands, even. He's the kindest soul I've ever met, despite what his rough exterior tries to camouflage.

"You and I both know you wouldn't have thrown ornaments at me," I say, my heart hovering somewhere between apprehensive and relieved. "You're not that mean, despite what you try to project with your shaggy hair and weird body art."

He smiles the softest smile, and I smile too. And all is right with the world. If only I could say the same about my heart. He rubs the back of his neck and looks at me through his lashes.

"Okay, maybe I wouldn't have thrown them at you. But I might have refused your gifts. You probably just bought a bunch of dumb things, anyway. Like Play-dough."

I blink, flustered and trying to work up some irritation all over again. "Stop being so critical. Now when are we opening gifts?" I'm a two-year-old again, because a tantrum is all I can manage right now and I bought stupid Play-dough like an idiot.

Caleb laughs. "Tomorrow. Now go in the kitchen and check on the tenderloin. It still has another hour to bake, but I don't want it to burn."

"And what am I supposed to do if it *is* burning?"

He shrugs. "I don't know. Take it out or something."

I roll my eyes and stomp toward the kitchen to the sounds of people coming and going. Just before I reach the doorway, I'm struck by a thought—something I realized on my way inside this building to-night—and I turn.

"Caleb?"

"Yeah?" He's helping the last little girl here into her coat; it's the same shade of cotton candy pink as mine. I doubt it comes with an agenda. When he finally looks at me, I ask.

"You're really not going to take it down, are you?" It's weird, his refusal to budge, and I can't keep a small amount of awe from creeping into my voice. When his eyebrows scrunch together in confusion, I elaborate. "The nativity scene. You're going to leave it up?"

He gives me slight smile. "Until New Year's Day. Maybe longer."

I just look at him a long moment, trying hard to process this guy who goes against the norm—who breaks all the rules with the confidence of someone much older, even with the whole world freaking out around him.

I guess I stare at him too long, because now he's asking the questions. "Why? You're looking at me like you think I'm crazy." Like I've sprouted a third arm and you're trying to guess what I'll do with it.

I slowly shake my head, unable to look away. "Not crazy. Just…different. Everyone always takes it down. Eventually, one of two things happen: either we manage to persuade them that making a small sacrifice is better than losing money, or they cave to the pressure of public outcry. People don't like pressure. Or the negative attention that comes with it."

He closes the door and drops the blinds, shutting us in for the night. Then he turns to me. "Well, that's the thing about me, Kate. I don't mind pressure. In fact, you can pretty much count on me doing the exact opposite of what's expected. Case in point—a pastor going to a bar, getting into a fistfight, then picking up a barely-dressed drunk girl and taking her home. Not a lot of church-going men would do that." He slides me a wink…one I feel to the tips of my toes. He means it as a joke, but to me it means…everything.

I swallow and force my voice to work. "That dress wasn't mine. I would never wear something that tacky on purpose. It was Lucy's."

"Why am I not surprised?" My heart flips at the way he grins at me. "It wasn't all bad, though. You looked pretty darn good in that dress."

I bite my lip and turn away before he can see me blush.

I like different.

I like different a lot.

"Tell me about your tattoo."

"You mean my weird body art?" He taps the toe of his shoe against mine. "What do you want to know?"

We're lying side by side on our backs at the edge of the gym floor with our elbows touching—whether accidental or otherwise I'm not sure—and we're looking up at the Christmas tree. Twinkling lights shine down on us like a thousand glittering stars, and I've never seen anything so pretty. I can't believe this hasn't been a yearly occurrence for me.

"Did it hurt when you got it?"

"Yes."

"Bad?" I cut my arm once on a table saw in my garage, and I can still remember the pain. I have a tiny scar just above my elbow to prove it.

"Like getting stitches without anesthetic. And that was the good part."

I turn my head to look at him. "Then why did you get it?"

He blinks at the lights, and for a moment his breathing stops. I know this because his chest, all this time rising up and down in a steady rhythm, stops moving completely. He swallows, and the sound drifts toward me. "As a reminder."

I know I shouldn't ask, and I know the reason is painful. Like the feeling you sometimes get when you're late for an appointment or miss a loved one's birthday and just before it hits you, unexplained panic sets in. That's how I feel right now. "A reminder of what?"

He sighs. "Of my mother."

His mother. Other than that brief talk about his stint in jail, it's the first time he's mentioned her, the first time he's allowed me a glimpse into his past. Something tells me it isn't pretty. Something also tells me not to say another word to keep the spell around us from breaking.

"She died when I was seven. I almost died, too, but I wasn't that lucky."

My heart breaks at those words, and as Caleb goes on to tell me the story of a kid abandoned as a baby—then left alone and bleeding at the bottom of a ravine—my eyes begin to sting. He talks of standing helpless as the life he once knew was ripped away before he lost his first tooth, of the way it left him isolated and lost and without anyone to love him. Of the carousel of foster homes and friends and schools that left him spinning without a handhold.

It all falls into place. These kids. Caleb's heart for service. His determination to keep this place together...to do whatever it takes to provide the children the best Christmas they've ever had. A single tear spills over as I listen, the first tear I remember in years. I've been raised to believe in the matter-of-fact. To suck up feelings and get onstage. Pointless nerves don't sell causes. Any good performer knows that.

My nerves are frazzled now.

"No wonder you were in jail. You must have lost your mind after she died." It takes work to keep my voice steady. And even though I'm still not sure he wants me to know about this part of his life, the quiet intimacy of the moment makes the timing seem appropriate. I hope with everything in me that I'm not wrong.

"I did lose my mind." He says it so softly it's like I'm not supposed to hear the words. "Lost it for years and years. But that isn't the reason I went to jail."

His tone carries the hint of caution, a warning to proceed carefully, as if he wants me to make sure I'm ready for answers before asking him anything else. But of course, I'm ready. I've been ready since the moment I found him wearing my pink robe.

"Then what was the reason? Why were you in jail, Caleb?"

He's quiet for so long that I'm not sure he's going to tell me. But then he does, and that's the moment I know. The moment I know that no matter how I was raised or what I believe or whether things work out between Caleb and me or we say goodbye tonight and never see each other again, I've lost myself. I've lost myself, and he's holding all the important pieces. Even if I run millions of miles from here, I'll never get them back.

"Five years ago, I caught my best friend having sex in the back seat of my car outside a bar in Tulsa. Except the girl wasn't awake. She was out cold, drugged up on so much alcohol and pills that she should have been dead." He stares at the ceiling as the implication hovers heavy between us. That was nearly me. In the same way he saved that girl, he saved me, too. Only with me, the timing was better. "I pulled him off her and beat the crap out of him. I nearly killed him—would have if I hadn't been so drunk that I stumbled and fell at the exact wrong moment—and he ran before I could finish the job. While I was trying to get her out of the car, she woke up enough to see me hovering over her and started screaming, and that's when the police came."

I just look at him until it all adds up, and I'm horrified. "And they thought you did it to her?"

He nods. "It was my car, and she was bruised pretty badly. Bleeding..." The roughness in his voice makes my own throat hurt. "It took over two dozen tests and forty-eight hours to clear me of the charges. Those might have been the worst hours of my life if it hadn't been for what I'd already been through with my mother."

Everything in me aches. My throat. My chest. My eyes. The pain of trying to control my tears and grab more than a shallow, ineffective breath becomes just too much. I can't ask him what kinds of tests. Or what happened to his friend. Or how he met Chris and Scott and everyone else who gave him a second chance and turned his life around. I just know that I want that same thing...a chance. A turnaround, except with my family intact. I don't know if it's possible, and I have no idea how to get it. But right then it occurs to me that Caleb of all people might be the one to show me.

I ask the only question that seems safe. The only one that might keep me from shattering right here on the old wooden floor as thoughts of family and faith and new ways of life dart through my brain.

"Why an eagle? How does that remind you of your mother?" My voice is thick with the worry of finding out.

He doesn't speak for a long moment, but then he finds my hand and squeezes it once, like he needs the encouragement to push forward. I squeeze back and link my fingers through his, giving it to him. "The day she died, the last thing my mother told me was to stay awake. To sit up and keep my eyes open until help came to rescue me. So I did. For three long hours I did, even though I was tired, even though it hurt, and even though she was dead in my lap and I wanted to join her. But the day I decided to follow God, I realized that I had never really stayed awake at all. All those years, I was sound asleep and wanting to die at the bottom of that ravine." He finally looks at me and smiles. His eyes are watery like mine. "But when I met God, I woke up. More than woke up, I soared. I think my mother would be proud that I finally did what she asked."

I'm under water, and I can't breathe. Trying physically hurts.

I think of my mother. My father. Of all the people in their organization and in the media who expect something from me…things I no longer have the energy to give. I think of everything about my life, every speech I've made and every flier I've handed out. I think of how I've felt dead forever, a puppet wearing pink in a show I no longer want to perform. I want to soar, but I have no idea how. I'm not sure I ever will. Or if I'll ever have the courage.

It doesn't take me long to figure out that I don't.

Or that I shouldn't have asked Caleb about his tattoo, which led to this entire conversation.

No longer able to hold my finger over the hole in the dam containing my tears, I let go, turn my head, and shatter right beside him.

29

Caleb

"A Long December"

—Counting Crows

*I*t's Christmas. The best day of the year out of three-hundred and sixty-
five options. The one day when adults can act like kids and kids can beg
for whatever toy they want without fear of being reprimanded. It's
Christmas. The day Jesus was born. The celebration of everything His
arrival represents.

Today is Christmas.

And I'm in love with an atheist.

"All we need to do is convert her to our side and you'll be the luckiest guy on the planet."

From the moment I woke up this morning, Scott's words have echoed in
my head, ricocheting through my mind like a childhood taunt. "You're
never the luckiest guy on the planet...never the luckiest guy..."

And it's true. Since the beginning of November, I've wanted only one
thing for Christmas this year. It wasn't until Kate left last night that I
realized might not ever happen.

"Happy Christmas Eve!" Mrs. Jenkins walks into the kitchen and
shouts this before I've even poured my first cup of coffee. The sound is
like the blare of a horn at two a.m.—rude and unwelcome. I reach for
the creamer, reminding myself for the hundredth time to get a working

coffee pot of my own. They cost twenty bucks, won't exactly break the bank, but I can't ever seem to remember.

"Happy Christmas Eve," I mutter back, pinching the space between my eyebrows. I'm still wearing pajama bottoms and an old t-shirt and haven't brushed my teeth—the two requirements that need to be met before engaging in conversation. It's a personal rule of mine.

"Happy Christmas Eve!" she says again when Scott walks into the room. I cringe, especially because what comes next is—

"Happy Christmas Eve!" Scott shouts back. I'm surrounded by Chihuahuas yapping in my ear. This family is insanely perky in the mornings, and right now I want to muzzle both of them and stick them inside an electric fence. Christmas might be my favorite holiday, but not before noon, and *not* on a day that I don't have to work.

"It's not even a real holiday yet," I say. "Could you both reign in the enthusiasm until tomorrow?"

They share an amused look, one I don't have to see to feel. Chris shuffles in and heads toward me—my only ally in this Disney World nightmare—to get his own liquid wake-up drug. The mugs clang together as he grabs one from the cabinet, further exacerbating my already cranky personality. I've been compared to Scrooge in the immediate hours after sunrise, and not just in December. It's a label I don't mind wearing. My inner Santa comes out after lunch.

"Happy Christmas Eve." Chris's voice is only marginally softer but somehow even more annoying.

"Not you too," I groan. It seems they've all succumbed to yapping this morning. I'm still too tired for it, and if I'm being honest, still torn up over the vision of Kate last night, quietly crying for what felt like hours while I held on to her hand. I'm still not sure how long we stayed that way, but at the time I just knew that nothing was worth letting go, not as long as she needed me. And when she didn't, she pulled her hand away.

I'm sorry, Caleb. I can't stay here.

And then she stood up and left.

When the door slammed behind her, all my prayers—all Scott's prayers—seemed to bounce off the ceiling of heaven and break apart at my feet. All thoughts of being on the same team, of sharing the same faith, of walking side by side with a girl I'd grown to love like the idiot I am, were gone just like that. I'm glad I never told her.

Now it's Christmas, my favorite time of year, and I just want to bury myself alive. I'm counting on the coffee to give me a reason not to.

"What's on tap for today?" Chris asks no one in particular as he leans against the counter.

"Bud Lite, hold the ice," I say. It's a lame joke, maybe the worst one I've ever told, but the sun has barely cracked the horizon and nothing is particularly funny.

The whole room groans. It serves them right for being so chipper. "We haven't heard a beer joke in months. We thought you'd forgotten." I hear the wistful edge in Mrs. Jenkins' voice, like it was a futile hope.

"Of course I haven't forgotten. I have a lot more where that came from."

"Lucky us," Scott pipes up, grabbing a bowl and a carton of eggs. He begins cracking them and I reach for a pan. Chris grabs a stack of plates from the cabinet and Mrs. Jenkins' opens the bacon, separating the strips one-by-one and laying them in the pan. She asks me about the kid's program tonight and I fill her in on the details. Before long I can *almost* forget about the turmoil surrounding Kate. Eventually the food preparation turns to eating and eating turns to cleaning and cleaning turns to talk of opening gifts.

Somehow I forget about my desire to head back to bed and skip this day, and my excitement returns, albeit only on a miniscule level. But miniscule is better than nothing, and I grab onto to it with everything I have. It's Christmas Eve morning. And even though it took me a while, I manage to find the joy.

Everything might have gone south the past two months, but I still have God. I still have my faith. I still have a family.

For now, for always, it's enough.

It doesn't take long for me to realize it isn't enough.

It should be, but right now it isn't and I can't take much more.

I'm in my apartment and my phone is taunting me with every minute it doesn't ring, so I shove it in the top drawer of my dresser to keep from staring at the black screen. I've eaten, showered, taken a nap, and straightened up—something I rarely do because who cares? I'm a bachelor. Messiness is expected. Still, I've wiped down the bathroom counter, rearranged my desk drawers, and located all the bags of lifesavers and candy canes I bought last-minute to fill the kid's stockings because someone has to play Santa for them.

I check my watch. Only two-thirty, but I've run out of stalling tactics. The kids will start arriving to the center at five. I might as well make sure they have something incredible to show up for. I've never actually worn a Santa suit and probably never will again, but this year will be the exception. This year, I'm going to find one.

With no idea where to start looking, I grab my keys off the dresser and head out to find Scott.

Because if I'm playing Santa, his skinny butt is playing an elf.

30

Kate

"It's My Life"
—Bon Jovi

It's a few minutes before five, and even though I know it's too early, I can almost hear the sound of children ripping Christmas paper from those packages. I can hear shrieks. Laughter. Even the sound of Mr. Jenkins' voice as he shares a message of hope just like the one he shared a couple of weeks ago while I stood in the shadows. I reach for my pillow and cover my head, but the phantom noise only intensifies. I shouldn't be lying in my bed, anyway. All of it is punishment for my laziness.

In the other room, my mother is making dinner. Lasagna, if she sticks with what she mentioned yesterday. It's my favorite, but it sounds awful—like a defiled Christmas feast I've never eaten before. Tenderloin. Tenderloin is what Caleb eats on Christmas Eve, and tenderloin is what I want, served on paper plates with plastic forks in a bleach-scented gym. It screams Christmas. Somehow I know this, even though—with the exception of that tiny tree in my apartment bedroom—Christmas has never spoken to me at all.

I push the pillow off my face and sit up, then reach for the novel I started reading earlier that morning—wanting to lose myself in the story of another person's life. I could've chosen better than this particular character's, but sometimes, like music, books are the best way to escape.

I've barely made it to the bottom of the page when someone knocks on my door. I'm in my old bedroom in the house I grew up in, sitting on the pink-flowered comforter bought new in the eighth grade. My apartment is only a mile away, and we don't celebrate this holiday, but I've always come home for Christmas, and always at my mother's request. This year is no different.

And that's when a strange thought begins to gnaw at me.

This year is no different.

By the time the door opens, I remember the tears my mother shed in the kitchen just a few days ago, and my heart is beating out an odd little rhythm that I can't quite decipher. When my mother comes in, I stop trying.

"What are you doing in here?" Wiping her hands on a dish towel, she walks over to sit. Angling her head lower, she takes in the book's title. "*Flowers in the Attic*. An...interesting book," she says.

"It's weird," I say, "but it passes the time." She looks at me then, but it's different, reserved. Almost...worried. She looks over her shoulder as if waiting for someone to jump out of a corner. I know she's checking to see if my father is around, but he isn't. For now, we're the only two at home.

"Are you going to stay in your room all night? Your father should be home any minute, and dinner is almost ready."

I sigh and drag the book off my lap and onto the bed. "I'm really not hungry. I think I'll skip dinner tonight, if that's okay. I'm not sure my stomach can handle it."

A flash of alarm. It's there, and then it's gone, replaced with her customary composure. "Kate, please don't skip. I made lasagna for you. Can't you at least sit with us? It isn't often that we get to eat dinner as a family anymore."

Of course she plays the guilt card. Isn't it what mother's do best? But my enthusiasm level is at an all-time low, and I can't muster up anything fake. Still, I don't want to hurt her feelings, because she's right. They're busy and I'm busy, and in recent years, family time has become all but extinct. I sigh and try to make peace.

"Maybe I could eat some leftovers later while we watch a movie?"

"But Kate, it's Chris—"

She looks away, and everything in the room goes still. The air. Our bodies. Even the clock on my bedside table that has spent the last seven years ticking off seconds. Nothing is as it was.

And then all at once, everything is.

Her silence when I told her about Caleb. Her tears and departure from the room instead of the stern lecture I'd been expecting. The fact that she rarely...almost never...makes a speech.

It only takes a moment for me to figure it out, for everything to fall into place and shine a spotlight on both of us. On my father too, even though he isn't home. It's as if duct tape has suddenly been ripped off my eyes and I see it. Really see it. I stare at my mother's shirt and it all makes sense. I've seen it for years. I've worn it as a child playing dress-up. I know it like the back of my hand, but this time I really see it.

My mother tries to cover it up with a hand to her neck.

"Mom, what is that?" I reach for the old brooch pinned underneath her collar and finger the edges, sharp and crooked, but smooth as butter. Made of eighteen karat gold and at least half-a-century old, it sparkles more today than it did when I was younger. "You wear it every year, but you've never told me what it is. What is it?"

I know what it is, but I want to hear her say it.

Her hand hides the entire brooch. "It's just an old brooch of my grandmothers. I like to wear it to remember her." She stands and walks toward the window to peer out. I suspect it's only to keep busy, because she fixes her eyes on one spot and doesn't move.

"Mom, what's that thing on your shirt?" I'm not asking. I'm trying not to explode.

She doesn't turn around.

"Kate, it isn't what you think. I just—"

"I think it's a manger? Am I right?" All these years, I've seen a gold pile of matchsticks on my mother's shirt—matchsticks and straw arranged in a formation of tiny x's just above her heart, but now I see it. When I narrow my eyes slightly, I can even make out the outline of a baby's face. A baby's face that, until now, looked like nothing more than a tiny orb set inside the sticks. Like an egg in a nest—only it's not.

"Kate, just let me—"

"Say it. After all these years and everything I've done for you and dad, you owe me that much."

My mother has aged twenty years in as many minutes. With resignation on her face, she slowly lowers herself to the bed, her eyes guarded. It takes only a moment for them to become red-rimmed and watery as well.

"I met your father in my church youth group my senior year of high school. My father was the pastor."

My blood chills; a shiver runs up my arm. "That isn't what you told me—"

But she's lost inside her memories and keeps going. "Your dad was a very charismatic boy, and by the time I figured out he wasn't there to learn about God—that he was there to learn the ins and outs of how a church works—I was too in love to care."

From there and almost in a trance-like state, my mother spins a tale of a teenage girl in over her head, of her parent's—my grandparents— heartbroken and pleading for their daughter to leave him. Of a girl on the verge of doing that very thing, until she discovered she was pregnant. Of a wedding…of silence and broken ties with everyone who loved her. Of a baby and a home and woman determined to make the best life for her and her child. Of a desire to keep the peace and strengthen her marriage—in with both feet despite monstrous misgivings.

All of it is news to me. All of it.

Minutes, hours, days go by before my mother stops talking. When she looks at me, I see fear behind her eyes. She hadn't meant to tell the story. Like unloading a flood of repressed memories on a therapist's sofa, she probably wasn't aware until it was over.

"Kate, you need to understand that I love your father," she says, her fingers absently caressing the brooch.

"I know you do," I whisper. "I've never doubted that for a minute. I love him too."

She nods. "He's a good man. He's provided a great life for me and for you…" Her voice trails off. I hear the love in her words. I hear the thankfulness.

And also the regret.

The need to reassure her rushes to my mind. "I've loved everything about my life," I say. "Everything…"

Mostly.

I look her in the eye. "But I told you about that man when I was little, Mom. At Target. How he came out of nowhere after I prayed." I silently challenge her to look away. She shifts uncomfortably. "You told me I was silly and not to speak about it again. So I didn't."

My mother blanches in front of me. In all my life, I've never seen someone lose color so quickly. "What else was I supposed to say, Kate? I couldn't have you questioning things, not with your father around. He has such strong beliefs…"

"What about your beliefs, Mom? What about mine?"

Shock passes her face in an instant. My mother glances at the doorway before turning to me again. Her gaze turns serious, imploring. Like she has something to say and only a few minutes to get it out and she wants me to pay attention to every word. So I do, forcing my mind to clear of everything but her, myself, and the expectation between us. Even the hum of the dryer on the other side of the wall goes silent.

"Are you telling me you suddenly believe in God?"

I swallow. Shake my head slowly back and forth. "I don't know what I believe anymore. I just…I'm not as sure as I used to be that He doesn't exist." I look up at her. "What if He does, Mom? What if all this time…" I can't finish that sentence. What if I've been wrong all along? What if we all have?

"Your father would be humiliated."

"This isn't about him. This is about me. What am I supposed to do? Forget about the organization and the lawsuit and the media? As my mother—tell me. What am I supposed to do?"

She picks up my hand and brings it to her lap. For a long moment I can see the struggle, the warring within her to both parent me and be loyal to my father. Finally, her shoulders sag. She looks tired, drawn—obvious by her long sigh.

"I can only tell you this, Kate. I never should have turned my back on my old life. I know that now—I've known it most of my adult life. As long as I live, it will be the one thing I'm ashamed of. The biggest mistake I've ever made." She's kneading my hand like bread dough as moisture gathers in the corners of her eyes. Even though it hurts a little, I let her keep going. She seems to need the distraction.

"Then why did you do it? After all this time, why do you continue to stand onstage with him and say all these things against perfectly good people?" Maybe I shouldn't be so harsh, but she owes me this. Besides, my hand is really starting to hurt.

"Because your father believes in this cause. And in a way, I guess I do, too. Faith can—and should—stay private. I've managed to keep mine that way all these years. And even if I didn't feel that way, it's too late to change things now."

I shake my head. "But Mom, it's not too late—"

"I've made my decision. I won't walk away from your father. He's built—*we've* built—too much to give up now." She tilts her head in thought, focusing on my wall. "In the oddest way, even though I know it's wrong, I'm still proud of what we've accomplished. Proud to know that we've made a difference in the way this country practices religion."

"Even if it means kids get thrown out onto the street?"

"There is always another place for kids to go when a center like this one closes. A Boys and Girls Club. After school programs…"

"Kids can't spend the night at either of those places."

"It's my understanding that not many spend the night at Caleb's place, either."

"Not many isn't the same as zero, Mom."

She says nothing, because there's really nothing to say. We blink at each other until one of us makes a move. That person is my mother, but she leads us right back to where we started.

"Kate, I turned my back on the way I was raised a long time ago. I hurt people. Your father hurt people. People who loved us both…some we haven't seen in over two decades. It's been exactly eleven years ago today since I've seen my own mother. We tried to keep a relationship going for a while, but it just didn't work. Too many differences." Again, her expression turns faraway. One tear slips out of her eye and glides down her nose. "She sure thought you were special, though. Do you remember the way she cried the first time she saw you? I think you were three at the time…"

I say nothing, because I don't remember it. Until now, I never knew we once had a relationship.

"I ran from everyone who loved me, and in turn, they eventually gave up on me." My mother swipes at her eyes and fixes her gaze on me. "That won't happen to you," she says, looking so momentarily resolute that it unnerves me. "If you choose to walk away from the way we've raised you, you'll never lose me. And I can promise you—*promise you*—that you won't lose your father, either."

I don't move as the implication of her words settles around me. It's as though she's known all along, as though her life is being lived out in reverse and she has a chance to redo it through me. She ran away from God to save her relationship.

And she's telling me to run toward Him to save mine.

Still, I grasp for an anchor. Something I know. Something to save me from that life-changing turnaround I wished for just last night with Caleb. Because up until now, life has been steady, and steady is comforting.

"What about the media? Everyone will talk. You and Dad and everyone in the organization will be ridiculed and—"

She stops me with a hand to my knee.

"Your father is a master at getting people to see things his way. Don't worry about him. He'll be upset at first, but he'll understand. Once I point out the irony of your situation being the exact opposite of ours, he won't have a choice."

Still, I'm not certain. "You're suing him; Caleb. His church. What makes you think he'll have anything to do with me after that?"

Guilt darts through her eyes. She covers it with a small smile. "He's known about the lawsuit for weeks. If he hasn't turned away from you yet, something tells me he never will."

My eyes burn with unshed tears as I weigh her statement and everything she's handed me. An out with them. An in with Caleb. The freedom to live my life the way I want to, and the promise that I'll be loved in spite of it.

It takes only a heartbeat to make my decision, and I'm off the bed, opening my closet and pulling out my coat. The pinkest, puffiest, furriest one I own. Even my mother grimaces through her tears, and she's the one who gave it to me.

"You're going to wear that?" She doesn't ask where I'm going. She already knows.

I grin and kiss her on the cheek. "Trust me. Caleb will like it."

My father walks in just as I make it to the kitchen. "Dinner smells good." He looks at me, takes in my attire. "Nice coat. Where is she going?" he asks my mother.

She and I share a look, and in that moment I know something else.

My mother has my back. She's always had my back, even as I stood on a stage giving speech after speech that I never plan to make again.

I realize something else.

No matter where I go—no matter how things turn out with Caleb—I'll never stand in front of a crowd again. My photo will never be on another pink flyer. In fact, after tonight, I'm done wearing pink for good.

And it's at this moment that I feel free. From expectations. From spectacles. From the spotlight. Even from fear.

For the first time in my life, I'm not afraid, and I'm not running anymore.

"She's going out for a bit," my mother says to my father, slipping me a quick wink as she snakes her arm around his waist.

I kiss my dad on the cheek. He is a good man. And if I've learned one thing lately, it's that there's always hope for men like him.

"I'm just going out," I tell him, repeating my mother. "But I'll be back. I'll definitely be back. Save me some lasagna."

"Don't count on it," he says, jabbing a knife into the first corner piece.

I smile and take a moment for this image to sear into my mind. My mom. My dad. My family. For years and years, the three of us against the world. Figuratively, and at times, literally.

For most of my life, I've loved it that way.

But now it's time to grow up and make my own way.

With one last glance behind me, I turn and walk out the door.

31

Caleb

"The Truth"
—Kris Allen

*T*here are four things I've learned in twenty-four years of living, three that I hope to pass on to my own son someday.

One: it sucks to be alone. I should know; I've been that way for most of my life. When my father left, when my mother died, when I was shuttled from one foster family to another because no one wanted me. When I was in jail—sitting in a dank cell with concrete walls so thick they closed in on my nineteen-year-old brain like a clamp determined to squeeze all thought process and emotion out of me. I'd never felt more abandoned than in that moment. Hope to never be in that place again.

Two: it never hurts to find a good friend.

Even a nerdy, scrawny, quiet one who likes church potlucks and chess and is nothing like you. After all, looks can be deceiving. Sometimes the chess player in the plaid shirt has the guts of a heavyweight and winds up being the person who saves your life. After he rips the heck out of your hand in a cheap move that scars you forever, that is.

Three: sometimes life requires abandonment, loneliness, scars, and a walk through a pit of awfulness to make a person appreciate the sweetness of true, lasting, unadulterated freedom. And I've learned the way to real freedom is to find God. To accept that He has a plan for your life. A strange plan, sometimes—not all of it is pretty, some of it isn't pleasant, and some of it seems downright weird. But I'll take His weird over my idea of perfect any day of the week. Because, I, Caleb Stiles, found God. I'm free for the first time in my life.

And four: life's a heck of a lot better with a hot girl on your arm.

Hey—I said this was for my son. I'd never say something that stupid to a daughter.

I've officially turned in my man-card, spit on my masculinity, kicked my ego to the dirt—and that was *before* I used make-up to cover the top half of my tattoo. Still, in the middle of all this chaos, it's hard to be embarrassed. Or to care. Because today—I'm Santa Claus.

But that doesn't mean I won't break every bone in Scott's hand if he shares that make-up part with anyone, because I will. I told him as much at least a dozen times earlier tonight as he spread layer after layer of Cover Girl on my chest. It's bad enough that I'm two hundred pounds underweight and didn't have time to find appropriate stuffing to fill this suit. Santa *cannot* show up with an eight-inch strip of black ink all over his chest.

Although, looking at Scott now, I doubt I have anything to worry about. The guy is wearing pointy green shoes with fuzzy red balls at the tips and a matching cone jingle bell hat that keeps flopping in his eye. I doubt even Will Ferrell would be caught dead wearing that get-up.

We both look like morons.

Happy ones, but still.

A person can't help being happy while surrounded by dozens of excited kids.

"Hold on a minute!" Scott says, giving me a look of pure exhaustion. He isn't fooling me. I haven't seen him this excited since last August when What's-His-Name chess player won the national title after a record-breaking round that exceeded last year's playoff by a whopping forty-seven minutes.

What can I say? Scott's a nerd. As straight-laced as they come. And the coolest guy I know.

"Listen to Scott!" I say above the screams. These kids are wild. Like last year's group on crack. Which is strange, because our numbers are up only by three. Not enough to create this kind of temporary madness. "I want everyone to sit down right now!"

I'm not sure if Santa is supposed to bellow more than the customary *Ho-Ho-Ho*, but this Santa does. It takes a couple of minutes, but the kids quiet down and slowly form a ring around my feet. The younger ones look wide-eyed at me, fear lacing their expressions that this angry Santa Claus will leave here without emptying his large white pillowcase of toys.

That isn't going to happen.

I take a deep breath, and when the noise dies down—*thank you, God*—I slowly open my bag.

"Okay, now. Who wants to go first?"

It's the wrong thing to say. A tarantula tossed onto the middle of the floor wouldn't draw as many gasps and squeals. Scott nails me with a look, but I ignore him. With more dramatic flair than should be allowed for a straight guy, I withdraw the first item. It's just a dollar-store jump rope, but the entire room spins into a frenzy as I hand it off to Shelley, a little blonde girl sitting partially on top of my left foot. She grasps it with both hands and toddles off to her case worker—her foster family was too busy to show up tonight.

I start to bristle with anger again before I remember that Santa is supposed to be jolly. Anger isn't part of the shtick.

I force a smile that turns into a real one when Scott trips over his shoes and almost lands headfirst into the tree. The room erupts in laughter and I reach for another toy to give to Matt, a precocious six-year-old currently hopping from one foot to the other in front of me. He's missing a shoe; I have no idea why. Maybe in his excitement, he started ridding himself of clothing.

"This one looks like it's for a boy," I say in my best baritone voice. Matt fist-pumps the air with both hands and lets out a whoop.

Christmas Eve is in full swing once again.

Kate

I expect to see a lot of things when I push through the door, but the sight of Caleb—and I can tell it's Caleb because never in the history of shopping-mall Santa's has one ever looked *that* good—in a fuzzy red suit wasn't it. It stops me in my tracks just inside the door, and I can't help the slow smile that works its way across my lips. He's holding a bulging pillowcase and doing a poor job of disguising his voice while he passes out gifts, but the children are loving it. A little boy wearing one shoe bounces excitedly in front of him while Caleb reaches into his bag. The missing shoe puzzles me until I see it a few feet behind him. I laugh softly to myself. Some kids like to be free from the confines of clothing. I used to be one of them.

While trying to stay as inconspicuous as I can in this hideous pink coat, I stand in the shadows and take in the room. It's my first Christmas ever, and I want to remember all of it.

The lights on the tree are brighter than I remember them being last night; definitely brighter than the ones in my little apartment. I watch them for a moment, the way they dance across the gleaming wooden floor that makes up the basketball court. Just beyond the room a sliver of the dining room is visible, candlelight casting shadows over the darkened walls. The tables look untouched, which means dinner hasn't been served.

I can make out the top of Ben's head as he sits in the middle of the large circle of kids. He raises his hand and I see the flash of a toy sword. I roll my eyes. It seems Santa isn't above handing out weapons to small children, especially when Santa's persona and his elf sidekick have been taken over by two men-children who are nearly as raucous as the kids.

Speaking of kids, I take in Santa's sidekick, a very awkward Scott who has tripped twice in the thirty seconds I've been here. In his defense, walking in high heels is hard enough. Walking in oversized floppy shoes would be next to impossible. Caleb laughs at him. So do I. I don't mean for the sound to come out so loud.

As Caleb hands off the gift to the little boy, his head comes up. Even if I hadn't been watching him, I would have noticed the stillness that settled over everyone in the room when he spotted me.

I wait. Hold my breath. Have second thoughts and wonder if I should leave.

But I won't.

He doesn't say anything and neither do I.

My being here says it all, and I can tell by the gleam in his eyes that Caleb thinks so, too.

Caleb

One minute everyone is laughing and everything is like every other Christmas I've experienced here for the past four years, and the next minute the sound of music drifts from the back of the room and spills into my chest. I know that laugh. I've heard the laugh. I didn't think I would ever hear it again, but I look up, straight into the eyes of Kate.

Kate, with her beautiful smile. Kate, with her blonde curls. Kate, with her ugly pink coat that I fully intend to either burn or convince her to donate to charity before the night is over. Except charity won't take something so hideous. Of that I am certain. So I'll just have to step up and take her—and it—instead.

I let the bag fall and walk toward her, feeling the eyes of everyone in the room on the two of us. Parents. Children. Case workers. Baffled co-workers wondering if I've lost my mind. I have. Plus my heart. I lost them both five weeks ago inside a seedy bar in downtown Oklahoma City and I haven't gotten them back. At this point, I'm one-hundred percent, all the way certain I never will. I'm in this for good. And because she's here right now, in spite of everything we've been through, it's easy to assume she is too.

It's also easy to assume she's changed her mind about God, but maybe I shouldn't assume so much.

"What are you doing here?" I say. It occurs to me that Santa's baritone voice has moved on an upward slide, but I can't fake anything. Not here. Not now. And definitely not with her.

"Nice suit." Her words sound bold, but I hear the tremor in her voice. She eyes me up and down to cover it, and even though I know what she's doing, and even though the velour fabric is as itchy as it is uncomfortable, I feel her stare like a zap to my spine. "I came to see you," she says.

That's all I need to hear. I grab her hand and pull her around a corner, away from prying eyes. Once we're out of earshot, I pull her to me so that I can look at her...really look at her...when I say everything I want to say.

"You came to see me?"

She nods. It's the prettiest nod I've ever seen.

Without removing my gloves, I pull off my hat and yank down my fake beard and reach for the awful white fur that lines her coat.

"It's cold outside," I say. "And we're inside a church, and last time we were here you ran out as fast as you could, so why would you come back?"

"Like I said, I came to see you." Her hand goes to my chest and stays there, and I'm pretty sure she can feel my heartbeat through the red coat. Heck, if I turn around, I'm certain Scott would tell me he hears it from across the room. "And you're right; I did run out last time I was here. But I'm back now, and I'm not leaving. If you'll let me stay."

I stare at her for a long moment, wanting to believe her words but also knowing that sometimes belief is fragile, especially when it's at the beginning stages. "What about your parents? What about the lawsuit? I'm a youth pastor. That won't change."

"I'm glad you're a pastor. It's one of the first things I liked about you, I just didn't know it until now." Her voice is so soft as she looks down and fiddles with a button at the edge of her coat. Without looking up, she continues. "As for the lawsuit—I can't stop it." It takes work, but she looks up at me, imploring. "I'm sorry, and I know you probably hate me for it, but—"

"I've never hated you for a second, not even the day I drove you to that rally and found out who you were." It's the truth. I might have been angry. I might have been offended. But I never, ever, hated her. From practically that very first day, it's been the opposite. And frankly, I'm tired of fighting it.

"And your parents?" It's the only question she hasn't answered—the one I still need to hear. I lost my parents years ago, and it's the loneliest feeling in the world. I could never live with myself if I caused that kind of grief for Kate's parents...or for her. I won't take her away from them no matter how much I want her with me, no matter how misguided their views might be, because goodbyes rip your heart out and leave you feeling worse than dead, especially when they're permanent.

"My mother is the one who told me to come here tonight," she says. The words leave me speechless. Of all the things I imagined she might say—a hundred reasons why her parents' approval didn't matter, all the ways we couldn't be together because of media scrutiny and pending litigation—this wasn't it. *Her mother told her to come?*

I don't verbalize my surprise. "What about your father?" For the first time, her confidence slips, and a glimmer of fear slides in the vacant space. She bites her lower lip and looks past my shoulder into the gym. A few dozen kids have their eyes trained on hers, but she doesn't see any of them.

She looks at me. "I'll...work on him."

"He might not ever understand."

For a long moment she says nothing, but when she finally speaks, it's with the fragile conviction of a woman who's lived with the man forever. "I think he will. Actually, I'm certain of it."

It isn't a promise, and he may never be okay with us, but I believe her. He may hate me forever and never forgive me for taking his daughter away from everything he's built, but I believe her, because she's new to real belief and she's afraid for the future and one of us needs not to be.

There's no place for fear inside a church on Christmas Eve. She needs to understand that, and I need to be the one to show her.

I'm not sure which one of us makes the first move, but my hands are in her hair and her lips are on mine, and we kiss each other with all the gentleness of two people who've waited for this moment. I want to savor it, breathe it in. Not because I think it's our last kiss, but because I think it's the first of many. I'm in this. I'm in this all the way. I pull her even closer and move deeper, wanting to touch her and feel her and absorb every part of her fear that I can through the layers of our equally horrible clothing choices.

I'm in this. I want her to know it.

But I stop, because I know I should. First, because we need to go slow. I don't want to risk damaging a relationship that God has handed me—only Someone with a divine sense of humor would put two people like Kate and me together—and I'll do everything I can to keep that from happening. Second, because the disgusted groans of twenty children and a half-dozen co-workers fill the once silent space behind us. I lean my forehead against hers and breathe in and out, feeling her do the same until we're in perfect sync.

Kate smiles the softest smile. "I realize I'm not up on my Christmas etiquette, but I don't think Santa is supposed to be kissing random girls who walk in off the street."

"Crap." I've made a colossal mistake, but there's really no way to fix it. "What can I say, Santa's a ladies man. A real sucker for women dressed like circus candy." That earns me a shove, but I'll take it. I'll take it again and again and never complain.

"Should we go over there?" She nods toward the group still staring at us from several feet away. "There's a couple of kids on the verge of a meltdown, and I think you need to give them a gift before it happens."

I look over my shoulder at the faces of two kids staring down at the abandoned bag, and I know she's right. It's Christmas. Time to spread some joy.

Caleb

She's been unnaturally quiet since dinner ended. If I think about it, I can almost convince myself that she regrets walking in here tonight. Maybe it was impulsive, maybe open curiosity. Maybe a test to see what I'm made of, or maybe just a dip into the unknown, kind of like the rush you get as you stand at the edge of an open airplane and allow yourself to fall. Sure, there's elation. Sure, adrenaline is pumping. But then you land on dry ground and grow stunned at your stupidity. Chastise yourself for your blatant disregard for safety.

I went skydiving once, and that's exactly how I felt.

She's sitting under the Christmas tree all alone, and I'm pretty sure she feels that way now.

I prop a folding chair against the wall next to a row of others and make my way across the floor. The gym is abandoned except for the two of us. I can hear the faints noises the janitor makes as he cleans the kitchen, but I've seen the mess; he'll be back there for a while.

It's the second time I've walked toward her tonight, but this time I'm much more nervous. Part of me has known from the beginning that our differences have drawn us together—her family against God, and me His staunch ally. I'm not stupid; I know there's something exciting about the forbidden; that like danger—in the beginning—it's something you can't get enough of. But something tells me the newness has worn off. Kate's had her Christmas, and now that she's experienced it, I'm worried she's through.

With all of it. With me.

It's the way my life has worked forever, and I'm prepared.

I come up behind her and lower myself to the floor. Maybe this night won't end the way I want it to, but I'm diving in. No matter how things wind up, we need this moment.

"So what did you think? Was your first Christmas everything you thought it would be?"

She pulls her gaze from the lights and focuses on me. "No."

My heart thuds. I give it a silent command to shape up or leave me the heck alone.

"Technically," she continues, "Christmas isn't for another…" she checks her watch, "…fifteen minutes. So, no. I'm still waiting to see what the first one will be like. So, what do you have planned for me tomorrow, Caleb? Because I don't know how you're going to top tonight, but I can't wait to see it." Her mouth just barely turns up at the corners.

My heart thuds again, but this time for a different reason. Tomorrow…she's planning to stick around.

"What if I can't wait until then?"

She tilts her head to look at me. "What do you mean?"

Without saying anything, I move toward the tree and pull out the last gift tucked inside the back. It's hidden well, away from questioning eyes. Sparing me from the sympathetic glances I might've received if Kate hadn't shown up tonight. I gambled that she would. A crapshoot for sure, but it paid off.

"This is for you," I say as I hand it to her.

Her eyes are round blue orbs as she takes in the gift, then focuses on me. "You got me a present?"

I can't help smile at her wonder. "I got you a present."

"But, what if I hadn't—"

"Then I would have burned it. Smashed it into a million pieces. Turns out I don't have to." I nod toward the package in her hands. "Well, are you going to open it?"

It's all the permission she needs. Without regard to Mrs. Jenkins' wrapping expertise—I'm a guy and can't wrap presents to save my life—she tears into the glittery red paper, ripping the bow to shreds in her eagerness. Something tells me she's never opened a Christmas gift before.

By the soft smile that tilts her mouth as she studies the opened present in front of her, something also tells me she likes it. "I don't have this one." She looks up at me, her eyes shining as a hundred different expressions cross her features at once. I love every single one of them, but I'll save that news for later.

"I kind of figured you didn't. You want to listen to it?"

At her eager nod, I stand up and head toward the record player that I brought from home and placed at the corner of the gym right behind the tree. Within seconds, the soft strains of Bing Crosby's *White Christmas* begin to play. I sit next to her again, this time a little closer, knee touching knee. It isn't enough contact, so I reach for her hand and bring it to my lap. For a long moment, neither of us speak. Kate is the first to break the silence.

"Can you do something for me?" Her voice is a whisper, laced with timidity. Yet at the same time, I can hear the resolve behind her soft words.

I want to tell her I'll do anything she wants. That I'll stay with her forever. That we'll listen to music in this gym, dance in my office, get married and have babies, and that life will be perfect, but I can't. I fully intend to one day, but I can't now. Instead, I simply answer, trying my best to keep my voice casual.

"Sure. What do you need?"

I look over at her, and she tells me.

Right then, casual goes by the wayside and everything inside me cracks—all the edges and sharp angles and hardened insides that have made me *me* since my mother died seventeen years ago. I'm melted; a pliable, liquefied version of the person who's lived inside me for so long. I can't believe the transformation hasn't happened before now, but it hasn't, like life was waiting for this moment, this exact time to really change me.

And I do what she asks.

"You really want to know?" I can hear the hope in my voice, the barely-controlled elation that comes through the words.

She smiles at me, the most beautiful smile I've ever seen. "I do."

And under a Christmas tree that's showing the wear of two-dozen excited kids…in a gym that smells strongly of antiseptic and the leftover remnants of beef tenderloin…at midnight on Christmas morning, a Tuesday morning that's barely just begun and will forever seal Tuesdays in my mind as the best day of the week…

I sit beside a princess and tell her about a King.

EPILOGUE

Caleb

"Jesus in the Southern Sky"
—Sleeping With Sirens

Two months later

I barely remember the nightmares, because they stopped abruptly almost eight weeks ago. It's almost as if on the night Kate walked into that gym, my former life ceased to exist and a new one slipped into its place. The dreams left. The loneliness fled. Even Starbucks runs have turned into something I enjoy. Kate likes Starbucks, so I try to swing by there a couple of times a week just to see her smile when I hand her a Grande soy caramel latte, hold the whip.

I can't believe she drinks that crap, but whatever.

Some might wonder why all this change didn't happen on the day I found God, but I don't question the reason. It's not up to me. As they say, God works in mysterious ways—a corny expression, but it turns out that sometimes it's appropriate.

Though you'll never hear me use that phrase, not on your life.

Today is Valentines' Day, but Kate isn't here. She's spending the morning with her parents while I finish up some work, though I use the word *work* in the loosest of terms. So far this morning, I've written a letter to Ben—he's moved in with his new family and all reports point to the fact that he's incredibly happy. I've straightened the stack of albums on my office floor, sent a few emails, counseled a troubled sixteen-year-old girl new to our church who's currently struggling with a relationship that's become too physical. And spent five minutes talking with Mrs. O'Hare.

I would give my right arm and both eyeballs to undo *that* conversation.

The woman has *got* to find a filter, but she's seventy. I have a feeling her personal one went missing on the day the Vietnam War started. Like she lost it somewhere in the pile of all the protest signs she and her friends hand-made in her parent's garage—which they did, because she's told me all about it at least a dozen times this year alone.

Still, I'd rather hear that story all over again than the one I just heard about her husband wearing leather pants and an open-collared puffy shirt and shaking his thing all over the salsa dance floor. I guess it's not my eyeballs I need to relinquish, after all. It's my ears.

I push in my desk drawer and stand, finished with the day and ready to leave. In an hour I'll pick up Kate, and just thinking about it has my heart pounding. I can't wait to see her. More than that, I can't wait to give her my latest gift. She'll be surprised. She might even be angry. She'll definitely cry. And I'm prepared for all of it.

I fist my keys and walk out the door.

"So what's the big secret?" she asks a few hours later. We're sitting in a booth at the back of the room, practically pressed against the wall because the restaurant is so crowded. For the dozenth time tonight, I thank God that I remembered to make a reservation. The stacks and stacks of people waiting in the lobby is just sad—the poor guys standing in rumpled shirts next to annoyed dates even sadder.

Clearly none of them are going to make out with their girls tonight. Not like me. I smile to myself just thinking about it.

"Caleb."

"What?" I blink, feeling like I've been caught doing something wrong. Which I haven't. Yet.

"What's the big secret?" She sets her fork down and leans on her elbows.

I pick up my glass and take a sip of water to bide time. "There's no secret."

"You're a terrible liar. There's a secret. Now tell me what it is." She plays with the blade of her knife. I'm pretty sure this is an innocent gesture, though it's just as likely to be a not-so-subtle threat. Good thing I'm my own man and don't give in to girlfriend pressure.

"Okay, I got you a gift."

I'm a wimp. A whipped, pathetic wimp.

As I expected, her eyes narrow. "We said we weren't buying each other gifts. You promised. What kind of man goes back on a promise?" She wraps her hand around the knife. I resist the urge to flinch. And then I tell myself to suck it up and be a man.

"Oh, put the knife down, Killer. I didn't pay anything for it, so it doesn't count." I catch my smile at the way her face falls. For all her fake-outrage, she's upset that it didn't cost money. "You'll like it, though," I add with a shrug. "You'll love it, in fact."

The smile returns as her palms go up and stretch toward me like a kid at a birthday party. "Then give it to me. I love gifts." Just as quickly her excitement fades again, and she frowns. "It's isn't something pink, is it? Like a purse or a robe or, God-forbid, a dress?"

I laugh, taking in the red dress she's wearing that clings to her in all the right places. Nothing is showing that shouldn't be, which somehow makes it even hotter. I focus on her eyes, where my gaze should remain. It takes some effort, but I manage.

"It isn't pink. It'll *never* be pink."

She sighs in relief. "Thank goodness. Then hand it over."

Taking my time so that I don't miss the look on her face, I slowly pull my gift out from under the table and place it in her hands. She gives a little gasp, knowing what it is without tearing a single strip of paper away. Eyes the size of saucers stare back at me. "Caleb, you need this. You can't give it to me, I won't take it." She gives the gift a little shove in my direction, but I'm stronger and push back. And then I lean back in my chair and tilt my head in appreciation.

"Well, as a matter of fact, it turns out I don't need it after all. And if you don't take it, I'll never speak to you again." It's an empty promise, kind of like my promise not to give her a gift, and she knows it.

"You call me every hour of the day, and if you don't, I call you, so we both know that isn't true," she says. Curiosity wins out and she pulls back a corner of the paper, tears a smooth strip off the front. The image of Bob Dylan's brown suede jacket appears from shoulder to hem. Through the remaining wrapping paper, she fingers the edge of the album she willingly gave to me three months ago—the kindest gesture, the nicest thing anyone has done for me ever or since—and she smiles. I see the tears even before she looks up at me. "Why don't you need it? Without state funding, how will you pay for meals and transportation and electricity and—"

I place my hand over hers to stop her. She's felt guilty since the ruling came down last month, but it's time for her to stop. That lawsuit is no more her fault than it is mine, and besides, some good has come from it. More good than she knows. More good than even I understand.

"I don't need it because from the moment we lost, private donations have been pouring in. All the free press didn't hurt. We have more than we need to operate for the next year, so don't worry," I explain. "The album is yours. I love you for giving it to me, but I don't want it back."

Her look goes soft. "I'll keep it, but if the donations ever stop then I want you to ask me for it again."

I lace my fingers through hers and tug on her arm. She knows what I want, and without a hint of embarrassment, she comes around the table to sit on my lap. She fits perfectly inside my arms, and I could sit this way forever. "The donations won't stop. I have no doubt in my mind that we will have everything we need without having to use any of your albums. But thank you. It meant everything to know you would give something like this up for me."

She threads a hand through my hair and leaves it on the back of my neck, then presses her forehead to mine. "I'd do anything for you, because I love you, Caleb. I hope you know that."

I do, and I tell her so. I tell her something else, too. Something I've been wanting to say since she walked into that bar wearing that tacky pink coat almost three months ago today. "Someday soon, I'm going to ask you to marry me. Be prepared to say yes, because I'm not taking no for an answer."

She raises an eyebrow in a challenge, but I see the hope behind it. "Then you'd better hurry before I change my mind and dump you for someone better." Her words are soft, breathless. Her lips are so close, and I can't take another second. Maybe we shouldn't kiss so publicaly in a restaurant, but it's Valentine's Day. It's expected. At least that's how I justify it.

When we break apart, she rests her head on my shoulder and traces the outline of my tattoo. The eagle means something to her now; like me, it's now her favorite verse.

"Sometimes I still can't believe we're together like this. Why do you think it happened, Caleb? Why do you think you rescued me from that guy at the bar? Sometimes I wonder if it was just a coincidence, or if the whole thing was designed by God Himself to bring us together."

I smile into her ear, press my lips to her hairline. "It was God, definitely, but I can't tell you why," I whisper. "The only thing I know for sure is that sometimes He works in mysterious ways."

Turns out I use that phrase after all.

I drove to Tulsa without telling anyone why. Scott knew I was leaving for the afternoon, but he thinks I came to see Ben. Which I did. Sort of.

I saw Ben and took him for ice cream, but I returned him to his parents after only an hour with a promise to come back next month. Although he gave me a condition: If I didn't bring the pretty lady, he wouldn't answer the front door. So I guess next time I'll bring Kate. Next time, I'll stay longer. Today, I didn't have time.

Thinking only of the hour and the fact that I'm a couple of minutes late, I pull into a lot across the street and park the car. I'll have to fight traffic at the crosswalk, which might put me there at the end, but I want to stay inconspicuous. It isn't that I'm ashamed; it's that I'm uncomfortable. But sometimes our comfort level needs to be stretched, as I've found out these past few months. Sometimes, it's the only way to make peace and effect real change.

Plus, even though I have my suspicions, I have to know for sure.

The crowd gets louder as I approach. Once I'm at the edge of it, I stop, wanting to stay behind the camera lenses and protest signs, behind the spectators and what has the potential to turn into a circus if I'm spotted. The media would have a field day with this, but all I want is a minute.

All I need is a minute.

His wife stands next to him as he delivers the last part of his speech, the part where *Kathy* would come up and add to everything he's just said. Except Kathy is no more. Only Kate exists now, though she's occasionally referred to as Princess by me.

Even the fliers have changed. I reach for one off the back table and study the yellow paper. Kathy's image has been replaced with the smiling faces of Mr. and Mrs. Hawkins; forever a team, forever bound by a cause I'm praying will fade with time. Not the entire movement, of course Just their involvement with it. It's the one thing that keeps Kate unsettled. The one thing that keeps her from being completely, without a doubt happy.

I remember the words she spoke on Christmas Eve: *My mother told me to come here tonight...my father will come around eventually.*

Kate told me the story of her mother; privately, the woman has already accepted me. It's only a matter of time before she comes back to her Creator, too.

Things have been harder with her father, but lately...lately, I'm starting to think things might be on the edge of change. Maybe one day soon—with lots and lots of prayer—he'll be swayed to this side of the fence.

Maybe.

He's delivering his closing lines when his wife spots me. Even though fifty feet of Baptist church property separates us, I know the moment her eyes land on mine, because she touches her husband's arm. She touches his arm, and he glances at her. One second later, he's looking at me and falters on the word *demand*. He gives the word another try, but again he doesn't quite get the word out. His standard catchphrase is *We demand some action*—against nativity scenes, against government funding, or in this case, against a church that erected a marble cross exactly three inches beyond their own property and onto the property of a public park—a mistake that will cost the church approximately one-hundred thousand dollars to move if they're forced to.

We demand some action…he mumbles again. But right now, at this moment, Kate's father can't seem to make even the smallest plea for it.

So he stares straight at me. While I stare back at him. I see the discomfort that forms on Mrs. Hawkins' features…the questioning look she throws her husband's way. But before she can question him, I produce the envelope from my back pocket and hold it up. Without hesitating, he does the one thing I came to see. The one thing that confirms it. The one thing I've suspected for a few weeks now, even though I thought for sure I was crazy for thinking it in the first place.

He nods.

Presses his lips together.

And then looks away.

At that moment, all the air I've been holding in my lungs escapes, and I shake my head and smile. That smile stays on my face as he tugs on his tie, clears his throat, and resumes his speech. I turn to head back to the car.

When I reach the door handle, out of everyone's sight except my own, I withdraw the check from the envelope.

Twenty-five thousand dollars. The third one—in the same hand-writing sent from a local bank in a name I don't recognize—I've received since Christmas. Signed simply: *For you, for taking your own action.*

Public funding might be gone, but at this rate, the foster center will be in business indefinitely.

Feeling the weight of worry lift off me and drift heavenward, I glance up.

"I get it, God. Mysterious ways…"

And with that, I hop in the car and close the door.

Though I know this bit of information needs to stay secret for now, and though I'm not dumb enough to think much will change in the days ahead—Mr. Hawkins has his convictions, and I have mine—it still gives me hope. The man is reaching out. The man is accepting me. The man just wants his daughter to be happy.

So do I. Suddenly, I'm hit with the familiar, overwhelming desire to see her.

So with the sun in front of me, I point my car west and drive toward Kate.

THE END

"But those who hope in the Lord will renew their strength. They will soar on wings like eagles; they will run and not grow weary, they will walk and not be faint."

—Isaiah 40:31

Thank you so much for reading *Sway*. If you enjoyed the book, please take a minute to leave a review on Goodreads. I appreciate it!

Made in the USA
Columbia, SC
30 November 2023

27482115R00157